D1644403

THE CONGO CONTRACT

A P BATEMAN

Facebook: @authorapbateman

www.apbateman.com

Rockhopper Publishing

ALSO BY A P BATEMAN

THE ALEX KING SERIES

The Contract Man
Lies and Retribution
Shadows of Good Friday
The Five
Reaper
Stormbound
Breakout
From the Shadows
Rogue
The Asset
Last Man Standing
Hunter Killer

ALSO BY A P BATEMAN

THE ROB STONE SERIES

The Ares Virus
The Town
The Island
Stone Cold

Standalone Novels
Hell's Mouth
Unforgotten

Novellas
The Perfect Murder?
Atonement
(an Alex King short story)

Further details of these titles can be found at
www.apbateman.com

DEDICATION

For Clair, Summer and Lewis, and their constant jokes
about the
'A P Bateman Show'
It never gets old...

PROLOGUE

Twenty years ago
Democratic Republic of Congo

KING DIDN'T WAIT for the man to stop groaning or moving, his legs twitching irritably as death slowly took hold. He wasn't going anywhere, and the rifle he had been struggling to get hold of was out of reach. Any last-ditch attempt to avenge his brothers or his own imminent death wasn't going to happen, no matter how much the man would want it. King wiped the blood off the blade of the knife on the man's shoulder, before sheathing it and picking up the FN rifle. The rifle was heavy and hot from the contact. King checked the magazine and breech then bent down and pulled two more magazines from the dying man's bandolier. The FN packed a punch in its full-fat 7.62x51mm. Heavy and cumbersome, the magazines were heavy, too. But the rifle tended to be a one shot, one kill weapon and he checked that the front and rear sights were square and undamaged

before shouldering the rifle. Ahead of him there was movement in the brush. The man beside him let out a moan, and
King pressed his hand over the man's mouth, pinching his
nose with his thumb and forefinger, keeping the weapon
aimed at the brush. The man barely struggled and was gone
inside a minute. King removed his hand from the man's face
and wrapped it around the fore end of the heavy rifle, glad
to take some of the weight off his right hand and shoulder.

The jungle glade was hot and humid, dank, and dark.
The sunlight broke through the fronds in the canopy in
multiple beams, like spotlights on the stage. A foot appeared
in one of those spotlights. It was followed by a leg and an
arm and part of the body. Dark skin, beads of sweat glistening in the light. The figure froze. Twenty metres from
King and unaware that he was standing in the middle of the
peep-sight of the SLR. His face still out of view. King waited.
A shoulder emerged from the darkness, illuminated in
bright sunlight. The man's vest was brown and torn and had
probably been white once. King slowly and steadily took a
knee, his entire form in the shadows. The man's face clipped
the light. Black and dripping with perspiration. The whites
of his eyes, big and bright. King's finger tightened on the
trigger. There would be others for sure. Directly behind
him. King had a choice. Take down the man in front of him
or wait and see how many more stepped out of the brush
and into the killing ground in front of him. King got his
answer as another figure stepped closer to the first, and a
boy soldier ducked around the second man. Ten years old if
he was a day, carrying the AK-47 on a sling around his neck
because the weapon was almost longer than he was tall.
King kept his aim steady. The presence of the boy didn't
change a thing. He'd seen enough to know that the boy
soldiers, the 'infantry' of the Southside Boys had been

trained to be fearsome, fearless killers. Snatched from their homes then beaten and abused, made dependant on mind-altering khat, indoctrinated into an existence of pure violence, and turned into soldiers before they even reached puberty. King did not want to kill a child, but he'd seen what had happened when a grown man had hesitated, and dead was dead in his book.

He would not make the same mistake.

Behind the backs of the men in front of him several shouts drew their attention. King had known the enemy would lack discipline, but he supposed what they lacked in tactical skills, they made up for in numbers and a complete and utter fearlessness, and the khat that made them feel invincible. The mind-altering state had certainly meant that the dead man behind him had put up a fearsome fight and had been butchered by King's blade before the inevitable loss of blood made even the invincible stop functioning. King was glad he now had the SLR in his hand. The FN, or the L1A1 as it had been known in British military service was certainly a more reassuring option than the 9mm Uzi he had ditched after running out of ammunition. Three of the Southside Boys had taken at least six rounds a piece before they had stopped moving.

The three hostiles were all looking behind them now, waiting for something. Another shout and the foliage beside them parted and two more men stepped out from cover and into the glade.

"So, what the fuck are we waiting for?" came the whisper. Not even a whisper, a barely audible hum.

King's heart raced as he realised that he hadn't heard the Scotsman creep up on him. He kept his aim, like he had known his mentor had been there all along. "More of them to show up," he replied in a low murmur.

"That FN is semi-auto only and the barrel is almost long enough to poke them with from here." Peter Stewart paused. "Too many more of them and your odds are lowering with every single swinging dick inviting themselves to the party..."

"The range lessons are over," replied King, as he lowered the rifle. He reached for the grenade attached to his belt and eased out the ring pin with his thumb. "Don't worry, old man. There'll be enough meat left for you..."

There was no quiet way to release the lever, and it sprang off its half hinge and clattered into the foliage. The lead man looked over, his wide eyes white in the beams of light parted by the fronds like a child's kaleidoscope. King silently counted, but Stewart blew their position when he dived for cover. King threw the grenade and followed Stewart into the brush, rolling around so he could lie prone with his rifle facing towards the enemy as he buried his face into the dirt and covered his head with his left hand. The concussive thud of the grenade was felt through their bodies – in the hollow of their chests and in their guts - and shrapnel, plant debris and body parts rained down around the glade. There were screams and groans, a child's scream turning into a sob. Stewart was up and pushing through the brush, his Uzi held out in front of him in his right hand, and he had characteristically drawn his knife and had it firmly clenched, blade downwards, in his left hand. King followed, taking Stewart's beaten path out into the clearing. The boy was sitting on his backside and was clearly dazed and confused by the concussive blast that had robbed him of both his legs. Stewart put a bullet into the boy's forehead without hesitation and King guessed that the action both gave the child a swift end and paid a debt for one of their own. But even though their losses had been great, King felt no better for it, no sense of vengeance or justice for the bullet he put into the next man, nor the one after that.

Stewart was charging through the clearing and King couldn't help thinking, for the second time on this mission, that his instructor and mentor taught the theories of close quarter battle procedures but forgot almost everything in the actual firefight. However, he still had one procedure down, and King could see that unless he quickened his own pace, the tough forty-something Scotsman would be leaving him behind again. To remain static in a close quarter battle was almost certainly to die, and Stewart was like a whirlwind, darting this way and that. He crouched and leapt, ducked, and dived and alternated the speed at which he cut through the men in front of him.

King could see that the man had taken down three more men in a volley of gunfire and with downward stabbing motions and slashes left and right with the Ka-Bar US Marine Corps knife until they had stopped moving. King fired at the men as they engaged, each shot aimed at the centre of the torso and taking a man to the jungle floor. Stewart buried his knife deep between a struggling man's shoulder blades, dropped onto one knee and changed magazines as the man fell to his knees. King watched Stewart heave himself up using the embedded knife as a handle, then tugged it free and resumed his charge into the enemy as the man he had just killed fell forwards onto his stomach.

King took a knee and reloaded the heavy rifle, then remained in his position and fired at a group of three men. When he looked up, Stewart was no longer there and the enemy were massing to the edge of the glade, torn between fighting, and fleeing into the cover of the jungle. King cursed Stewart and got moving again. There were twenty men ahead of him, many of them boy soldiers. He was in it now. To show mercy was to die. He had been told of the things he would see in this profession, and until he had landed in Angola, he had killed just one man in his time with MI6. That man had been a rogue agent, and he had been trying to kill King at the time. He had killed before, two men in a bar fight, and that had started a chain of events that started his path with MI6 and ultimately saw him about to die in a jungle at the hands of boy soldiers high on khat and with a bloodlust in their eyes.

King dived onto his stomach, taking cover behind a dying man as he changed the magazine in the FN rifle. He was aware of his movements being painfully slow, the enemy advancing, their aim getting closer with every shot fired until dirt flicked up into his face as the bullets drew dangerously near to him. Several bullets hit the wounded man that he was taking cover behind, and he groaned and lurched then went still. King got the rifle up to his shoulder and rolled several times, much as a child would down a meadow hillside, then stopped himself when he was ten feet away from the body and on the edge of the glade. He started to fire at them, picking just the closest person to him, or the man who seemed most in control of his weapon. Gunfire erupted from behind them, and Stewart appeared from the edge of the jungle some twenty-five metres from where King had last seen him. In jungle warfare, Stewart had taught what he had casually called the 'peek-a-boo' technique and was using it to good effect. He disappeared again, and after a few seconds, he emerged ten metres to the right, now flanking the men after he had sprayed them with gunfire from behind. King rolled into the thick foliage, scrambled to his feet, and ran as fast as he could through the brush to mimic Stewart's tried and tested technique. He almost stumbled into a boy of ten or eleven years, crawling through the brush. King shouldered the rifle and the boy looked up at him, his eyes fearful and his hands held up in front of his face as if they could offer protection to a 7.62mm bullet. Futile, but hopeful. King could see that the boy had lost his weapon. He must have come close to Stewart too because there was a six-inch gash running from one side of his forehead to the opposite side of his chin, just missing his eye but making up for it by putting a lateral cross over his mouth. His lips were hanging loose, and blood had turned his dirty T-shirt red. King cursed himself for hesitating. He had shown a young boy soldier mercy just two days before. Allowed him to run, scared and defeated. But at what cost? Your mistakes shape your future. King had made a costly mistake and one of their team had died. Stewart had primed them all to show no mercy, give no quarter. And the old bastard had been right all along. King had thought him wrong to play God, but there really was no other safe option. Without further hesitation he squeezed the trigger and moved on. The nightmares, drink and darkness would surely take hold of him now. He would become just like the tough Scotsman who had trained him. He had gone down the road from which there was no return, no salvation.

King pounded on, his mind in a fog, not even sure if the fight was worth the cost. He worked his way to his right, and eventually came out into the glade slightly behind the line of men, mindful to stay out of Stewart's arc of fire. King fired the weapon for all he was worth, bracing his weight behind the mighty recoil and aiming at each man through the peepsights. The melee lasted a few seconds and when every man was down, King could see Stewart reloading at the edge of the clearing and drawing his pistol. King changed over to his last magazine and tried to ignore the Scotsman as he worked his way through the clearing giving a bullet to the heads of both men and boys with his 9mm Browning pistol, regardless of whether they were moving and breathing, or lying quite still.

King was fighting for breath, his chest heaving. He felt unsteady on his feet and sucked in lungful after lungful of precious, dank air. He hadn't eaten in two days and the effect was taking its toll.

"You're forgetting to breathe in the contact," Stewart observed. "When you were boxing, I bet you didn't hold your breath..."

King nodded. He had done, and his trainer had always nagged at him, telling him he couldn't always win in the first round and that breathing kept the fight in you to last the distance. He had put King up against hardened distance fighters to teach him the lesson or swapped over sparring partners after each round until he had got the message. Out here, he had done the same thing and high on adrenalin, he had probably only taken a couple of breaths throughout the entire battle.

"Hydrate," Stewart snapped, but King noted that the man was drinking from his own hipflask and water and glucose was the last thing he'd find in there.

King sipped from his own camel pack. Water was plentiful in the jungle, and he'd soon find some more water and drop a few purifiers into it for a sickly cocktail of sterilised mud, water, and dead parasites. He sealed the drinking tube, his eyes on the bullet hole in the child's forehead. He looked at the boy's legless corpse, knowing that it was the grenade that had done for the boy what Stewart had finished. Without any warning, King retched and vomited next to the child's body.

"That's a fucking waste of good water, lad," the Scotsman

called out harshly. King wiped his mouth with the back of his hand and spat on the ground. "Must be the adrenalin, son."

"I think so," King lied.

"Aye..." Stewart shrugged. "The little bastard would think nothing of slicing off your own dick and shoving it down your throat, so don't waste your tears... or the contents of your stomach... on him."

King looked away from the body of the boy and watched as Stewart took his second swig of whisky. "There'll be more of them coming soon," he said.

"I'm counting on it," the Scotsman replied. "The more the better. Let them come after us while Dimitri heads south. We need to buy them some time."

King looked around the clearing. The bodies were strewn in a grotesque display of angles. Of splayed limbs, broken skulls and the ground had soaked red, the penetrating light through the canopy highlighting the macabre scene that he knew he would see as a snapshot in twenty years' time. If indeed, he was lucky to live that long. But after following the crazy Scotsman, he seriously doubted that. He did not want to count the bodies, better he didn't know. Early on, Stewart had told him never to put a number on it. That had not been possible before this mission. He knew the numbers. Both before his service and since he had signed his life away. He could have counted his death toll on one hand, and still have a couple of digits spare. And two of those souls had been unintentional. A stupid argument fuelled by alcohol and ego. But now? After just one week, he had no idea how many people he had sent to their graves. And he knew he wasn't out of this yet.

Stewart picked up an AK-47 and ejected the empty magazine, tossing it onto one of the bodies. He started checking through the dead and soon had four fully loaded magazines shoved into the pockets of his bandolier and had decided to ditch the UZI machine-pistol for the rifle. King found the body of a man who had been carrying an FN SLR and started helping himself to ammunition and magazines. He already knew the weapon worked, so he wasn't bothered about the veritable display of hardware strewn before him. He looked down at the teen's body. The SLR rifle in his hand had earned the moniker, 'The right arm of the free world...' But not for this guy. His world had not been free. His fight had not been just, and had not lasted long, either.

Both men froze as they heard shouts further down the trail. Stewart was already ducking into the brush, and King followed suit, stepping backwards, and disappearing from the glade when he was less than a foot into the foliage. Perspiration stung his eyes and he ignored it, as well as the biting flies that were after his sweat, and crawling insects that were working their way between the top of his boot and where his combat trouser leg had become untucked. King took a deep breath to steady his nerves as he shouldered the rifle and readied himself for the second wave.

1

One week earlier
London

PETER STEWART KNEW ENOUGH about situations such as this to expect no more than a ten-by-ten briefing room on a lower floor. No wood panelling, no imposing mahogany desk and no twelve-year-old Macallan whisky aged in sherry oak casks and poured into cut crystal glasses to toast in the mission, like the current Director General of MI6 had a reputation for. Not so much as a cup of tea at this level. He looked at the station table, usually there would be a coffee machine, a teasmade, and a few cups. But not today. The table hadn't been prepared. This meeting was going to be an in and out. Stewart didn't even imagine there would be anything recorded. He had been on a few of these jobs, and he knew he would be deniable and that no help would be heading his way if it all went to hell in a handcart. But, that said, he often welcomed the freehand such missions gave him.

The door opened and a tall and rather humourless man in his late thirties walked in. He carried a folder in one hand and his mobile phone in the other. It was a sleek *Motorola Razr*, not quite the blocky and heavy Nokia that Stewart had been issued the year before and was still using. Armstrong thought it made him look sophisticated, but he obviously hadn't heard that estate agents, city traders and car salesmen were all about the flip-phones. Or perhaps he had. Perhaps that was why he was wearing the navy pinstripe suits these days. He was followed by a stern forty-something woman with wiry greyish brown hair pulled back in a severe bun. Her name was Felicity Willmott, but behind her back everyone knew her as one of the 'Emilies'. Emily was the Soviet name given in the sixties to women of a certain age who had married the British Secret Services instead of a husband, and whom they would target with thirty-some-thing men who could wine and dine them with flattering conversation and who mirrored Adonis in looks. They would take them to bed and use pillow talk in the comfort-able time which invariably ensued after sex, in a relaxed and unguarded state of intimacy. Emily had been the chosen name because its Russian equivalent was considered boring and suited the personality of a spinster in such a job. MI6 had labelled these men 'Ivans', and before long they were feeding the 'Emilies' with false information for their Russian lovers to send back to Moscow.

"Take a seat..." Armstrong said without looking at him. He was checking his text messages.

Felicity Willmott remained impassive, having barely acknowledged Stewart, who was used to this after twenty years of doing the dirty work for MI6. He had found that he was both feared and revered in equal measures and that suited him just fine.

Stewart pulled out a chair and studied the man in front of him as he sat down. He was greying at his temples. The position did that to people. He'd give the man until he was forty before he reached for the *Just for Men*. Another five before he started to lose it altogether. His hairline was starting to recede already. Armstrong snapped the phone shut and Stewart said, "Beam me up, Scotty..." with a smile.

"What?"

"Your phone."

"What about it?"

"It's like they used in *Star Trek*."

Armstrong shook his head and said quite seriously. "No, that must have been something else. This is a brand-new model."

Stewart smirked and shrugged his shoulders. "Of course..."

"You've seen the news?" Felicity asked.

"Aye."

"There's a problem," said Armstrong. "As you will know, Angola has just come out of a civil war that has been raging since nineteen-seventy-five. That's twenty-seven years of sporadic, on and off fighting. A Cold War proxy battle between Cuba and the Soviet Union backing the People's Movement for the Liberation of Angola, and the US and the South Africans backing the anti-communist National Union for the Total Independence of Angola." He paused. "After UNITA won and the reds left for Russia and Fidel's Caribbean, taking their financial and logistical support with them, the Angolan president showed his appreciation by granting lovely *official* oil contracts to both the US and ourselves."

"Oil and blood can always be found on the same fields..."

"Don't get all sanctimonious on me, Stewart. You go where we tell you to, and you've spilt enough of other peoples' blood for Britain's interests to come down from any moral high horse you elect to ride upon." Armstrong paused. "It would pay you to gen up on the region. Especially now."

"I think I'm pretty well *genned* up on Angola," Stewart smiled mirthlessly. "I'm aware of the situation in Angola, Michael, perhaps more than anybody else in this godforsaken building. And I've spilt enough of my *own* blood for Britain's interests, as well. And as for morality, well I've helped our country's oil interests along in the past, so to speak. Far more than the cause of freedom at least." He paused. "Angola was a dirty little war, leaving half a million people dead and a further million wretched souls displaced. But we got what we wanted from the instability and eventual ceasefire. BP are drilling already, both inland and offshore. Exxon are estimating that they will pull out more oil there than they do currently in the Gulf of Mexico. And we got to stiff the South Africans into the deal, too. They provided munitions and commandos and training and have yet to sign an oil deal with the Angolan government. And it doesn't look likely, either."

"Yes, shame," Felicity Willmott said uncommittedly. "Well, there's only so much to go around. And we always look after our own interests first."

Stewart was used to this type of meeting. Feared and revered also meant that he never went into a meeting one-to-one, and he knew that whatever was said and agreed upon, if it all ended up going south, then the two against one approach was the way of the institution he served.

When all was said and done, his end of the stick always had some shit on it.

"Anyway, shall we forget the history lesson and get on to why I'm here?" Stewart stared at them both and added, "Angola and the Democratic Republic of Congo aren't responding to our government's offer, or request, to send in the boys from Hereford."

"Indeed," Armstrong nodded. "These idiots from the Congo have taken seven OPEC inspectors and six employees from BP. They are demanding an inordinate amount of money, as well as American rapper Fifty Cent to put on a concert for them." He chuckled and shook his head. "These bloody imbeciles are tripping on acid, by the sounds of it..."

"Khat," Stewart interrupted. "It's a weed they chew. It's an amphetamine, stimulates them and makes them feel invincible. At least in the amounts they consume." He paused. "And of course, they're all ganja heads, too. So, paranoid, unstable and lethargic. Like two sides of a coin."

"I couldn't give a damn about any of that, Peter," said Armstrong. "But we need those hostages back and we need the Southside Boys of Da Congo... oh, for God's sake, I can't even say their name seriously... put out of business."

"Aye, they sound like a really shit troop of rappers, but they're making a big name for themselves, and they are feared by the local population and government forces alike." He paused, his normally cold eyes seeming to show a rare glint of emotion. "Because they take young boys from villages, indoctrinate them, use them for laying landmines and executing prisoners, and the Southside Boys themselves enjoy nothing more than rape and murder. And they excel in chopping off the limbs of their victims while they are still alive. There are people who now do a roaring trade in crutches and artificial limbs out there. It's not all because of the landmines. The Southside Boys even crossed the border in one of their raiding party events and sliced the right legs off the Angolan national football team. The 'B' team. All eleven of them, just below the knee. The bus driver, the assistant manager and the coach all lost an arm..."

Armstrong cleared his throat, and straightened his tie before saying, "Well, rather you than me, that's all I'll say on the matter," he said, apparently uninterested, but Stewart could see the man was disturbed by the story. "Because I want you to put a small team of deniable men together and get the hostages back." He paused, tossing the folder across the table. "Especially those three."

Stewart picked up the file and opened it. "And what's the news on a ransom? Can this guy Fifty Cent come and perform?"

"Don't be ridiculous!" Felicity chided.

"My dear, I think Peter is baiting us..."

"Oh..."

Stewart smirked as he looked through the file. There were three single sheets with a few typed lines on each, a short bio really, and a photo clipped to each sheet. Stewart read the pages unhurriedly. He didn't particularly like Armstrong and thought the man could wait, given his lack of sentiment. He eventually looked up and said, "We had assets in the OPEC delegation?"

"Naturally. One SIS officer, an officer with the Security Service and a low-ranking civil servant who was on a fact-finding mission. All three are known to one another, so it's only a matter of time before these wannabe gangsters make one of them talk and the dominoes fall, and Great Britain PLC will have egg on its face, and the Southside Boys *of Da Congo*..." He emphasised the last part with contempt. "...

have more than a request for several million dollars and an American rapper to perform a concert."

"Who the hell is this Fifty Cent, anyway?" Stewart asked tersely.

"Curtis James Jackson the third, apparently. He's an American hip-hop star, or rapper. That black music with bad lyrics and lots of gold jewellery. He's huge, but I'd never heard of him," said the man who played Andrew Lloyd Webber CDs in his car on his commute. "Wants to get into the movie business. God forbid…"

"Right," Stewart frowned. "And they *really* want a concert?"

"Yes."

"Then give them one. And send a couple of Tomahawk cruise missiles in before the headline act gets there…"

"It's certainly a thought. But it's not even on the table." Armstrong shook his head. "But it just shows that these Southside Boys are off their heads with drugs, completely delusional, which means the hostages don't have much time. And God help them while they're there."

Stewart rose from his chair and said, "I'll get a plan in place."

"Don't break the bank," Armstrong replied.

"And all of this is deniable?"

"If you fuck up it will be," Felicity replied. "Naturally, we'll deny your existence."

"And if I succeed?" he asked wryly.

"Then, tea and medals all round, old chap," Armstrong said lightly.

"It'll be your baby, then." Stewart paused. "Another one of your successes."

"That's how it works. You should be used to it by now," Felicity replied.

"Right..." Stewart sneered. He knew the two were intentionally working together like a tag-team, but he had never got comfortable with it.

Armstrong watched him head for the door then said, "Get that new chap on it. It will be good for him."

"King?"

"Yes, I believe that's his assumed name."

Stewart frowned. He had recruited the man, trained him, but his last mission had left the senior MI6 operations officer in doubt as to whether he'd made the right choice. "Are you sure?"

"Beirut wasn't his fault, Stewart. You know that. It could have happened to anybody."

"Yeah, but shit sticks. He got away, the asset was killed, as was another agent." He shrugged. "I don't think he's ready."

"He made it out of a hostile situation, pursued through the streets by fifty or more terrorists with a bloodlust. I think that shows he's got the tools for the job."

"But that thing with the rogue IRA cell. The safecracker fled from France with the money. King couldn't find him, turned up blanks for months afterwards."

Armstrong nodded. "Unfortunate, but he rooted out Ian Forsyth as a man of questionable morals and his plans to *lose* the money."

"Forsyth tried to kill King, but he failed. King was lucky." Stewart paused. "The guy was a light-heavyweight boxer, and he underwent tactical training with the SAS and our facility at *The Farm* in Norfolk. Ian Forsyth was a liaison officer, a handler. If King couldn't kill Forsyth in an out and out brawl, then he should never have been in the job."

"Yes, but Forsyth was armed and had already killed two IRA terrorists and that career criminal that was dealing with

them, and King killed Forsyth with his bare hands."
Armstrong paused. "What's the problem, Peter? You went
out of your way to recruit him, spring him from prison and
wipe the slate clean. New identities are expensive, as is three
years of elite training."

"You can be wrong about some people. King's a brawler,
nothing more."

"He scored a one-seventy-two IQ. More than any of us
sitting around this table. Possibly more than anyone else in
this building. Maybe even in this postcode. The man could
put people on Mars or cure cancer in another life..." He
shook his head. "No, give the man another chance. That's an
order." Stewart nodded. There was no point arguing his
point with a man like Armstrong, but there were other ways
to deal with the likes of King. Accidents happen. During
battle, bullets went astray. A fragmentation grenade had
solved problems for many a company of soldiers over the
years. An overzealous officer out for medals and glory at the
expense of his men often got 'fragged' on the battlefield. He
would give King a chance, but he wouldn't allow a third
mistake to go unpunished. Stewart reached for the
doorhandle and Armstrong added, "Oh, and Peter... It's
vitally important to retrieve the hostages, but not as important as keeping Britain's future oil plans for Angola and the
Congo quiet. Do you understand?"

Stewart hesitated but did not look back at the MI6
mandarin. He understood. The hostages' lives were para-
mount. Right up until they were no longer viable, and then
dead was better than them becoming a pawn that could
change the game on the chessboard. "Loud and clear,
Michael. Loud and fucking clear..."

2

L ambeth, South London

LEANNE JEFFRIES WAS IN DEEP. She knew there was no way out, but peer pressure and street survival had made her do it. Now they wanted more. She had seen how it went for girls like her. She'd been put into care after her mother had overdosed. She hadn't meant to do it, of course, but that was drug addiction for you, and nobody meant to do the things they did when they were high. For her mother, she supposed she took a hit to make life easier, make the act of going down on a man in the front seats of a car for twenty or thirty pounds a little more tolerable. Sometimes she had taken men back to their council flat and done so much more. They had usually eaten well for a few days after that, but sooner or later the money would end up snorted up her mother's nose or flushed through her veins and then she would be out for longer, occasionally spending the nights in a police cell or in hospital. She worked through the bruises. Some men would not be bothered about such things. Others insisted she drop the price.

She had three brothers and a sister when she had been taken into care. Her youngest brother was mixed race, and had been adopted by a black family, the thinking being that he would be more culturally nurtured, despite never knowing his father and being brought up within a white family. Her sister and younger brother had found a temporary placement with a nice foster couple in Devon and had integrated well. Her older brother Mark had been in and out of trouble. He had put more meals on their table from the age of fourteen than their mother had managed to do, and he had looked after them in other ways, too. He had his own demons, skirted the law, and found himself in and out of young offenders, then prison. He fought in a few boxing matches and prize fights but left when two organised crime gangs took a financial hit when he had refused to take a dive in an early round. She had heard that he died while trying to escape from Dartmoor Prison. Drowned in one of the many hidden bogs on the moor. That had made her sad, he always seemed like he could have gone further and done more with his life, but their mother's failings had shaped them all. Mark had tried to earn money, but without qualifications and direction, he had fallen foul to the law. And now, alone in the world, Leanne Jeffries lived back on the same streets that had taken her mother and with the company she was now keeping, she could foresee her mirroring her mother's life. The apple never falls far from the tree. But she had kicked the habit, only for how long, she did not know. It was only a matter of time before she took a hit again, became addicted once more. That was the price of the company she kept. The world around her.

He was watching from the edge of one of the tower blocks. The buildings were brutal in design, nothing but greyness and depressing concrete. There were plans in place to fit blue and green cladding to the outside of the tower blocks in the whole of South London, and it would no doubt offer a little respite to the harshness in design. It would be a start, but until the council stopped piling people into tower blocks, the area would still have its problems. It hadn't changed since he had lived here all those years ago, and until they were torn down, he doubted it ever would.

He heard the Vauxhall Astra before he saw it. He knew little about wattage and amps and sub-woofers, but he knew that the vehicle had a lot of them and even with the windows wound up, the music was loud on another level. The exhaust had been swapped over to a sports model which competed with the music decibels, but probably did little to enhance performance. The windows were tinted on the illegal side of dark and the bright orange paintwork was gleaming with iridescence. Black marijuana leaf decals had been stuck to the rear quarters of the vehicle. The windows rolled down beside the girl and the decibels increased dramatically. He knew the girl to be eighteen, and that had been her ticket out of foster care and back to her old life. She headed over and bent down, the volume of the rap music booming out of the vehicle was lowered while the discussion took place. As she straightened up and tucked the thick envelope inside her shoulder bag, the Astra sped off with front wheel-spin and a rasp of exhaust note which competed for decibels as it was cranked up.

Not subtle.

For a drug dealer and his crew, the car was on the notice-able side. But that was what boys like this did. They oper-ated with invincibility, right up until they went down for a ten-year stretch. They owned the streets for a while but were quickly replaced with equally unsubtle and stupid young men. But there were plenty of drugs and plenty of idiots willing to move them, like the youths in the car, and the girl on the street.

"The deal was you walk away..."

King turned, startled by the silent arrival of Peter Stewart. "How did you know you'd find me here?" he asked, watching his sister enter the tower block. When she disappeared inside, he turned around and looked at him.

"You're on thin ice, son."

King sighed. "She's in trouble. She was in foster care, but she's old enough to leave now."

"Shit happens."

"She's going to go down the same road as our mum."

"Her choice. There's always another road to go down."

King shrugged. "I can't leave it like this."

"You're not Mark Jeffries anymore. That guy is dead." Stewart paused. "That guy was a bum. A petty criminal who bit off more than he could chew and paid the price. But Alex King has the chance for a new life. One that has whitewashed over his past and has given him a worthwhile future. You're in your mid-twenties. You've had a second chance and have got plenty of miles left on the clock." He swept a hand towards the tower block opposite them. "That's your past. Not even *your* past. Some loser called Mark Jeffries. And you're taking a stupid fucking risk being here. You've only been gone three years, you could be recognised!" King subconsciously pulled up the hoodie top he was wearing under his leather jacket. "I'm glad all that training hasn't gone to waste," Stewart scoffed.

"What are you doing here?"

Stewart smiled and lifted the flap of his jacket to reveal a pistol tucked into his waistband. "The world can't see you again, King." His smile waned and his eyes seemed to penetrate him. "I won't tell you again. This isn't your life anymore. Step away from it, and any thoughts you have about seeing your sister and do what you have been recruited and trained to do. Starting right now."

King stared at the butt of the pistol poking out of his waistband, and then back at the man's cold, unwavering eyes. The man had seen death and its spectre lived on in his eyes. King hoped his own eyes would never look as cold and grey and threatening. But he knew what he had gotten into and guessed it was just a matter of time. "Okay, I'm listening..."

"We've got a job on. Go home and pack. Hot climate, travel light."

"Just a Speedo then..."

"Think jungle and scrubland. Like the Serengeti."

King nodded. He had seen the news. "Where and when?"

"Three hours, Terminal three, Heathrow. We'll do the briefing out there."

"And where is *there*, exactly?"

"Angola."

3

Luanda, Angola

"THE CEASEFIRE HAS BEEN in place for three months now," said Stewart. "Jonas Savimbi, the leader of UNITA, or the National Union for the Total Independence of Angola... that's a fucking mouthful... got himself killed on the battlefield against pro-Portuguese colonialists. There's talk of democratic elections taking place, but frankly these people have been fighting for twenty-seven years so that will remain to be seen."

"Portuguese?" King asked, still looking out of the window of the taxi as the delights of Luanda swept past. By delights, there were plenty of dead dogs in the gutter and children begging for food on the street, but the UK had brokered major oil deals – with both sides of the warring factions, naturally – so it couldn't have been that bad a place. "What has Portugal got to do with it?"

"Fuck me, read a book once in a while, King." Stewart paused. "Angola was a Portuguese colony. They rocked up in Africa in the mid fourteen-hundreds, expanded the slave trade between here and Brazil – another Portuguese colony - in the late fourteen-hundreds and hung onto it until the nineteen-seventies. Five-hundred years. Since then, pro-Portuguese and Angolan independents have fought over the place. Fuck knows why because it's a proper shithole..." Peter Stewart dug into his bag and retrieved a thick, worn paperback. King could see the pages had been dog-eared and some had even come loose. "Start by reading these. We must work on your further education. Once you fall in love with reading, you'll never stop, and every book you read afterwards is another lesson that may well help you later in life. Read *anything* and you learn *something*." King flicked through the book. It was a collection of Dickens novels. He frowned and for a moment it looked as if he was about to lob it out of the window. Stewart smiled. "Give it a chance. I guarantee you'll get into the stories, and you will unwind when you have some downtime. Better than television any rate."

King did not seem convinced, but he had furthered himself considerably since his recruitment, and had found something of a father figure in the tough Scotsman, although the sentiment hadn't been reciprocated. "Thanks," he said, placing the book in his own leather carry-on. He remembered his own Christmases being like the poor family in *A Christmas Carol*, if only for the poverty and without the love. Perhaps he'd give the book a go. He hadn't read any since school, and he'd left at fifteen.

The taxi slowed and pulled into a quiet side street where two women were talking animatedly, and children played nearby in the gutter. They were poking an injured cat with sticks and laughing as the cat swiped at the tips of the sticks with its good front paw. Stewart frowned and the taxi driver slowed and parked at the kerb. He flashed a look at King in the mirror, who checked behind them, then looked back at his mentor.

"There's a pickup truck with several men in it driving up to us," said King.

"How many?"

"Four in the back, two up front."

"What the fuck's going on?" Stewart rasped at the driver.

"Local tax. You pay. Everything OK as long as you give money..."

"Shit!" Stewart cursed loudly. The taxi driver made to reach for the glovebox, but Stewart reached forward grabbed him by his shoulders and snatched him back in his seat, he caught hold of the seatbelt, reeled it out its full length and wound it several times around the man's neck and pulled tightly. "Check the fucking glovebox! Now!"

King thrust himself between the front seats and pulled the glovebox open. He grabbed the battered and worn CZ-75 9mm pistol and checked the breech and magazine. The first of their would-be robbers was standing at the window, a revolver in his hands. King did not have time to aim as he fell back into his seat and double tapped the man, centre mass, through the glass. The window shattered and the man went down onto his knees, clutching his gut. His head was momentarily at the same level as the pistol when King fired a third shot and the man's head popped into a pink mist. Stewart was putting his back into it, having pressed his foot into the back of the driver's seat. He pulled with all his might, the driver gargling and grunting like a truffling pig. Contrary to Hollywood's best efforts in portrayal, the man's neck did not 'crack' as it broke, but a squishy, wet noise reminiscent of scrapping large chunks off the inside of a pumpkin, was clearly audible as the throat was ruptured and the vertebrae popped out and severed the spinal cord. King was already moving, and he kicked the door wide open and rolled out into a crouch. He snatched up the .38 Smith & Wesson the dead man had been holding and tossed it into Stewart's lap. The Scotsman didn't have time to check the cylinder and he spun around in his seat and aimed out through the rear windscreen at the nearest of the other men. He fired and the man bent double. Stewart used the muzzle of the revolver to knock out the glass, but King had already dropped the wounded man with a double tap. He was up and moving, crouching briefly at the rear quarter of the Toyota Corolla taxi as he fired upon the driver of the pickup, then he bolted out and covered the twenty feet in three easy paces, taking down the passenger in the front seat and the driver in a volley of six shots. The fifth man was working the cocking lever on an AK-47. He should have made the weapon ready before they made their move, but King shot him square in the forehead and he dropped the rifle and sprawled in the rear bed of the pickup. A sixth man was sprinting down the road. King aimed but couldn't see a weapon in the man's hands and lowered the pistol. He wasn't going to shoot an unarmed, fleeing man in the back. He watched the man as he ran, but visibly flinched as the gunshot rang out just inches from his left ear. The man sprawled and skidded onto his knees in the dusty road. King looked to his left, then watched as Stewart walked around the pickup and calmly strolled over to the man he had just shot. The man had started to crawl in the dirt. Instinct kicking in and fighting for survival. He did not see the stocky Scotsman walk up to him, but he kept crawling, smearing the blood trail with his stomach from the through and through shot to the centre of his back. Stewart shot the man in the back of his head and turned around and stared at King.

King checked the pistol, more for the distraction from Stewart's glare than to check how many rounds he had remaining.

"When you let a man go..." Stewart said coldly as he joined King at the front of the pickup. "... you'd better be certain he doesn't live on to kill you and yours..."

King nodded. Across the street the two women, both with babies strapped to their backs with ingeniously folded blankets, watched them silently, then continued to talk as though nothing out of the ordinary had happened. The children still played with their sticks, poking at the injured cat on the side of the road. One of the women shouted at them and they ran away laughing, the cat seeing its chance and limping off into the bushes.

"They just don't care..." said King quietly.

"That's life out here, son. They've had war in one form or another for twenty-seven years. Now, get that piece-of-shit driver out of the seat and get us to the hotel. The sooner we're out of here, the better."

4

For a country that had been war-torn for such a long time, the hotel kept an impressively well stocked pool bar and the pool itself was both clean and clear, and two women were doing gentle lengths as they talked, sunglasses pulled up on top of their heads and doing what King would have called 'old lady stroke', or breast-stroke. Two men wearing dark *Ray-Bans* drank beer in tall glasses and frequently watched the two women as they talked. There were empty chairs with towels laid on them at their table and King guessed the two women were spoken for. One of the women glanced up at him and he raised his glass of beer an inch higher and smiled. He was a free agent and didn't give a damn about other people's perceptions of conventions. It was their problem to work through. If the woman was with one of those men, then it was up to her to say that she wasn't interested in him, and he certainly wouldn't listen to the man's take on it. The woman with glossy brunette hair glanced up at him again and smiled, her red-headed friend still in full flow about a long-running dispute between her and her husband. King smiled and looked up at the two men. One of them put down his beer and got up from the table. King sat back in his chair and waited for the inevitable, but it never came. The man was heading for the lavatories beside the bar. He looked back at the brunette, who was now climbing the steps and smoothing back her wet hair. The sunglasses were down, and she was heading towards King.

"Buy you a drink?" King said amiably as she neared his table.

"What?"

"I'd like to buy you a drink."

"Why would you want to do that?"

"I'm a humanitarian and you look thirsty," he replied. "It's important to remain hydrated in this climate. I feel it's my duty to get you a drink."

She smiled. "From your lack of suntan, I'd suggest you were new to the delights of Africa." She paused, placing her hands on her hips. The straps on her tiny bikini bottoms were riding below her hip bones. "Clearly you have a lack of sunscreen going on from the way you're slowly turning into a boiled lobster. Perhaps I should be worried about *you*?" She pointed to his two empty glasses and said, "But at least you're working on that hydrating thing. I'm Lucinda."

"Alex," King said, the name never quite sounding right to him somehow.

"Are you here for the hostages?"

"What?" King frowned, glad that his sunglasses would have hidden his terrible poker face.

She shrugged. "I'm a freelance journalist." She nodded towards the two men. "That's Roger Siegfried with The Times. He's the one coming back from the loos. Probably snorted a line of coke while he was in there. Genius writers and artists always needs a muse, and Roger's personal favourite is cocaine. Byron had his women; Hemingway had his booze, fishing and guns, and Wilde had his own self-loathing and young men," she smiled. "But that's writers. An odd bunch. Rebecca, here..." She nodded towards the woman in the pool who had now placed her sunglasses on the pool edge and had graduated from 'old lady stroke' to a fearsomely professional front crawl, or freestyle. "... she's with The Telegraph. That's her photographer sitting with Roger Siegfried. I think he wants to jump ship to be honest. He'd do anything to work with someone like Siegfried."

"So, you and Siegfried take you own photos?"

"I do. I write and photograph, but I'm just a lowly free-lancer working my way up. I suppose I'm lucky to have been accepted in that company. Although it may have something to do with Roger Siegfried wanting to sleep with me," she smiled, cocking her head at a suggestive angle. "Siegfried's photographer is sleeping off the mother of all hangovers. He's a genius too, but he only functions when he's completely drunk. Again, his muse. Couldn't photograph the tower of Pisa and get the angle to show when he's sober..."

King laughed. "So, are there many stories to be found beside a hotel pool?"

"*You* tell me. What's your story?"

He hadn't worked on a cover story. Stewart was meeting a fixer and they were still waiting for some 'approved' mercenaries to make their way up from South Africa. King had ditched the taxi, but he needn't have worried, the police were difficult to find and easily bribed in the city.

"I'm in security," he replied. "There are some OPEC execs coming in to try and bring a quick resolution to the hostage situation and they are going to need looking after."

"And you look after people?"

"When they let me." A waiter drew near, and King waved him over. He ordered another beer and nodded for her to order.

"A white wine spritzer, please. No ice." She paused as the waiter went away, pausing to clear some glasses at the correspondents' table. "Here's a little tip, don't have ice in your drink. You can't drink the water, either. Guaranteed case of dysentery if you do."

"I'll be sure not to." King nodded, but he knew that the water would be getting a damned sight dirtier where he was going. "How long have you been here?" he asked. "Given that wonderful all-over tan of yours."

"You noticed?"

"Hard not to, what with that bikini of yours. Tell me, do Colgate make swimming costumes out of dental floss now?"

Lucinda smiled. "I've been having some downtime for the past two days. Hence the tan. Before that, I was digging into accounts of war crimes in the Congo. Most of us have been, but since the Southside Boys snatched those oil execs, I suppose the press have been congregating on Luanda and working out where to go next. This hotel is one of just a few that are considered safe in the city."

King nodded. There had been two armed guards outside the foyer, but other than that it appeared to be wide open. "So, there will be more members of the press coming?"

She nodded. "Undoubtedly." The waiter arrived and she smiled as her wine and soda was placed in front of her. The barman had topped it with ice and lemon and there was a glace cherry in it, skewered on a cocktail stick. King guessed not many people visiting Luanda drank white wine spritzers. King drained his beer and placed it on the tray as the waiter put down a fresh one. It was cold and didn't have a cherry in it. Lucinda picked up her glass, scooped out the ice and tutted as she tossed the ice into a nearby flower bed. "They can't get a bloody thing right. Just wait until dinner... Anyway, it's been tempting to head up to where the hostages were taken, but it needs a bit of planning. I suppose I was waiting to see what the old hands did next, and then tag along. What are we drinking to?"

"To thirst," King smiled.

"Well, that's as good a thing to drink to as any." She raised her glass and they clinked them together. "Are you here alone?" she asked after taking a sip.

"Travelling with a colleague."

She nodded and leaned comfortably back in the chair. King eyed her under his dark glasses. She had a good figure without looking like she worked out. He imagined she ate on the go, got her exercise by being busy and lived out of a suitcase. Her bikini wouldn't have taken up much room at any rate. He smiled to himself, the thought that he was meeting a different class of woman on his travels. Luanda wasn't paradise, but at least it was warm, and the skies were clear, and he could meet attractive women in skimpy bikinis on pool terraces while sipping a cold beer. It was certainly better than his native Lambeth, Brixton, and Peckham where he had spent his formative years.

"I'm planning on heading up to Cafunfo tomorrow. Or trying to organise something," she said. "You'll probably be heading there soon."

"What's at Cafunfo?"

"Nothing. But it's where the OPEC delegation were taken before they were abducted."

"I thought that was Hu?"

"Well, Hu is near Cafunfo and from what I can gather, Hu has little more than mud huts and chickens pecking about in the road. Anyway, it's near the Farcasi oil deposits."

She frowned. "It's a good place to start for a story. I'm just waiting on my ticket. Roger Siegfried made the call."

"Ticket?"

"For the airplane. There's an airport there. Well, I say airport... but it's just a little dirt landing strip. They probably have to herd cows and goats off it before a plane can land."

"And you need a ticket for that?"

"Not really, but somebody needs to get paid to find a pilot that needs paying. Then, we must wait for the pilot to get here, then wait for a bloody R in the day just to be sure, and no doubt end up paying some more money. TIA."

"TIA?"

"My god, you really are an Africa rookie, aren't you?" she laughed. "TIA. This Is Africa... It's what you say when things that would normally happen anywhere else on the planet, don't. Or when something wholly unacceptable on every other continent, is just the norm."

"TIA..." King mused. "I like it. Anyway, why do you think I'll be going to Cafunfo soon?"

Lucinda smiled, took another sip of her drink, and lifted her sunglasses. Her eyes were soft and brown and warm and the whites were the brightest King had ever seen, and they glinted with a sparkle of something King couldn't quite put his finger on. Intelligence, perhaps. Or alertness. "Because your story is BS," she said quietly. "You're not in close protection, so you're not here to look after some OPEC executives, or whatever the hell your cover story is..."

"I'm not?" King asked warily, regretting even asking her to join him. His eyes drifted down to her firm breasts, only just restrained by the loosely woven fabric of the wet bikini. Maybe he didn't regret it too much. "Why do you think that?"

"I read people, Alex," she said matter-of-factly. "I've seen plenty of bodyguards. You're too young, for a start. Most are in their thirties to fifties, having had at least ten years in the military or police force. Usually military, because of the work they get on the African continent. You're what, twenty-three, twenty-five?" She paused. "I'm thirty, so I know a younger man when I see one up close..."

King raised his glass. "Now, there's a thought..."

"Stop it!" she chided, but she was smiling, nonetheless. "Anyway, fit and strapping as those bodyguards usually are, they also spend hours and hours a day standing around waiting, and hours and hours a day sat on their backsides in vehicles, on planes or in hotel rooms. They don't look like you."

"Me?" King asked, now thoroughly confused. As part of his role within MI6 he had provided security to defectors and visiting dignitaries alike.

"You're a killer, Alex. Yes, you're all very amiable and I must say, delightful and encouraging company after spending the day with Roger Siegfried..." She smiled, pulling a face which made King laugh. "But you're all bone and muscle and sinew and I'd have you down as a special forces soldier in his prime..." She paused, sudden enlightenment spreading across her pretty face. "... that, or an intelligence agent."

"I..."

"What the fuck is this, happy hour?" Stewart strode up to the table and said, "My room Alex, now." He glanced at Lucinda and said, "Drink up lovely and shake your pretty little arse back to those old hacks. I need him for some business. You'll have to get your gutter press story someplace else..." He tossed one of the hotel's pool towels at her, covering her breasts and knocking the sunglasses off the top of her head and skewwhiff across her face. "Here, cover your tits up luv, you'll catch your death of cold in that thing…"

He half pulled King out of his chair, but King snatched his arm away and said, "All right, boss. I'll be up in a minute." His tone was low and gruff and when Stewart pulled at him again, he gave the angry Scotsman a shove and said, "I'll be with you in a minute…" Stewart glared at him, then nodded and walked back to the entrance to the foyer.

"Nice man," Lucinda commented as she straightened up her sunglasses, tossed the towel onto the ground and finished her drink.

"My boss," explained King.

"Now, he looks *nothing* like a bodyguard. More like a regimental sergeant major," she laughed. "I should know, my father was one. And that man has Parachute Regiment written all over him…"

King finished his beer. He knew Peter Stewart had served in the paras before working for MI6, but he said nothing and merely smiled down at her. "Well, it was nice chatting to you…"

"Take me with you," she said hurriedly. "Let me be there to photograph the release of the hostages…"

"I'm not connected to that," King said quickly. "I'm here to protect OPEC executives when they arrive."

"And I still call bullshit. You're either with the SAS or you're here in another capacity, but I can see that you're more than a bullet catcher. You're a special forces solider or an intelligence agent. I've been in the game long enough to recognise the type. And that rude Scottish gentleman is either your commanding officer or he's a case handler… something to do with a hostage rescue and certainly the man in charge on the ground."

King looked at Stewart who was standing impatiently in the shade of a canopy, his eyes firmly on the two of them. "Look, it's better you don't ask anything more, and certainly better you don't say anything to that grumpy git over there." He paused. "I've got to be going. It was nice to chat." He turned and headed towards the hotel, pulling on his T-shirt as he walked.

"You should know better than to talk to members of the press," Stewart growled.

"I didn't know who she was," King replied.

Stewart nodded towards the two men and the woman with red hair at the other end of the pool. The woman was drying her hair with a towel and Lucinda was joining them. "That ginger bitch drying her hair works for The Telegraph and the wanker with the coke twitch is Roger Siegfried who writes for The Times." Stewart shook his head. "Never mind that fucking book I lent you, you should start by reading the fucking papers..." He scoffed. "What did you tell her?"

"I said I was security waiting for some OPEC execs to come here."

Stewart's expression softened. "Okay, that's actually pretty good," he conceded. "Did she buy it?"

"Yes," King lied.

Stewart nodded then turned and headed inside. "Okay, well if you fuck her tonight, don't let the cover story slip."

King flushed a little as he followed and said, "I don't think that's on the cards..."

"You'd be surprised at those journalist chicks," he said. "They court danger and ride on a giant ego. A good scoop, some decent writing and an exclusive front page and she'd ride you like you'd entered the Grand National. They're all the same. especially the TV lot if there's a humanitarian story or something with war crimes, they need to feel loved after a report like that..."

King didn't know if the man was joking, but he doubted it. He thought about Lucinda and her micro bikini and the fact she'd been covering the situation in the Congo. He presumed she had meant the Democratic Republic of the Congo. Zimbabwe and Uganda had just started to pull their troops out and there were reports of war crimes on all sides. Rape was a common weapon in the African nations. Multiple men would rape women for days on end until they couldn't walk, couldn't control their bladders, and often bled to death – it was a reprehensible method of eradicating ethnicities and was so much more than making women pregnant and destroying ethnic bloodlines. It was about total dominance. King thought that was just the type of story Lucinda would be interested in writing but couldn't see her endearing herself to men and having an affair just to further her career anytime soon. She was well-researched about the hostages, the Southside Boys and had King down as a potential rescuer. King felt naïve. Maybe she had merely sat and had a drink with him for a lead to a story. He caught sight of himself in a wall of mirrors as they headed off the foyer and into the corridor leading to the stairs. A shade under six feet tall and around fourteen stone of muscle, but his eyes were cold, and his mouth looked a little cruel, and he had a pugilist's brow and a face that had taken a few punches in its time. He supposed he could have looked ruggedly handsome to the opposite sex, but he wasn't so sure.

"Where are we going?" King asked as they reached the stairs.

"You go and get changed and meet me in my room in

twenty minutes," said Stewart. "We're moving tomorrow, so don't get too comfortable."

"Where are we going?"

"Some piece of shit, fly-bitten speck on the map in the middle of this godforsaken country. A place called Cafunfo."

5

Stewart wasn't big on introductions and the men in this game weren't usually a talkative bunch. Ego had its part to play in that respect. That and the fact that mercenaries could easily incriminate themselves for what could easily be considered as previous indiscretions if they said too much. When those 'indiscretions' could often be classed by governments as war crimes, they tended to say even less. Dates and times and locations could cost them their freedom, and occasionally their lives. And, as many mercenaries worked for opposite sides to the same conflict, it could also trigger retribution.

King entered and saw that there was nowhere to sit. He didn't feel right sitting on Stewart's bed, so he perched on the table and nodded to those who glanced his way.

"Tom is on weapons," said Stewart. He looked at a tall, lanky figure with closely cropped greying hair and dark, sunken eye sockets. "What have we got, Tom?"

The man's accent was laced with such a thick and guttural Afrikaans accent, King struggled to understand a word he said. "My contact will get most things, just let me know what you want. I know he's got Uzi submachineguns, Heckler and Koch MP5s. The jungle is thick up there, so range isn't an issue and nine-millimetre will get the job done well enough. He's also got Browning, Sig, Glock, and a few Colt pistols. But I recommend staying with nine millimetres so you can interchange ammo if we have to."

"What about all the khat and crap they smoke and chew on?" asked a short, stocky man with an Australian accent. "They may need a bit more firepower, mate."

Tom shrugged. "You'll have to Mozambique them."

"Mozambique?" King asked.

"Eh, we got a rookie here, eh?" another South African smirked. He stood up and shook King's hand. "The name's Piers..."

"Alex." King shook his hand firmly.

"When you Mozambique someone, you fire two shots to the chest and one into the head. Most likely, you'll get two somewhere in the centre and the third in the throat or face, but hey, it gets the job done..." Piers paused. "The term was first coined when Rhodesian mercenary Mike Rousseau first did it in the Mozambican War of Independence. Rousseau rounded a corner and encountered an enemy combatant, armed with an AK-47 assault rifle, at ten paces. Rousseau brought up his Browning pistol and fired two bullets into the guy's upper chest. Hell, that's usually enough to kill a kaffir outright, eh? Even if he is off his head on go-go weed. Anyway, Rousseau sees that it isn't enough and attempted a head shot that hit the guy through the base of his neck, severing the spinal cord. Rousseau tells the story to an acquaintance who happens to be small arms expert Jeff Cooper who ran a shooting academy. He then incorporated the *Mozambique Drill* into his modern technique shooting method." He paused. "All his students learned how to Mozambique a hostile, just in case. I'm surprised you haven't heard of it, what with your line of work."

King shrugged and sipped on the bottle of water he had brought with him. He had accepted that he had agreed to kill for his country, but it didn't sit right with him talking about it. This afternoon, he had killed, but those men had been about to rob them and robberies in southern and western Africa tended to mean murder or abduction, and negotiations only ever went one way out here.

"We don't teach it," said Stewart. "It's bullshit anyway. Most times that third shot, aimed at a far smaller target, will be moving as your enemy is falling, advancing, or fleeing. You can't teach a drill for such a variable scenario." He looked at King and said, "Just do as you've been taught and fire until they stop moving, lad."

King felt his neck bristle and cheeks starting to flush. He was feeling like the underdog, but he'd wager his training had been at the hands of more professional soldiers and agents than these mercenaries had ever experienced. These men undoubtedly had a higher number of kills, but they were also the type of men who had faced off against untrained natives who had been equipped with old and outdated scavenged equipment. How difficult could that be? King sipped the water more for a distraction than to slake his thirst. He looked at the fourth man, a quiet individual who looked more smartly turned out than the other two. "So, who are you?"

"Just call me Reece," the man replied in a neutral English accent.

King shrugged, deciding not to press it. He looked back at the Australian and said, "I didn't catch your name either."

"Didn't fucking throw it, mate."

"Well, we'll be working together, so a name would be good."

"Make it Bruce, then." He smirked and turned to Tom, apparently uninterested in King. "What have you got for support?"

"A GPMG and an Accuracy International Rifle in seven-point-six-two. Again, interchangeable with the GPMG's ammunition if we need it."

"I'll take the rifle," the Australian told him. "Let the young fella lug the heavy machine gun." King stared at him, his heartrate increasing and his fists momentarily clench-ing. He took a deep breath to stop himself from striding across the room and punching him there and then. "Hah! Just fucking with you, kid! Hey boys, we've got to watch this one, looks like he wants to knock my bloody block off!" He stood up slowly, hands on his hips and his chin stuck out belligerently. "Anytime you fancy a go, me old cobbler..."

"Fucking well sit down," Stewart said quietly. "You too, King." He looked at the Australian and said, "Age may well give you experience, Jim. But I'll wager my lad will knock your bloody block off alright. So, leave it right there and let's get on with the briefing, we've got a job to do, and you fellas are only getting twenty percent upfront..."

"Hey, just kidding, mate," the Australian replied, but there was a flicker in the man's eyes that told a different story.

King had already made a note that he wouldn't make the mistake of trusting this man, but he said anyway, "So, what is it? Bruce or Jim?" He paused. "I may need you out there. Shit, you may need me, too."

The man shrugged. "It's Jim. And if I need you, it will probably be to hold my dick while I take a piss..." He grinned. "The doctor said I shouldn't lift heavy weights..."

There were jeers all round, but King couldn't help thinking the man was merely trying to save face, having lost it so quickly thanks to Stewart. He let the man have his moment and sipped calmly from his bottle of water. "Those jeans are pretty tight from where I'm sitting, *mate*. Are you sure you haven't got a fanny in there instead?"

The jeers were louder this time and Piers whistled loudly, slow clapping and watching the Australian.

"Right, that's enough," said Stewart.

"So, what does everybody want?"

"A Glock and an H and K MP5," said Reece. "A Glock seventeen if possible. The nineteen is too short to maintain an adequate velocity for khat-chewing crackheads."

Tom noted it down and looked at Piers and Jim. "Fellas?"

"Browning and an Uzi," said Jim. "Spray and pray! And make sure I've got plenty of mags for each. See if there are any of the twenty-round magazines for the Browning."

"Yeah, me too. The more magazines, the better, that is. But I'll take a Sig Sauer pistol and an H and K, fixed stock, if possible. The retractable is okay for storming a building, but it makes too much noise in the bush," Piers said. "Anyway, anything but an Uzi because I don't want an open breech with all the debris getting in. Closed bolt only for me."

"The Uzi has worked well for the Israelis. Nothing but sand and dust up there. It makes them easy to clean, too," Tom commented as he noted down his fellow countryman's choice. He looked at Stewart and said, "Boss?"

Stewart shrugged. "Anything," he said with notable disinterest.

"Come on, bro, I've got the good stuff!" He grinned. "My contact tells me they're practically brand new!"

"And I said, anything," Stewart replied somewhat tersely. "Weapons are tools, and I'll use whatever you get for me, but I've not got a hard-on for makes, models and accessories."

The South African looked as if the wind had been knocked out of his sails. He didn't make a note on his list and turned to King indignantly.

King shrugged and said, "A Browning, but just the one mag. I'll take either make of submachinegun. Four magazines will do."

"You not fixing on getting into a fight, mate," Jim asked, his Australian twang an octave higher than the rest of them. More so when he asked a question. "Or are you worried about carrying the GPMG?"

"No, I can handle the Gimpy," King paused. "But if we have a contact up close, there'll be weapons on the ground soon enough and we don't yet know how far we'll have to tab through the bush. Also, I did a little checking up on the area and deforestation has been huge these last few years, so there are vast areas of plains, and the jungle has been thinned in places, so if I can get my hands on an assault rifle, I'll be happier than I would be with a machine pistol."

"Get a load of National Geographic, here," Jim scoffed loudly.

Tom nodded. "I was up there a few years back and the place was like Gabon. And they call that place the lungs of the fucking earth. Hundreds of miles of nothing but stinking jungle." He shrugged like it didn't matter and that they'd wasted enough time talking about something he knew more than King about. "And you just want one mag for the Browning?" he asked dubiously.

King nodded, with as much disinterest as Stewart had mustered. "If I get to the point where I need a pistol up against this lot, I'll be well and truly in the shit by then anyway..."

"Piers, put the map up and let's get on with this, shall we?" Stewart said tersely.

Piers nodded and unfolded a map and started to secure it to the wall with *Blu-Tack*. Stewart handed out envelopes and the men each took one. King watched the men open them, so followed suit. He could tell that the other men were used to the way things were being done. King upended the envelope and a series of papers slipped out, along with a sheet of portrait shots of the hostages with their names printed underneath, and a copy of the map that was now secured to the wall. There was also a sheet of photographs of varying angles, distance, and quality of only black faces.

"Those men are to be considered high value targets. If we see any of those faces, we should treat them with extreme prejudice." Stewart paused. "They'll only try something again, and by identifying them and taking them out, we're looking after our future interests."

"Speak for yourself, bro," said Piers. "South Africa hasn't had so much as a look in with the Angolan's, what with you lot and the seppos vying for the oil business."

"Seppos?" asked King incredulously.

"Yeah, septic tanks, Yanks," replied Piers.

Tom held up his list of known Southside Boys. "Good luck identifying them, eh bro?" he spurted in his guttural Afrikaans accent. "They all look the fucking same..."

King frowned and studied the sheet. He'd grown up on estates where he was one of a hundred ethnicities. He could already differentiate the squashed and broad noses from the more aquiline and there were varying hairlines, scars, bright eyes, and yellowed eyes from malaria. Gold teeth, missing teeth, oversized teeth as white and straight as piano keys. Every face was different from the other and he already knew he could recognise the first three men, ordered in rank of importance, in a crowd anywhere. King took out a small digital camera and took a picture of the sheet. The camera had a small display screen and could be manipulated with four arrow buttons to view the individual images more closely.

"Don't bother with that, fella," Piers said quietly. "The only good kaffir is a dead kaffir, eh? No sense in being picky, just let your Uzi do the talking."

"My younger brother is mixed-race..." King said coldly. "And I'm here to rescue hostages, not act out my prejudices."

Piers stared at him for a moment, then shrugged. "You need friends in this game, rookie. You've already put a big black mark on your crib sheet with our Australian friend, and I'm guessing Tom, my fellow South African brother in arms, isn't going to warm to you now either."

"Well, it's not a fucking pyjama party," Stewart growled. "We have a job to do, so let's get on with it. One, we travel to Cafunfo. There, we meet a contact who has information on the region where the hostages have been taken and will provide us with a guide. Two, we hike out to the area and attempt a reconnaissance. Three, we regroup, share intel, and put together a plan. Four, we accept that when the first shot is fired, the plan goes to shit, and we take it from there..." He smiled and everybody except King chuckled as they continued to either read the notes or study the photographs. "The CIA have agreed to re-task a satellite for us and hopefully by tomorrow morning we will have some aerial footage of the area. GCHQ will have a sweep later in the day and hopefully our contact in Cafunfo will have a fax machine for them to send it to us." He paused. "I suspect email and a secure connection and use of a computer terminal won't be an option."

"That's a lot of hopefully," said Reece, who until now

had done no more than give his name. King wasn't even sure that had been true. "My experience of the area that is jungle, is that the satellite images won't show us anything. The jungle is so dense in places that planes can fly right over encampments that are hidden by the canopy." He shrugged. "If what King said is true, and there are plenty of savannah and deforested areas there too, then maybe the satellite will get lucky and pick them up moving between jungles."

"We'll see." Stewart nodded. "But note the first man on that list. His name is Julius Lombobo. He's an imposing son-of-a-bitch, so there will be no mistaking him. He gets a bullet. It's as simple as that. If we can find them, that is."

"When we get close to them, we'll smell them," said Piers.

"Smell them?" King asked.

Piers nodded. "These guys will know what I mean. The blacks shit on the ground right there in their own camp, and don't wash from one month to the next."

"Yeah," said Tom. "When you get close to a troop of baboons or jungle dwelling kaffirs, it will all smell the same."

"Except the baboons are better eating, eh?" Piers chipped in and the others laughed. All except Reece and Stewart, who looked at King as if gauging what his reaction would be. "Only joking, my rookie friend..." The South African chuckled, then said, "They all taste about the same, to be fair..."

King said nothing. He was feeling the outsider and couldn't think of a way to fit in, but he wasn't entirely sure he wanted to. He just wanted to get the job done and get the hell out of Africa. Right now, as much as he had loathed it, riding a desk in the basement of the River House since his last assignment was a more agreeable option than this.

"Okay, boss," Reece said. "So, we get to Cafunfo, meet your contact, pick up our guide and go hunting in the woods." He paused. "What's our exfil? We can't yomp through the jungle with a load of civvies in tow. It may be a hard tab, we may be under fire the entire way."

"I'm working on it," said Stewart. "I'm giving you the facts. There are thirteen hostages, and we need to bring them all home. We don't yet know the terrain. If the satellite images don't show the camp, it will at least show clearings where we could arrange for helicopter evacuation."

"We're gunna need two, mate," Jim said quickly. "And they'd have to be big, Hueys at least."

Stewart nodded. "Well, time is of the essence. There are female hostages, and my betting is if they haven't all been raped already, then they soon will be. Hopefully, there will be a sane member of the Southside Boys who appreciates the value of looking after their hostages, but I seriously doubt it. When they took a couple of American missionaries hostage a few months ago, they cut them into pieces, then gave their ransom demands. When they were asked for proof of life it all fell apart for them."

"So, they're stupid," said Jim. "That makes it a whole lot easier."

"No," King replied. "They're reckless and unstable and that makes them about a dozen times more dangerous than stupid."

"Ah! The rookie is suddenly an expert!" Jim sneered. "When you've carved up as many blacks on this continent as I have, then you can give me some of your psychological bullshit. But until then, you're not the bloody expert."

"I'm glad I'm not an expert in what you say you've done."

King shook his head disparagingly. "But I'm smart enough to see past the obvious."

"We'll see," the Australian sneered.

"What about comms?" Reece asked, easing the tension a little.

"Motorola portable radios with ten channels. Channel seven will have limited range but is keyed in as the standard emergency channel, for what good that will do us. We'll use channel three as standard, switch up in odd numbers if the sets are compromised." He paused. "If we hit channel nine, go to ten than back up through in even numbers."

"But we'll all be fucked by then, if that's the case," Tom commented with a wry smile.

Stewart shrugged. "Long before that, I'd imagine." He paused, looking at each of the men in turn. "This is cobbled together because those hostages don't have much time and both the interim, puppet governments of both the Democratic Republic of the Congo and Angola are not willing to grant the UK use of our special forces on their soil as it could be seen as an official collaboration with the United Kingdom after the wars. Who knows, this time next week, and the political landscape will likely have changed. But those poor souls will likely be dead by then. So, we go in silently, strike hard and get out quick. By the time we leave on the plane for Cafunfo, we'll know the lay of the land, and whether using helicopters will be an option. If they are, I have a contact in Namibia who will get the job done for us." He paused. "That's all we can do for now, so head back to your rooms, order what you want on room service or in the dining room, but if you get drunk, then you're out and you can wave goodbye to your bounty. We're dry from now on." The men all got up and made their way to the door as Stewart said, "King, stay behind."

King shrugged, finished his water, and watched as the other men left the room, talking amongst themselves. He saw Reece glance backwards, noted the bulk of something in the small of his back and figured it was a handgun of some description. As they stepped out into the corridor, he noticed Reece seemed to have more situational awareness. The two South Africans were sharing a joke and Jim was doing his best to ruin the punchline for them.

Stewart closed the door and locked it. "What the hell was that?"

"What?" King asked, somewhat bemused.

"The fucking family sob story!" Stewart snapped. "Some dead criminal named Mark Jeffries had a mixed-race brother... Alex King is an only child! You can't slip back to your previous life, King. You're in it now and any mistake you make now can be used against you in the future. One comment about a mixed-race brother because those South Africans are blatantly racist, and now you've tainted your cover." He paused. "People talk, people find anomalies and they do their research."

"Okay..." King replied, irked not only by the admonishment, but by his own carelessness.

"You're off to a bad start. You should have laughed at their jokes, shrugged off their casual racism, because if you step on a bloody landmine, it's one of those men who'll be making the decision whether to patch you up and carry you on their back for days and miles, or just leave you to bleed out on the jungle floor." Stewart paused, looking intently at King. "We use mercenaries when we have to, but they're a different breed. You rent their loyalty, but you never truly buy it."

King nodded. Something told him that even if he caught them up, bought them a beer or two, it still wouldn't make any difference. He sighed. "Okay. Lesson learned." He shrugged, then said, "Reece is different, though. What's his story?"

Stewart nodded. "He's a good man. And, certainly your best bet for working with now that you've burned your bridges with the colonials. You'll have to prove yourself to them, though. Reece was in the army. Light Infantry, Fusiliers. He then passed selection and went into the SAS for ten years, but he screwed something up. He's done his penance and he's a sound bloke."

"What did he screw up?" King asked.

"The details are blurry," Stewart replied tersely. "He was on a mission in Iraq. It was a dangerous situation, and they had the goat herder scenario." King nodded. He'd heard the term before. The goat herder scenario was almost the default excuse for when special forces soldiers made a mistake operating in the Middle East, and their mission was compromised. It started in the Gulf War with Bravo Two Zero, the ill-fated call signal for the patrol who were discovered by a goat herder, a boy looking after his family's wandering goats. It may well have been true in that case, but there had been so many failed missions by allied forces since that had been put down to a chance discovery by a goat herder that there really couldn't be enough goats in the country or any other occupation in the entire region. "They were discovered and because of the proximity of the enemy, all the members of the patrol agreed they should kill the boy. They reasoned he was most likely eighteen and therefore an adult. Reece insisted that they should release the boy and abort the mission. It was debated long enough for Reece to make a sound case and after what was a tense hour or so, they all came around and remembered they were soldiers, not murderers."

King shrugged. "It was the right thing to do."

"Was it?" Stewart sat down in his chair and picked up another file. "The boy told the village elders, the enemy massed in numbers and seven members of the SAS were killed. Reece was the only man to escape. The regiment top brass knew it was the right thing to do, but the friends and families of the dead soldiers never let him forget it and nobody wanted to work with him again, and I gather just shopping in the local Tesco was difficult. Hereford is a small place, after all. He had to leave the regiment. He didn't tell the brass what was going on and said he had survivor's guilt and couldn't do the job anymore."

King stared into the middle distance. When killing was your business, nothing was ever black and white.

Stewart opened the file and handed King a sheet of paper with three photographs printed above a short bio.

King studied them. "We have agents in that delegation?" he asked, not hiding his surprise.

Stewart nodded. "Joanne Egerton, David Willis and Jane Hargreaves. As you can see, Joanne Egerton is one of us. She's an MI6 officer. She specialises in recruiting and handling agents in places where we'd like to know more. David Willis is a Whitehall civil servant. He's worked on projects with both MI5 and MI6 in the past, and he will likely be an intelligence mandarin in either service within a decade or so. He's advising the government on security requirements surrounding the British oil companies."

"I suppose he'll need to rewrite his report now..." King said somewhat mordantly as he read the man's bio. "What about Jane Hargreaves?"

"Yes. That's a strange one," Stewart said, looking at her picture. "She's something else, isn't she?"

King did not reply. He studied the picture and could see

that Stewart had a point. She was twenty-five, had shoulder-length brown hair with naturally blonde highlights, hazel eyes, and a dazzling smile. There was something about her, as if her personality left the page and hit you square in the eyes. King realised that the more he looked at her picture, the more he thought it would be impossible not to like her in person. "Why is she a strange one?"

"The strange thing is that she's out here at all. She's a member of MI5, and their remit is damned clear at present. They gather intelligence on UK shores and our territories and stop terrorism on those same shores. Angola isn't the sort of place they should be, but I gather it was something that David Willis was working on."

"Are they in a relationship?"

"Willis is married, Jane Hargreaves is not thought to be in a relationship. Not beyond dating at least."

"That hardly answers the question. Were they having an affair?"

"Couldn't say, don't know."

King nodded. "You've shown the other men these faces, but only as part of the hostage list. Why are you singling them out to me?"

Stewart opened the desk drawer and pulled out a bottle of Macallan whisky.

"I guess we're not dry, after all…"

"As if," Stewart chortled. "I just don't want those dick-heads getting bladdered and mouthing off all night." He pulled the two empty water glasses towards him and poured a couple of fingers' worth into both glasses, before sliding King's closer to him. King reached for his and took a sip. Stewart was a big drinker, and King had seen the man knock back a Scotch instead of breakfast before. King had never been bothered by drink but had started on a few beers since arriving and was secretly looking forward to a couple more later. He was still picturing the men they had killed in the side street, and he wondered whether he would be drinking as heavily as Stewart in ten or twenty-years' time, or whether he would be able to live with his actions and need no more than a cup of tea. That is, if he survived that long.

"Britain isn't going to be compromised if this goes wrong," Stewart said matter-of-factly. "Our orders are to see that those three people do not divulge what they know. There are still red elements here. The Soviet-Russian and Cuban insurgents lost, but there are spies all over. If the Russians get wind that there are two British intelligence agents being held, along with a Whitehall civil servant, then they will approach the Southside Boys for a trade, and money, or weapons and equipment will be no object."

"So, you mean..." King stood up, placing the Scotch back on the table. "Kill them?"

Stewart nodded. "If we can't get them out, then we can't allow them to talk..."

"Jesus Christ!"

"We don't give the orders or make the rules, son," Stewart replied. "But we *do* follow them."

"So, why tell me and not the other four?"

Stewart shrugged and cracked a mirthless smile. "Because, King, they're mercenaries. And with mercenaries there are two things you never do." He paused, taking another sip of his whisky. "You never give them all the facts."

King nodded. "And what's the second thing?"

"You never trust them completely."

6

Democratic Republic of the Congo

THEY HAD TRAVELLED for three days to get there, and they had lost one of their own along the way. His name had been Brian Hanson and he had been a fifty-year-old OPEC executive studying new seismic drilling practices being carried out by BP. OPEC, or the Organization of the Petroleum Exporting Countries, was an intercountry governmental level organization and had sent its executives to vet the suitability of both the Congo and Angola as member states. Both countries had recently installed new governments and already expressed an interest in joining OPEC to make way for their own drilling, rather than simply take what the likes of Shell and BP would pay them in royalties. Good for the two African countries and OPEC, not so good for the largest oil refineries all floating on the FTSE 100 Index and Dow Jones. But OPEC wouldn't grant membership and trade incentives unless Angola and the DROC could control security, which did not look to be the case.

Jane Hargreaves was determined that she would not be killed or raped by the animals who had called themselves the Southside Boys. She had kept her eyes to the ground and concentrated on living from one minute to the other. Brian Hanson had struggled from the beginning. Overweight, unfit, and struggling with the terrain in flat soled shoes and his torn suit, he had started to fall behind. Each time he did, one of their captors would beat him with the flat of their machete blade. Halfway through the second day, whilst slipping over for the hundredth time, cut to ribbons by thorns and stung by leaves seemingly like nettles, but with stings a hundred times worse, the man who had beaten him black and blue with the flat of his blade on the first day had turned the blade edge towards him and hacked for what seemed like minutes. The hostages had screamed, some had tried to flee but were stopped when bullets were fired at their feet. Huddled together, shivering in terror, they had watched the fifty-year-old man cut to pieces while he screamed. Hands, feet, legs, and arms had separated before his screams had been silenced by several savage chops to his neck. And that had been that. Where a terrified and exhausted man with a wife and two children had once fallen to his knees, a mass of body parts remained, blood dripping from the leaves above them, and the jungle floor a blanket of red. Many of the Southside Boys had huddled around the remains, and Jane had not looked at what they had been doing, but the men and boys had finally shrieked triumphantly as one of them held the whole liver high, skewered on the tip of a machete blade. The man holding the liver placed it on the bloody carcass and sliced pieces off, tossing them to the boy soldiers first, then to the older boys and finally to the rest of the men. They snatched and caught their morsels and ate hungrily. Chewing and laughing, occasionally glaring at the terrified hostages on the ground. One of the Southside Boys had explained, with the eloquence and voice projection of a great orator – blood around his mouth and dripping from his chin - that the liver of their enemies gave them strength and invincibility. By this point, Jane had barely been able to hear, her own pulse thudding in her ears and her heart feeling as if it would simply give out if it beat any faster. Their captors had not tethered their hands – if they thought that the hostages were all too terrified to attempt escaping before Brian had been killed – then they could be certain that nobody would try to escape now. They all needed their hands anyway, all of them had fallen a dozen times or more. And where could they hope to escape to? The jungle was dense and alive with snakes and spiders, the sounds of rock baboons near the clearings and troops of chimpanzees announcing the presence of leopards on the bush telegraph. Jane had no idea what dangerous creatures were out there, but she had heard a roar to remind her that deadly prey roamed the shadows.

The Southside Boys were wiry and fit. They ate little and offered no food or water to their captives. On the second day they had all fallen face first into a small stream and laid on their bellies as they drank all they could. As Jane filled herself with precious water, she could feel it saving her life. Her organs functioned better, her mind felt less foggy, and her eyesight had become less blurred. When they had finally arrived at the camp, the hostages had collapsed on the hard, compacted earth, and buckets of water had been provided with ladles to drink from. Most of them had used their hands to sup the water and cared not whether it was murky and full of debris. The hostages were suffering from cramp and could hardly move as they were jabbed with machete tips and herded into three huts made from sticks with palm roofs. The stick walls had been patched with animal dung, grass, and mud, but much of it had been poorly maintained and shafts of light shone through enough to illuminate their faces, muddy and bathed in sweat. Some rotting fruit and bowls of *posho* – a tasteless maize porridge slaked with water – had been tossed on the floor. The bowls upturned and the posho did not move, such was its consistency. Jane helped herself as the others did, without ceremony, snatching at what she could help herself to and not caring if her companions had a share. Three days, fifty miles and close to exhaustion and death when they arrived, and they had been broken down into animalistic behaviour. Using her filthy hands to scoop out the vile tasting porridge, she filled her mouth and licked her fingers clean, still clutching the soft mango close to her chest as she quietly sobbed and silently prayed for her life to be spared.

7

L uanda, Angola

KING HAD HEADED down to the bar, ordered a beer and taken himself off to a quiet corner on the terrace. He had ignored Stewart's orders that they should be dry from now on. He suspected the Scotsman would be getting through the bottle of Macallan and filling his hip flask tonight. The sun was low in the sky and the views of the sea afforded by the terrace were spectacular. He watched the sun-kissed horizon and sipped from the frosted glass. The Atlantic Ocean looked clear and choppy near the shore, becoming blue a hundred metres out and deeper in colour all the way to the horizon until it vanished under a golden blanket laid down by the sunset. He never tired of a good sunset, and he realised he had been almost sixteen before he had seen one. Until then, all he had seen was just tantalising glimmers of yellow and orange through a crowded London skyline. Now he never wasted a sunset if he could help it.

"Beautiful, isn't it?"

King looked up. He hadn't been aware of Lucinda standing to his left, a cocktail in her hand and the bikini replaced by a white summer dress. She wore simple tan leather wedges, and they matched the small crocodile skin handbag which hung from her shoulder on a thin plaited leather strap. "Stunning," he said, without taking his eyes off her.

She smiled radiantly and said, "Mind if I join you?" She paused. "Rebecca is having a crisis talk with her editor on the phone in the foyer and Roger seems to be finding his muse with the white powder..."

"Sit down and share my view," said King.

"Has your boss calmed down yet?"

King smiled. "No, he's always angry, that one."

"He'll end up having a stroke."

"I seriously doubt that," King replied. "He's a tough bloke. I expect him to go out in memorable fashion..."

"And he's a *bodyguard*, too?"

King smiled and sipped his beer. "Dinner?"

"You're being evasive."

"And you're digging..."

"It's my job."

"Then take a night off."

"Okay," she said, raising her glass. "Besides thirst, what are we drinking to now?"

"You raised the glass, you make the toast."

She smiled and said, "Chance encounters and happy endings."

King raised his glass. "I can drink to that."

Their glasses clinked and they drank, King watching Lucinda the entire time. She was attractive and intelligent and King liked what he saw. He wondered whether she liked him back, but the cynical voice inside his head told him to be careful. And that same cynical voice was brusque and Scottish and was to the point and went a good way to killing his mood.

"Do you know where they are being held?"

"Not yet," King replied.

"So, you *are* here to get them out!" she leaned forward conspiratorially. "I bloody well knew it!"

King looked around him before saying, "Shall we order?"

"What?" she frowned, then looked at him knowingly. "Just as long as you know that I'm not going to sleep with you to get a story..."

"I know," he smiled. "Dinner first."

"Hey!" she shook her head. "I mean it, I'm a serious journalist. I won't sleep with you to further my career."

King shrugged. "I don't think there's anything your *friends* wouldn't do. The coke head from The Times would sell his own mother..."

She nodded. "I suspect you're right."

"Is that why you're freelance?"

"What do you mean?"

"Well," King shrugged. "Do you lack the killer instinct that puts someone like Roger Siegfried at the top of his game?"

"Piss off!" she snapped, glaring at him, but her expression seemed to soften at once and she took another sip of her cocktail before she said, "Oh, possibly I suppose..."

"I didn't mean to offend," he offered by way of apology.

"The top journos seem to have a selfish demeanour that I don't see with you. I think their egos need to be fed on a diet of validation and praise. A selfish desire to beat everyone to the scoop and get the front page, or the headline TV news." He paused. "Simply put, you're too nice for this game. Why don't you write a book about the things you're passionate about instead?"

"It's that easy..."

"Right, I suppose not."

"You're just downing on everything I've worked on," she said rather solemnly.

"I'm sorry. I didn't mean to. It's just you seem so different."

"But you don't know me."

"I know," he reasoned. "You're absolutely right. And you don't know me either. You probably wouldn't still be sitting here if you did..."

"So, tell me about yourself."

King thought for a moment. His life had been terrible right up until he had met Stewart and been handed a lifeline. The oldest of five children, King had stepped in and provided when his mother had failed. She hadn't always been a failure, but she had always skirted it with reckless abandon. The children had never known their fathers, although they had plenty of father figures to choose from over the years. None of them reliable or a suitable example to follow. When his mother had made the transition from heavy drinker and casual drug user to full-blown addict, things had become far worse. She had fallen into prostitution and life and nature, circumstance and the drugs hadn't given her the goods, or the looks, to charge above the going rate for street corner whores in the area, which had meant she had often taken her next fix as payment instead. When that failed to put food on the table or clothe them, King had stepped up and worked in various jobs after school, started thieving to make ends meet and had bought what he and his siblings needed, as to give it to his mother was to go hungry, as she injected, snorted, or smoked all she earned. He had left school at fifteen to work full-time and then what had once been a promising amateur career as a boxer had turned into prize fights. They had all gone into care after she had died. King was older and fell in and out of homes and eventually into young offenders and short sentences in prison. King had never seen his siblings again, not until just before this mission when some casual enquiries had shown his sister going down the same path as their mother.

King looked at the woman beside him. He had read in a magazine that if a woman sat beside a man, instead of opposite, it meant that she was interested in him physically. For the first time, it truly dawned on King that he could wipe the slate clean and be whoever he wanted to be. He did not need to talk about Lambeth or Peckham, of tower blocks and council estate hardships. He wasn't Mark Jeffries. He was Alex King, and he was whoever he wanted to be. His cover had been that of a man with no siblings, his parents both dying in a car accident when he was eighteen. His father had been a construction engineer, his mother a former dental nurse but in later years she had merely been a housewife. They had lived in a quiet residential cul-de-sac on the outskirts of Epsom in Surrey. All King had known was that the 'real' Alex King had dropped out of college to go travelling in Asia and Australia. When his parents had died in a road traffic collision a year later, the Foreign and Commonwealth Office had not been able to find any trace of him to deliver the bad news. Stewart had kept the probate on hold and waited until he could use such a clean cover. Mark Jeffries had been recruited and sprung from Dartmoor a year after that. At the same time, an unfortunate soul fitting Jeffries' height, build and hair colour, who had been living on the streets in Cardiff had died in a cold snap and had no living next of kin. Stewart had claimed the body and it had later been placed in a bog on Dartmoor the night of Mark Jeffries' 'escape'. Fingerprints and dental records had been doctored and with the help and guidance of Peter Stewart, Jeffries had then become Alex King. To this day, the real Alex King had not been found, despite a red flag notice being put on him. It was suspected that he had ventured into the drugs scene in Bangkok, headed into the Golden Triangle to organise a drugs deal and never returned. King had inherited a semi-detached house in Epsom and just under twenty-thousand pounds. He had sold the property, invested the proceeds, and rented a flat in London. The 'real' Alex King had been an outsider and had drifted from his few childhood friends long before he went travelling and besides, King wouldn't be opening a *Friends Reunited* profile anytime soon. Alex King was just a guy who people once knew and never thought about again.

The realisation that after just three years of living a lie he could finally erase his past was liberating. He smiled at Lucinda and for the first time since he had bounced across Dartmoor in the back of an old and battered Land Rover on a cold and wintry night, unsure what he had got himself into, he felt truly liberated.

"What?" she asked coyly. "You're staring at me..."

"I'm admiring you," he said.

"I don't know what to say..."

"I have a tremendous appetite," he said decisively.

"We'd better order something then."

"Not for food," said King. He leaned in towards her and she didn't move. "For you..."

She smiled, touched his knee, and said, "I thought you said dinner first?"

"I changed my mind..."

8

Lucinda had been an experienced lover and King had allowed her to take the lead at first. Good love making always came from someone asserting some dominance and dictating the pace. The best love making happened when both partners could swap roles, interject, and react to one another. A shared, almost telepathic ability to sense what the other wanted, and how best to give it to them. King had used his strength and fitness to pin her against the wall as she undressed, and she writhed and bucked to climax, returning the attention to him when she pushed him down onto the bed. She was a tease, which King appreciated, but she also knew how far to take it and what he needed at the right moment.

Spent and satisfied, they eventually collapsed back down on the bed two hours after they had entered the room full of anticipation and passion.

"I need a drink," said Lucinda breathlessly.

"I'll get some room service," King replied, reaching for the phone. "Hungry?"

"Famished."

"Wine?"

"Of course."

King ordered club sandwiches and fries to go with a bottle of white wine and two beers. He asked for an ice bucket for the wine and the beers, and some bottled water to slake their thirst, but didn't hold out much hope from the response. "You can judge every hotel in the world by its club sandwich," he grinned. "Every hotel seems to have one on its room service menu, like it's international law, or something..."

"What's the big no-no you've had so far?"

"I had one with scrambled egg and dried white fish in it instead of chicken in Beirut," he replied, screwing up his face in distaste. "It went everywhere at the first bite, then in the bin... I hope you don't mind me ordering sandwiches. This is the kind of place where I'd give the oysters a wide berth..."

"Sounds a safe bet to me." She paused. "Finger food for a sinful and decadent bed picnic..."

"Sinful?"

She looked at him awkwardly and shrugged. "Things are... complicated..."

"I'm guessing there's a boyfriend back in England," King said casually, but he was irked. He hadn't experienced sex like it before and had started to fall for the woman.

"A husband..."

"Shit..."

"It doesn't really affect *you*, does it?"

"Ouch..."

"Oh, come on!" she chided. "You were hardly going to propose after a one-night stand!" She paused. "Oh, God, you're not one of those obsessive stalkers, are you?"

"Had a few, have you?"

"Meaning?"

"Stalkers."

"Oh." She looked flustered. "I thought you meant, men..."

King chuckled. "I'm not a prude," he said. "And I don't want your running total. I was just surprised that you were married, that's all."

"Don't I look the marrying type?"

King shrugged. "You're in Africa and you don't have a tan line on your ring finger. Nor indentations where one has ever been."

"I prefer not to wear one," she said, a little aloofly. "And you noticed?"

King said nothing.

There was a knock at the door, and it went a good way to lifting the mood, although the last thing he felt like doing now was to lounge on the bed with club sandwiches and fries. Her marriage had put up a barrier where the getting to know you stage now seemed a sticking point. Maybe the mood would settle once the food arrived. King wrapped a towel around his waist and checked the spy hole. He looked into the man's face, the perspective skewed and distorted in the fisheye lens. The man was standing with the tray on the flat of his hand, hovering near his shoulder. Quite a skill, and King suspected he had received classical training from a French maître d'hôtel at some time in his career. The man's other hand was free, and King supposed the bucket of ice had been out of the question. The training wouldn't have helped if supply and demand was not there. King unlocked the door and stepped aside. The waiter smiled and walked in with the tray. Lucinda had flung a robe on, and it was several sizes too large for her slender frame, but it enabled her to cover herself up to her chin. She smiled at the waiter, then looked back at the hotel literature which she had picked up as some sort of prop. King could tell that she wasn't interested in it, but it was clear what they had been doing and she should have known that hotel staff have heard and seen it all. There were literally no surprises to be had after a few years in the job.

"No wine or beer?" King asked. "Don't worry if you haven't got an ice bucket," he said, feeling his request must seem ridiculous to someone whose nation had been at war for almost thirty years.

"It is on the way up, Sir," the man replied, but he had trouble holding King's gaze. "Is there anything else?"

"No, only this..." King slipped the man a US five dollar note. He did not have kwanzas on him, but he knew the monthly wage to be approximately five times this amount. The man stared at the note in his hand and looked up into King's eyes, somewhere between gratitude and sorrow. King supposed the sorrow came from realising how much better life was in the West. "Thank you," King added.

"Sir, thank you very much..." the man said quietly. He backed away to the door and struggled to maintain eye contact.

King let the man out and closed the door. He walked back to the tray and picked up a chip. "Do you want to get dressed?" he asked before biting it in half.

"No," Lucinda replied. "Why would I?"

King would have preferred to go back downstairs, watch the moon over the sea and take his meal on the terrace. He couldn't see them having a second round and for some reason, now that he had discovered she was married, he felt less inclined. He shrugged and said, "I don't want to get in the way of anything."

"Alex, I'm a big girl. I know what I'm doing." She paused.

"I haven't stepped outside of my marriage very often. Yes, there have been a couple of men, and no, my husband doesn't know. But it's just sex. You enjoyed it, didn't you?"

"Of course."

"Then that's enough." She smiled and took one of the chips for herself. "Now, let's eat our sinful bed picnic, have another drink when they arrive and see where it takes us." She touched his thigh and rubbed tantalisingly close to his groin. "I'm hoping to the same place as before..." She trailed off at the sound of the abrupt knock on the door. "Thank goodness for that, I really am quite parched..."

King paced to the door and opened it wide for the waiter to come in with their drinks. The muzzle of the sub-machinegun almost touched King's cheek, and he swatted it aside and the burst of gunfire trailed across the wall and into their tray of food. The muzzle flash engulfed King's face and the flame licked at his cheek painfully and the noise in the confines of the room was deafening. King could not hear Lucinda's screams, nor much of the second burst of fire, his ears ringing, and the sound almost completely muffled. He realised that he had caught hold of the short barrel, but even with the palm of his hand almost cooking with the heat of the discharge, he kept control of the weapon and kept it away from his body as the bullets peppered the wall and penetrated the neighbouring room. King kicked out, but the towel hampered his movements and the gunman barged forwards and cannoned into King, lifting him off his feet and throwing him onto the bed, on top of Lucinda, who was screaming and trying to free herself under King's weight.

King had taken in the ill-fitting uniform of the hotel front of house staff, and the man's stubbled face. As he fought the man off him, he had already discounted him as being a member of the hotel staff. He had also had the presence of mind to check if the man was alone or had back-up. Thankfully, King realised that it was just the one man, but the man in question was as strong as an ox and smelled twice as bad. King still had control of the weapon, but the man was now pummelling King with a barrage of punches, although the man did not know how to maximise his power this close to his target. King tensed his entire torso, well-muscled and used to taking blows in the training Stewart favoured for his recruits. He tucked his head, gritted his teeth, and took all the man could give, until he saw his opening. King lashed out with his left hand, a solid punch. It glanced off the man's chin without any discernible effect. King punched again, but he could tell that the man was on something – khat or speed or cocaine. King jabbed the man in the throat, but his neck was thick with muscle, and he missed the windpipe. The man continued to punch down with his left hand. He had the advantage of reach and gravity and in King's desperation to hold onto the weapon, he could not strike and block the man's attacking blows. He needed to end this now. He lashed out with his index finger, deep into the man's right eye, bent his finger and hooked the eyeball free of the socket. The man wailed, instantly gave up the fight, and released his grip on the weapon. King upturned the sub-machinegun and put the muzzle under the man's chin and squeezed the trigger. The weapon dry-clicked – either empty or jammed - and King instantly used it as a club, battering the man across the side of the head and bucking him off him. He followed up with what he thought would be a knockout blow with the butt of the weapon but knew he had overcooked it when the man's skull cracked open like a coconut, and he fell limply onto the floor.

"Jesus Christ!" Lucinda wailed. "What the fuck just happened?" King said nothing. He looked down at the body on the floor, its left foot twitching wildly. "Is... is he dead?" she asked quietly.

"Yes."

"Who was he?"

"No idea," he said. "But that waiter's attitude was all wrong when I tipped him. He knew this was going to happen. Whoever this guy is, he paid or intimidated the man to come up later with the drinks and catch us off guard." He winced, shaking his hand. "Damn, that hurts..."

Lucinda stared at his hand, then hurried off into the bathroom and returned with a soaking wet hand towel. "Here, this should help..." She pressed it into the palm of his hand to ease the burning. "What do you mean by... us?"

King shrugged. "You covered war crimes in the Congo. There are people who will want you dead. And I'm here to..." He trailed off, checking the machinegun in case it was a stoppage that had rendered it useless, but it was empty. He dropped it on the floor and closed the door.

"To what?" she asked, looking at him intently. But she quickly relented. "Shit, I can't be found here in your room!" she exclaimed, hastily picking up her dress and shoes and underwear. "I'll be in my room. Two-seventeen. Come and find me when you know more. But be aware that Roger Siegfried and the other journos will be all over this like a bloody rash."

King nodded. "That's what I'm worried about." He gathered his clothes and started to get dressed. "But I'll likely be making a run for it. The police are too corrupt to risk staying. They can always be bribed, but then that only means someone could have paid them off first."

"You didn't do anything wrong," she said. "The man barged in and tried to shoot us."

King shook his head. "I can't risk it. I have a job to do, and it cannot be jeopardised at any cost."

9

Stewart put down the phone and cursed as he took a swig of his Macallan. King looked at him expectantly and said, "Are they on it?"

"Aye, lad." Stewart paused. "I doubt the bastard waiter is still on shift, though."

"He knew," said King. "There's no doubt about that. He brought up the food, and something wasn't quite right. The guy who attacked me was following him up with the drinks."

"Had yourself quite the little party, did you?"

King shrugged. "I could die tomorrow, just making hay, boss."

"You almost died *tonight*. Probably because you were too busy making hay and didn't have your head in the game." Stewart paused. "Why the hell did you have to kill him? We could have interrogated him and discovered who he was working for."

King thought about the incident, the man's bull-like strength, the whites of his eyes – as if he was high on something – King's hand gripping desperately to the scalding barrel of the submachinegun to keep it away from both himself and Lucinda. It could have ended very differently. King would never admit to Stewart that he had been scared, but for a moment, as he had been overwhelmed by surprise and at a disadvantage on his back with the man's weight pinning him down, he had wondered if that had been it. When he had seen the opportunity, he had taken it. Gruesome, but necessary. And after he had redressed the balance, he hadn't meant to kill the man, but he had certainly wanted to hurt him. Hurt him enough to stop him in his tracks. He had given a good swing, but it wasn't exactly a science. Or perhaps it was. Force had met resistance and force had won.

"This is about as bad as it bloody well gets," Stewart added. "The police here are far too corruptible. They don't understand political world affairs, the bigger picture." He paused, finishing his drink. "But worse than that, it means that somebody knows we are here and that we intend to do something about the hostages."

"It may have just been a robbery," King suggested. "These people only earn a few hundred quid a year. If he paid off the room service waiter, then he would still be in profit with what both Lucinda and I were carrying on us. Not to mention jewellery or watches..." He glanced at his own Rolex Submariner. The watch had cost him almost three months' salary, but he had always coveted such a thing, especially as there had been so many poor-quality fakes doing the rounds in the pubs he had frequented in south London. "He would have scored a fortune if he'd got away with it..."

"Lucinda..." Stewart mused. "How much do you know about her?"

King shrugged. "She's a freelance journalist."

"Married?"

King regarded him closely. Stewart would make a decent professional poker player because he gave nothing away. "I imagine you already know..."

"Well, she is."

"You've checked up on her?"

"No," he said curtly. "But I do know all *about* her."

"And?"

"You're playing with fire, son." Stewart picked up the bottle of Macallan. King could see that a few fingers' worth had disappeared since they had taken their drink together earlier. He poured a measure into both glasses, slid the smaller of the two across to King. "You are on a mission, son," he reminded him before taking a sip. "Mixing business and pleasure is not a good idea for most people in most professions. But for an intelligence operative operating in a hostile environment, it's a fucking terrible idea. You've already let your guard down and it nearly cost you dear. And with a bloody journalist, no less. I don't think I need to spell it out, but people in our game don't give the press anything. Let alone the end of your dick. And especially not the back end..."

"If you're worried about pillow talk..."

"Pillow talk!" Stewart snapped. "It's fucking inevitable!" He shook his head and said, "But worse than that... the woman's husband is a politician. He's a member of the cabinet! Christ King, you need to read a bloody newspaper once in a while!"

"Oh, right..." King closed his eyes. "I didn't put the two and two together..."

"Well, you two put *something* together..." Stewart shook his head. "She's called Lucinda Davenport and she kept her maiden name when they married. She wanted to make it in the world of journalism on her own. Her husband, Hugo Truscott is the Business Secretary. A controversial decision on behalf of the Prime Minister because Truscott holds multiple interests in capital investments, and if some of the companies whose boards he sits on gets oil contracts in Angola, the Congo and Namibia, then he will do very well indeed. But if it is ever discovered that you had connection..."

"I shagged his wife, it's hardly a viable connection."

"Really? You're that naïve?" Stewart scowled. "The press would have a field day. And the opposition? Forget it. The House of Commons would be debating this until the cows came home. You could even end up bringing down the government." Stewart paused, shaking his head before finishing off his glass. "The journalist wife reporting in the region, her secret agent lover tasked with rescuing kidnapped OPEC officials and the politician who sits on the board of companies with oil interests in West Africa and has everything to lose if OPEC doesn't grant the drilling licences."

"Oh." King sighed.

"Oh, indeed." He looked up as his phone played a few bars from Francisco Tárrega's *Gran Vals*, now synonymous with the Nokia ringtone. "Yes?" Stewart listened, nodded then said, "OK, we'll be there." King looked at the Scotsman inquisitively. Stewart opened his leather duffle bag and took out his combat knife, tucking it down his waistband. "Piers has found our waiter," he said. "I'm sure you'll want some answers..."

10

Questions and answers. It was rarely ever that simple. People lied. The answers they gave were rarely ever the answers you wanted. You could threaten. But threats were idle unless acted upon, and most people knew that. There was coercion. But coercion only muddied the water. Coercion could intimidate, and most interrogators considered threats, strongarming and a few slaps as coercion. Many people could get through some physical persuasion and still hold onto their secrets.

The two South African men had skipped the threats and coercion and gone straight to torture. When King and Stewart arrived at Tom's room, where they had taken the man whom they now knew as Horácio Bartolomeu he was tied to a plain wooden chair, his hands and ankles bound with electrical flex which had been pulled out of the portable television set and his mouth clearly stuffed with something bulky. Strips of the man's shirt had been cut off and wrapped around his mouth and neck. Bartolomeu's eyes were wide, and the man was clearly terrified, his nose bleeding and cuts around his eyebrows were open and raw.

"What's going on?" Stewart asked, but it did not exactly need explaining.

"Just softening the fucking kaffir up, eh?" Tom grinned.

"If someone is onto us, then I want to know," said Piers. "If they know we're coming, then you're on your fucking own. I'll take my twenty percent and the next plane out of here."

"He can't exactly tell us anything while he's gagged," said King, stepping forward to remove the strips of material. Tom blocked his path. He was a big man, but not as broad and muscular as King. "Get out of my way," King said coldly.

"Can't do that..." Tom pressed a finger into King's chest. "The black bastard took a bribe. I want to know from who..." He jabbed the finger into King's chest as he spoke, emphasising each word with a prod.

"That's your trigger finger," King said measuredly. "Remove it, or I'll snap it in two."

"I'd like to see you try..."

King snatched the man's finger and yanked it back towards him. There was an audible 'crack' and a gasp from Tom, his expression not only one of surprise, but the sudden realisation that he had just baited a predator and come off worse. King jabbed the man in the throat with the edge of his left hand for good measure, and before any counterattack could be mustered, the South African staggered backwards clutching his throat with his left hand and staring at his twisted finger.

"Well, that's fucking spiffing, son..." Stewart said to King as he stepped between the two men, but he needn't have bothered. Tom was still struggling to breathe and was staring at his crooked finger. Stewart walked over to the South African and caught hold of his hand. He studied the man's digit, then took hold of his wrist, pressed his own elbow into the crook of the man's elbow and said, "This is going to hurt, but it's better now rather than later. Your adrenaline is your best friend right now..." He did not give the man time to answer and pulled his wrist and yanked hard on the finger and once it stretched the ligament and became pliable, he manipulated it back in place amid the man's screams. It had taken so much effort that when Stewart released his grip and straightened his back, he was perspiring profusely and breathing heavily. "Get some ice on it as soon as you can and strap it up for a couple of days..."

Tom stared at King but said nothing. King stared back and the South African looked away first.

Stewart turned his attention back to Horácio Bartolomeu, who had been watching intently, but now looked terrified once more. He looked across the room at Piers, who had watched the incident between King and his fellow countryman noncommittedly. "Ungag him," Stewart ordered. He watched as the South African untied the strips of ripped shirt, then waited for the Angolan to open his mouth wider. Piers hooked out the lightbulb that they had both forced into the man's mouth, which was still remarkably in one piece.

Piers looked at Stewart and shrugged. "He'll be ready to talk now." He paused. "Otherwise, it goes back in, and I'll slap him around his cheeks until it explodes..." He stared down at the terrified man and said, "And we all know what a mess a shattered lightbulb makes when it goes pop..."

"You fucking dickheads..." King said quietly, unable to hide his distaste.

"Big boys' games," Tom said briskly, regaining some composure and walking closer.

King shook his head. He walked across the room and picked up a bottle of water. He twisted off the cap then took it over to the Angolan and held it up for him to sip from. The man drank thirstily. His eyes showing the true terror he was feeling.

"The man's soft," said Tom derisively. "Too soft for this work."

"He wasn't so fucking soft when he dislocated your finger," Stewart commented flatly. He turned to the Angolan and said, "No fucking about, pal. I want to know who paid you and what you have told them."

"I don't know!"

"You don't know what you told them?"

"No! I don't know who it was!"

"You let your employer's down. You betrayed a guest. It will cost you your job."

"No!" The man shook his head. "I need my job..."

Stewart looked at Piers and said, "You found him here?"

"Out back. On a smoko..." Piers shrugged. "We paid the duty manager to tell us who delivered King's food. Asked him where we could find him..."

"Shit, the trail is getting easier to read," said Stewart. "Let's just hope this duty manager can keep his gob shut when the police come calling."

"It's sorted," Piers replied. "But it's going to cost you five thousand US dollars. The duty manager has made some calls and right now the gunman is heading down the coast and up a river to a spot where the crocs got a taste for human flesh during the civil war. Both sides just tossed prisoners into the river from bridges and the crocs did the rest. He's got a couple of maintenance men to sort the plaster and paint in both rooms – the bullets went right through the wall - and King's room is being deep cleaned as well. He'll likely pay out a few hundred dollars, but the guy has retirement plans and I think he'll see that it's all done right."

"Perfect," Stewart replied. "Just as long as he keeps quiet."

"Jim's shadowing the guy," said Piers.

"Where's Reece?"

"Fuck knows. Having a beer in his room would be my guess."

"You didn't tell him?"

"We had it covered," Tom said gruffly.

"OK," Stewart nodded.

"We'll be out of here tomorrow, anyway," said Piers. "It's as tidy as we could hope for."

"That just leaves this guy," said Tom. He looked hot and troubled, his finger clearly causing him some discomfort.

Stewart looked at the terrified Angolan and said, "If you don't tell us what you told him, you'll have a hell of a lot more to worry about than losing your job..." Stewart paused. "My colleagues here..." He waved a hand towards Piers and Tom. "... are not fans of people of your skin colour at the best of times. Let alone someone who has taken money to lead an assassin to their door."

"I did not know what he was going to do!"

"Bullshit!" Stewart snapped. "How much did he pay you?"

"I..."

"You got him into the hotel. You supplied him with a uniform. You told him the room number, more than likely you led him through the hotel to his door!" He pointed at King. "The man tried to kill him!" Stewart glared back at Bartolomeu and said, "How much?"

The Angolan bowed his head. "Nothing." He paused. "Three men with guns came to my home. Two of the men stayed with my family. One of the men went with me to the hotel. They said they would kill my family if I did not help them."

King stepped closer, offered the man some more of the water, which he drank down greedily. When King pulled the bottle away, he said, "So, these men are still there?"

The man nodded. "Yes. They are very bad men. My wife, my daughters... they cannot stay there with such men..."

"Tough shit, kaffir," Tom sneered at the man. "I bet they've all had a good fucking by now. Your wife may not even want you back now..."

Bartolomeu looked up at them pleadingly. "I did not have a choice. I told the man where to find you," he said, looking at King. "You are a decent man. You gave me a large tip... it wasn't personal... I am sorry."

"I bet you want that tip back now, eh?" Tom smirked at King. "Maybe he'll let you have a go on his wife to compensate you?" He looked back at the Angolan and smiled. "But she's probably a bit sore now, but who gives a shit...?"

"Dickhead..." King said quietly, shaking his head.

"Want to say that again, pal?" Tom took a pace closer and stared.

"I'm all the way over here, *pal*. There's no need to stop walking..." King growled. "You've got plenty more fingers for me to work my way through..."

"For fuck's sake," Stewart shook his head despairingly. He looked at Tom and said, "Untie this piece of shit." He turned to Piers and said, "I need a piece. Make it two, King can come with me."

"What are we doing, boss?" King asked.

Stewart watched the Angolan rubbing his wrists. "We're

going to have a little chat with the men holding his family," the Scotsman said quietly.

11

S tewart had paid the duty manager in cash from his operation fund. The man had taken his money, promised that everything would be put right before the general manager came on duty in the morning, and provided them with two drivers. Stewart wasn't happy with the arrangement. He would rather have had their own cars and driven themselves, but time was critical, and the drivers would know their way around Luanda, and they would get there far more quickly than if they had sourced vehicles on their own, and besides, Angola wasn't overrun with Hertz or Avis rental offices. The vehicles in question were a Toyota Corolla saloon and a Mercedes E Class estate and they had both seen better days. At least ten years old, battered, and dusty having probably never been washed, and both vehicles had cracked windscreens that had spider-webbed across the entire screen and the headlights from oncoming vehicles made it blindingly difficult to judge.

The apartment block was in the north of the city and despite appearing dilapidated, was far more luxurious accommodation than most of the citizens of the nation's capital could ever hope for. Across the street a shanty village had grown with people sleeping under plastic sheeting and cardboard, and fires burned fiercely in old forty-gallon oil drums with many turned into communal firepits for cooking on. There was the heady aroma of cooking meat, spices, burnt flatbread, sweat and human excrement on the air. A hum of people talking, children crying and of dogs barking in the hope of some scraps of food. A miasma to the senses of the uninitiated, but which Stewart ignored as he stepped out of the car and looked around him. Horácio Bartolomeu ignored the shanty village. It was nothing new to him.

King was taken in by the sights and sounds of the shanty village. It took up the entire pavement for over a hundred metres and the smell was nauseating. He watched as the two South Africans stepped out of the Toyota, both ignoring the sight like it was an everyday experience for them. But then, they had worked all over the African continent and he supposed they had seen far worse. The thought that King would likely see worse over the years left him feeling some-what cold and indifferent.

They had yet to pick up their weapons from Piers' contact, but both the South Africans carried Browning 9mm pistols, tucked into the waistband of their trousers, with their shirts untucked to conceal the bulky weapons. King carried his K-Bar knife, strapped to his belt and like the South Africans, concealed under his untucked shirt. The knife had been designed for the United States military during World War Two and had a razor sharp seven-inch blackened blade with a leather handle and metal cross guard. A blood groove ran along the length of the blade to allow easy withdrawal if used for stabbing. But it was all theory. King had trained to use a knife in close quarter combat engagements, but the thought of using it as his primary weapon had suddenly filled him with dread. He looked across at Stewart. The man's shirt wasn't untucked, and he knew that Stewart had not precured a firearm and had insisted that the weapons they had liberated from their attackers be disposed of. King had tossed the handguns into a drainage culvert when he had ditched the taxi, and the machine pistol used to attack King had been dealt with by the duty manager.

Two gunshots echoed through the night. King crouched beside a low wall, searching for the direction of the sound. A dog barked in the ensuing silence. He looked at the other three men, noticing that they had not flinched at the sound. To his consternation, he saw that Tom had seen him crouch and was now smirking. Another four gunshots rang out and more dogs started to bark but quietened down after twenty seconds or so. Perhaps they were used to it.

"We shouldn't have left Jim at the hotel as fucking nursemaid to that hotel manager," said Piers as he drew his pistol and cocked the hammer. "Someone should stay with the cars." He paused. "If they're not here when we come back out..."

"The rookie can sit this one out," Tom sneered. "He's practically shitting himself..."

King stared at him but said nothing. But he had to agree that they suddenly seemed undermanned, and Reece had seemed to have gone AWOL. His room had been empty, and he had not been in the bar.

"King goes with me," Stewart replied. "Tom, you can stay. Give King your weapon."

"Fuck you," Tom growled. "I'll stay, but I'm not guarding the cars without a weapon..."

"It's OK, boss," said King. "They don't know we're coming, and we want one of them alive to find out how they knew where we were, and what we are here to do." He paused, looking at the Angolan. "How big is the apartment?"

The man shrugged. "Maybe four metres by five metres where we live. And then there are two bedrooms each three metres by two metres. And the *banheiro*..." He paused, struggling for the translation. "...the toilet and the place of bathing..."

"The bathroom," King nodded.

"Yes," the Angolan replied nervously.

"Sounds like a proper shithole, eh?" Tom grinned mirthlessly. "Well, it's certainly close quarters. Not enough room to swing a cat, eh? But plenty of space for them to root some pussy..."

King snatched the Browning out from the man's waistband at the same time as he shoved him hard in the chest. Tom sprawled towards the Mercedes and the man behind the wheel looked up from the stuffed flatbread he was eating, but lost interest almost as quickly. "You need to keep your mouth shut," King said coldly.

Tom squared up to King, his cheeks flushed and breathing heavily. "Give me back my fucking gun," he replied. He was angry, but King noticed a hesitancy in his expression. But then again, he no longer had the gun.

Stewart stepped between King and Piers to pre-empt an escalation but noted that the man hadn't raised his weapon in defence of his compatriot. "King..."

King ignored the Scotsman, staring back at Tom. "I'll double your fee if you can take it off me..."

"King..." Stewart prompted.

Again, King ignored him and kept his eyes on the South African's, which were boring into his own with such intensity that the whites were clearly visible in the darkness. The man subconsciously picked at the tape around his broken index finger, then his composure relaxed a little as he realised that he had been beaten. "Stay by the cars. Make sure they're still here when we get back," King said, turning towards Bartolomeu. "And you... lead the way..."

Stewart smiled as he watched King assume command of the situation. Tom was seething, but had relented and had turned to the drivers, berating them should they decide to drive off without them.

King kept the Browning held down beside his right leg. The area was dark, and people were sleeping in doorways and in dried drainage culverts. King supposed they knew the risks of flash flooding hundreds of miles inland which could unleash a tsunami of water, but beggars could not be choosers. Ahead of them an old car sped off an area of grassy waste ground and left a hubcap spinning in the road. It was not using its lights and as it sped into the distance, its brake lights illuminated its backend, but it was impossible to make out the make and model.

"Somebody's up to no good," said Stewart.

"Besides us?" King shot him a sideways glance.

"Crime is all there is around here," the Scotsman continued. "Too many years of war and civil unrest. Nobody knows how to do an honest job anymore."

King was about to question that fact, pointing out the employees at the hotel, but as he watched as the Angolan led the way to his apartment, he was quickly reminded that Stewart's words may well be true, considering what had led them to be here, and that the duty manager's clean-up operation was an all-time lesson in lawlessness and bribery.

Horácio Bartolomeu's apartment was on the eighth floor. Washing draped from the stairwell and doors to the other apartments were open filling the stairwell with noise and cooking smells. The Angolan explained that the apartments were so small that most people left their doors open so that the children could spill out onto the landings and the open doors would create a flow of air in the searing heat. But as they climbed the stairs and drew closer, the man looked worried and eventually said, "Something is very wrong..." His pace quickened and King shot Stewart another glance. There were people ahead and when they saw Bartolomeu at the top of the stairs the voices were loud and frantic and the Angolan looked back at King and Stewart frantically and said, "It is my family...!"

Stewart turned to Piers and said, "Wait here, watch our backs!" The South African obliged, leaned back against the wall and pulled up his shirt, making it easier to get to his pistol. Stewart said to King, "Give me the gun..."

"Fuck off..."

"King..."

"No, boss. I'm armed and it's staying that way. I can have the same discussion with you as I did with Tom..."

The Scotsman shook his head irritably as he took out his knife. "It may well end up differently for you..." he said, but he shook his head and started after the Angolan, before stopping in his stride and turning back to King. "Well, go on then! You've got the weapon, lead the fucking way, son..."

Horácio Bartolomeu stopped as several people swarmed around him, and the man was deluged in chatter. King pressed on, guided the man past and towards the apartment. "They... they are saying that my family are dead..." he said tearfully, his shoulders sagging and his pace slowing as if he was walking in treacle.

King ignored the man, but he could feel him sag under his grip. He lifted him, kept the man moving in front of him, selfishly using him as a shield as much as to keep him walking. When he pushed Bartolomeu through the open doorway he shouted at everybody on the landing and inside the room to get out. Stewart took King's lead and barked orders to go, shoving men and women alike and clipping a couple of inquisitive children around the ear. The people were subservient to authority and did as they were told. The gun in King's hand was enough to stop them questioning them further, and Stewart swiped the air with his knife, the blade glinting in the light from bare, low watt bulbs.

The Angolan was on his knees beside the body of his wife. She was naked from the waist down and it was evident she had been raped. Bartolomeu had two daughters barely into their teens and both girls were huddled together. Naked. Dead. A bullet hole in their foreheads. The man's son had been strangled. He looked no older than ten.

"Jesus, Mary and Joseph..." Stewart said quietly as he closed the door behind them.

Both men lay dead on the floor. A bullet hole in their foreheads and two more dead centre in the chests. The 'Mozambique drill'. Both men looked similar to the man King had killed in his hotel room. The same few days' stubble on their chin, eyes yellowed by malaria. Tough and wiry and muscled. Both men carried short versions of the AK-74 assault rifle, the AKS-74U with folding metal stocks and shortened barrels.

"What do we think?" Stewart asked.

The woman and her daughters showed all the signs imaginable with rape. Both men had been caught with their trousers down. King said, "These two scumbags had their fun. Probably strangled the boy in front of his mother before they started. Maybe to coerce them, more than likely to torture them further," he said. He stalked off into the bedroom and returned with some sheets. He dropped one over the boy's body, covered the two girls with another. "But these bastards didn't kill the women." He paused, respectfully laying the last sheet over the man's wife as he sobbed quietly beside her. King stood up and looked at Stewart. "But I don't know who did."

"What makes you so sure they didn't just kill the women after they'd had their fun?"

King shrugged. "The AK rounds would have topped them like boiled eggs. Those headshots were made with something small. Likewise, the men have the same sized bullet holes in their skulls, with no exit wounds. I'm thinking a seven-point-six-five of some sort or perhaps even a Makarov. Nothing too potent. There would be no shortage of Makarov pistols around here after the Cubans and Russians were here for so long."

"So, our shitbags here strangled the boy, did their raping and God only knows what else, and someone shot them, but also shot all three of the women..." He paused. "A Makarov would have needed reloading for that."

"Girls," King corrected him. "A woman and two girls..."

Stewart shrugged like it didn't matter and that getting hung up on their ages was just semantics. "We heard gunshots on the street. These bodies are fresh. I'll bet my last twelve-year-old bottle of Macallan that the car that raced out onto the street had the gunman inside."

"I won't take that bet," said King. "I think it's a given."

"What a cluster fuck," Stewart said quietly. He looked at King and whispered, "Our friend here is a problem..."

"How so?"

"The hotel is being cleaned. The body is being disposed of... do I need to spell it out further?"

"The man is in bits," King retorted.

"And that means he is unstable," Stewart paused. "He's a link to what happened at the hotel, and that means he's a link to us." Stewart shook his head irritably. "Give me the Browning."

"No."

"Do you want to do it, then?"

King said nothing. He looked at the Angolan sobbing on the floor. He had moved to his son and was praying quietly. The man had taken a bribe to look the other way and it had cost him everything he had. "No, I don't," King replied solemnly.

Stewart held out his hand impatiently. "Get those people off the landing and back into their rooms. Then, go back to the cars with Piers and make sure that piece-of-shit Tom is ready to move, or hasn't done anything stupid..." King lifted the pistol slowly from where it had been hanging loosely in his hand beside him and Stewart snatched it off him and nodded to the door. "Now go..."

King left the room. He shouted for two children and a young woman to get back inside their rooms and pushed past Piers at the top of the stairs. "Come on, we're going," he said without stopping.

"Where?"

"Boss's orders, just come on!" King snapped tersely.

King had barely taken the first flight of stairs when the muffled gunshot echoed behind them. He could tell that Stewart had used something to quieten the gunshot – most likely a folded blanket pressed up against Horácio Bartolomeu's skull and the muzzle of the 9mm pistol – and it was only because of King's training and that he had known what was going to happen, that he recognised it as a gunshot at all. It was no louder than a champagne cork popping, but admittedly he doubted a bottle of champagne had ever been in this part of the city, let alone this building.

As King crossed the dark ground to the two parked cars, he realised that his night vision had gone. He didn't see Tom stride up to him until it was too late. "Give me back my pistol..." the man said aggressively. King ignored him and went to walk around him, but the South African got into his face. "Now!"

"The boss has got it," King replied. "Now get out of my way."

"I say you make me..."

The man did not finish his sentence. King's knee had connected with the man's balls, and he doubled over caught between that agonising moment familiar to all men when breathing becomes an issue and the pain cannot be quantified. King could have finished him in any number of ways. The man's head and neck had been presented to him, a gift to a fighter, but he chose to walk around him and headed back to the car.

King had served time in prison. He had only survived because he had not allowed himself to be pushed around. And he wouldn't do it here. He knew that both he and Tom had got off on the wrong foot, but there was nothing to be gained from backing down. He leaned against the car and watched as the South African slowly forced himself upright. Stewart emerged from the darkness. He looked as if he was about to hand the pistol to him, but looked at King, then at Piers, who shook his head and held out his hand for the man's pistol. Both men had read the situation right enough. Only King wondered how things might change when they picked up their weapons and started on the trail tomorrow. The feeling that his battles could now be on two fronts made him uneasy. Like it or not, he had made an enemy out of the man who should have his back. King was a fighter, and a survivor. He looked at the South African as he shuffled back towards the cars. He would let the man sleep on it. But if he continued down this path, King knew what had to be done.

12

T he water was cool and refreshing. They had been assured that there were no crocodiles in the vicinity and the way the local children used a length of rope suspended from a precarious overhanging branch to swing far out into the pool, plummeting into the depths to the whoops and delighted screams of each other would confirm this. The water is too clear, apparently. Crocodiles like to hide in dirty water, camouflaged until the very last second before they strike. The pool was too high up as well, and the waterfall at the end of the pool was a natural barrier for the crocodiles, although she knew them to inhabit the river further upstream. But sometimes you had to go along with local knowledge and for the people of Hu, the pool was a haven for collecting water and cooling off in the blistering heat.

"It's the steep walls and rocks," someone had said. She cannot remember whom now. "The cattle can't drink here, so they piss and shit elsewhere, further downstream."

She had felt the cool water wash over her, deliciously cooler the deeper she swam. At around ten feet deep, she rolled onto her back and blew bubble rings to the surface. That was when she heard the gunshots, muffled and distant. Except they were not distant. They were deathly close. The water deadened the report. The bubble rings had stolen her air and she could not swim away and was forced to surface into the midst of the carnage. Pandemonium greeted her as she surfaced and stole a breath. Torn between fleeing and staring helplessly at the commotion, she snatched a breath and swam underwater for the opposite bank. She could not have seen such things, it could not be happening. People rounded up like cattle, men firing their automatic weapons into the air, bodies strewn across the sloping rocks, clearly gunned down as they had attempted to climb towards freedom. She rose for breath, snatched a lungful and dived down again. Suddenly she is aware of a shoal of fish in the water, streaking downwards. And then, to her horror, she realises that they are not fish, but bullets. Impossibly fast for the first few feet, then slowing drastically until at ten feet in depth, the brass projectiles tumble and fall to the bed like stones tossed from above. She cannot dive deeper, cannot risk coming to the surface for air. She changes course, but remembers how crystal clear the water is, how they had seen crayfish scurrying on the bottom. She knows that there is no escape and yet, she cannot stay. The overriding need for air kicks in and her body is fighting for the surface. She has no choice and when she surfaces with a splash, she snatches a breath clearly expecting it to be her last...

Jane Hargreaves jerked awake. She now knew that it was poor old Brian Hanson who had told her about the clear water and the fact that the cattle could not reach it and contaminate it. Poor old Brian. Except he had not been that old. Just a fifty-something man who hadn't exercised in a decade and who couldn't keep up with the fearsome pace set by the captors and had succumbed to heat and thirst. A kindly man who had always stood the first round at the bar, talked too much and too soon about his wife and children. Even proudly showed off photographs of his teenage children like new fathers did with their new-born babies. A man hacked to death and whose liver had been eaten by these animals now holding them prisoner. She was hot and parched, but there was no water inside the hut. She had tucked her knees to her chest, but her muscles were starting to cramp. As she straightened her legs, something scurried over her shins and her legs shot back up in the darkness. She closed her eyes but could only picture the bodies on the bank of the pool. The women and children had been taken off into the bush by some of the boy soldiers. The Westerners, those who had survived, had been rounded up and led off another way. Across the border and away from the bush and savannah, and into the jungle, and with every fifty paces travelled the jungle had become more and more dense, until there was little light shining through the jungle canopy and the noise of bugs and God only knew what else had started to dominate the senses. But her thoughts had lingered on the scene of chaos and barbarity. Some of the women from the village had been gang raped on the rocky edge of the pond, then dragged to their feet to follow their own children to their fate. She had researched the tribal gangs of the neighbouring Congo before leaving London. Most of it seemed unbelievable. That the fact that humans could act in such a manner felt as if it had been used as an exercise in propaganda. How could people behave in such a way? With such savage barbarity? Well, she knew now that they did. She knew that such reports were not exaggeration from governments or districts venturing for assistance from the civilised world. The threat was real. And now she was living it.

Shrieks pierced the night. Somebody – a woman – was screaming. There were shouts of protest, immediately followed by screams and groans of pain. Jane fought the cramps in her legs to press her face up against the side of the hut. She tore her fingers into the mud and reeds that had acted as a primitive patch and lath. There was enough moonlight to make out a group of young men, one of them dragging a woman down the wooden steps of the neighbouring hut by her hair. Her heart raced, the moonlight too dim to make out her features. Long hair – either Kathy McLeish, PA to Malcom Palmer, one of the OPEC delegates – or Joanne Egerton, the woman with MI6, with whom Jane Hargreaves was liaising. Part of her hoped it wasn't Joanne – a solidarity between intelligence officers – but the thought made her feel repulsed that she should therefore be wishing such a thing on a young woman who had been less inclined to know the risks, forced by her position to follow her boss wherever he went. At least Egerton had known the risks before she had accepted the assignment.

"Oh, God no..." a voice broke the silence of the hut.

Jane glanced to her left to see a few of her fellow prisoners each squinting through holes in the wall. She said nothing, almost embarrassed to have been watching the poor woman's ordeal.

Two of the young men were unfastening their shorts and the other three had the woman subdued on the ground, her legs spread and rough hands pinning her elbows and knees to the ground. The woman had stopped screaming. Jane had observed that in times of great trauma and with the inevitability of a violent act bestowed upon them almost certainly unavoidable, people concentrated on the here and now, of breathing and bracing for pain. The women of the Cafunfo and Hu region had certainly suffered in silence.

And the thought of quiet acceptance made it all the more unbearable as she watched tearfully, then bowed her head and closed her eyes. There were shouts. Deeper, authoritative and in a dialect of French that was difficult to understand. A sing-song patter that was distinctly African in its rounding of feminine accent. Jane pressed her eye back to the slit in the wall. A large man carrying a machete kicked two of the men aside and slapped one across the backside with the flat of the large blade in his hand. The woman was kicking in the dirt. She closed her legs quickly, and she was looking to keep them that way. The man kicked another of the young men like a dog, and like a dog the young man darted away and cowered at a distance, eyes not meeting the alpha male.

"Jesus... that was just in time... poor girl..." the same voice continued with their running commentary.

Jane did not reply, but the man had a point. She watched the large man outside as he pulled the woman to her feet and jabbed at her with the tip of the machete, herding her unceremoniously back inside the hut. Her skill was in reading people. And she knew from the way the man had admonished the youths that he was in charge. The men had been highly aroused – animalistic in their fervour and zeal to commit such a sexual attack – and yet they had melted in front of him. He had clearly been at the top of the pecking order. The harsh way he had jabbed at the traumatised woman with the machete also told Jane Hargreaves that he was no saviour, either. He did not care about the fate of the woman, but he did care about her usefulness as a hostage and bargaining chip.

She watched as the man locked the door and dropped effortlessly down the uneven steps, dressed in three quarter length jeans and a white vest. Like many of the men he walked barefoot, but unlike most of them, he wore several thick gold chains around his neck and a white, oversized watch loosely on his left wrist. He had a swagger and confidence to him. And then she knew. The man was Julius Lombobo, leader of the *Southside Boys of Da Congo* – and from what she could see, not the drug-addled mindless madman he had been depicted to be.

13

The plaster was still soft in King's room, the paint still wet. King wasn't convinced of the handy man's work, but he supposed the filled bullet holes would dry and be undetectable in the morning. He guessed it wouldn't be that important, as the rest of his room looked well-worn, but at least the bullet holes had been addressed. His bedding had been changed and there was a damp patch on the carpet that smelled of chemical cleaner.

Serviceable or not, King wasn't staying here. He packed his things in his leather holdall and stopped by the bar for a bottle of wine and two glasses. He was done with room service. It was a bit of a reach, but when he knocked on Lucinda's door, she answered wearing nothing but a hotel bathrobe, her hair wet from the shower. She smelled of peaches and cream and King liked it.

"Just a minute," she whispered, then spoke into her mobile phone. "... No, just room service... I know it's late, I fancied a drink, that's all... it's been quite a day... oh, nothing, just getting arrangements in place for the flight to Cafunfo tomorrow morning." She waved King inside, smiled when she saw the wine. "... No, Roger's heading up there in the morning as well, not sure about Rebecca from The Telegraph, but Siegfried's snapper will be going, providing he's drunk enough. I suppose it's going to be a media circus in a day or two anyway, so we'd better make the first move, but I may have an in..." She smiled quite blatantly at King and shrugged. "No, a friend... okay, well I've got to go now... love you too, darling..." She ended the call and tossed the phone onto the table. "I'm guessing your room is out of order..." she said seriously, looking at the leather holdall on the floor.

"No, it's all good. I just wondered whether you could do with some company and a drink." He paused. "I know I could..."

She nodded. "That was quite a thing earlier..."

"Indeed."

"You handled it well," she said. "But I suppose that goes with the territory."

"When it's a case of kill or be killed, most people can step up..."

"I imagine you're correct on that count."

"Husband?" King nodded towards the mobile phone on the table.

"You're good," she replied, her tone laced with sarcasm. "Perhaps you should be a detective?"

King said nothing, just worked on the cork with his Swiss Army knife and poured the wine into the two glasses. He wasn't a wine drinker, but wine drinkers often did not like kissing beer drinkers, so he'd hedged his bets. "I can try and get another room," he ventured, handing her a glass. "But I'll be taking this intriguing bottle of Moroccan red with me..."

"Well, that settles it. How can I miss out on that?" she

laughed. "And there's me celebrating *Le Beaujolais nouveau est arrivé!* each season with a case from my husband's wine merchant." King smiled, then blew out a whistle and stroked his hand over his head, just an inch from his closely cropped hair. She laughed. "Oh, well at least you're honest about that going over your head!"

"Oh, there's over my head, and then there's that," he smiled. "Anyway, this wine might not be so bad." He looked around the room and smiled. "There appears to just be the one bed..."

"I've got a long day tomorrow."

"Agreed."

"And I've just showered. I'm all nice and clean. Everywhere."

"Sounds thoroughly inviting..."

"You're a naughty man," she said with a hint of mock protest. "And I've just put down the phone on my husband." She paused. "You must be very sure of yourself..."

King wasn't great at flirting. He wasn't great at beating around the bush, either. He finished his wine, put down the glass, then wrapped his arm around her waist and pulled her close to him. He was strong and she couldn't resist, but he looked her in the eyes long enough to give her the chance to protest before kissing her hard and full on the lips. She responded passionately and when they both pulled up for air, she tore off her bathrobe and let it drop to the floor. She stood stock-still, as if waiting for an appraisal. King swept her up in his arms and dropped her gently on the bed, then tugged at his own clothes. She smiled, as he inadvertently seemed to stand for a moment for his own appraisal, then bent down and lowered himself gently on top of her. Lucinda had her own plans for what she wanted him to do and pushed down on his shoulders, kicking her legs out and around him, but continuing to push him further downwards, until she cradled the back of his head with both hands and guided him to where she wanted him.

They made love for the next hour. Both attentive, both grateful. Exhausted, King crashed on his front, his arms wrapped around the pillow and his face buried deeply in the surprisingly soft cotton sheet. Lucinda lay on her back, the sheet pulled partially over her hips. The merest hint of covering but allowing more than a glimpse of her toned body.

"I'm done," she said.

"You have been," King grinned.

She cracked a smile, but King guessed she wasn't one for innuendo or crude humour. She looked at him intently and said, "I hope you don't snore."

"Never had any complaints."

She touched him softly, running a hand across his buttock. "I bet..."

Perhaps he had been too quick to judge on the innuendo front. "Early start tomorrow."

"It will be. I've already set my alarm," she said. "So, feel free to sleep on."

"Nah, I'll be away early, too."

"Roger Siegfried has a lead," she said lightly. "He's sharing, but he gets first dibs on the angle of the story and gets to file his story first."

"I wouldn't think him the type of journalist to share. And not with one so much younger, and dare I say, more junior."

"Me neither." She paused. "But he seems serious."

"He's tossing you the scraps, while he gets the meat."

Lucinda sighed. "I'm sure he is. But he's big enough for me to hang on his coat tails and still make a name for myself."

King did not respond. She needed to make her own choices. Perhaps the fact she was the wife of a prominent politician meant she would never truly get a fair crack of the whip in her profession. "What's his lead?" he asked.

"Well, I could tell you what *we* have, if you tell me what *you* know."

"Sounds intriguing."

"So?"

King rolled onto his side. She mirrored him, her breasts uncovered as she propped herself up on her elbow, her face just inches from his own. "Okay... we're securing the area for OPEC and Angolan government ministers to assess the situation around Hu and down to Cafunfo, until a task force can be sent in."

"A task force?"

"British special forces and Angolan national soldiers."

"I had no idea," she said quietly. "So, they must have a fair assumption where the hostages are being held?"

King nodded, tapping the end of his nose in secrecy. "Now, what's your lead?"

She shrugged, still mulling over his revelation. "Roger has made contact with somebody in the Southside Boys. He has requested to do a piece on them. Tonight, he heard back from them."

King tried not to sit bolt upright. He reached out and stroked her hips, followed the drastic contour down to her waist, then back up towards her ribcage. He smiled and said, "And?"

"And they've gone for it." She paused. "I may have to hang onto the arrogant bastard's coat tails, but it looks like I could be taken into the heart of the Southside Boys organisation if I do."

"When you say, into the heart of their organisation, do

you mean you're meeting with some of their leaders?" King paused, his heart racing and ever conscious not to give himself away. "Or do you mean to where they are keeping the hostages?"

Lucinda smiled. "I thought that would pique your interest..." She paused, aware that King had stopped caressing her and that he was paying her his full attention. "Roger is a cunning old sod," she said. "I imagine he's pulled off a serious coup. He was fairly drunk and had definitely snorted a line or two of coke, but he said this was a pinnacle moment for him, a career ultimate."

"And he's sharing that with you?" King asked somewhat dubiously. "I didn't think that's how journalists work."

"They don't," she replied. "But Roger has been trying to get me into the sack for as long as I've been scribbling. He also wants some of my husband's contacts and personal introductions for a series of biographies he has planned." She paused. "I guess he's willing to share."

"Your husband must be an important man," King ventured, hoping to steer the conversation. Stewart had told him what the man did for a living, and the fact Lucinda used her maiden name professionally. A little more information wouldn't go amiss.

"He thinks he is," she replied a little offhandedly. "He's always telling me so..."

"Roger or your husband?"

"Well, both, actually. But mainly my husband." She sighed. "Politics is a strange game... and that's exactly what it is... a game. It's not a profession, like being a doctor or a teacher, there's an element of truism there, but those are roles for professionals who lean towards a vocation. Politics is filled with ego, power, narcissism, and self-interest. I'm sure most people get into it through altruistic and philanthropic reasons, but it soon fades, and I doubt there is a single honest politician after a year or two of having been elected. I reckon every cabinet member has lied in their role at some point."

King wondered whether his role was a profession or a vocation. He doubted it was either. Although he believed it to be vital. Sometimes reprehensible, but absolutely necessary. "And are you going to give Roger Siegfried what he wants?" King asked, a little awkwardly. He realised he had stopped caressing her and gently moved his hand back down towards her hips, but the mood was changing, and Lucinda rolled onto her back, her arms crossed over herself, shielding her breasts from view. He couldn't believe it, but he was a little jealous of Roger Siegfried's advances and intentions. It was crazy, because she was married, and the jealousy wasn't his to feel.

"I'll give him the introduction," she replied. "But he's not getting me. I don't work like that. Besides, I love my husband..."

King couldn't work that one out, but he wasn't about to question what the hell they were doing in her bed.

Lucinda switched off her light and said, "I need some sleep..."

King switched off the light on his side and the room was plunged into darkness. He was spent, and somewhat selfishly hoped she was, too. He rolled over and wandered what the etiquette was with a married woman who had only just declared her love for her husband. He risked spooning, his hand covering her right breast, but she moved a little too quickly. It had just been sex, and now it was clear she just wanted to sleep. King rolled onto his back and closed his eyes. After a few minutes, he could hear her breathing change and realised that she was asleep. An hour later, and after checking his watch for the twentieth time, the luminous dials seemingly moving in slow motion through the hour, he got up and slipped out of bed. He bunched up his clothes and headed into the bathroom, where he took a cold shower and dressed quickly. Lucinda was still breathing fitfully, REM sleep going on and taking her into the depths of her subconscious imagination. King wondered whether she was accepting a Pulitzer Prize, but now that he thought about it, wasn't that American? Now he wasn't sure what prestigious award the British Press coveted and made a mental note to check. Maybe she simply craved the front page with a two-page follow-up. Or simply to prove she could be a respected journalist without people thinking that her husband's position provided her with a helping hand. King watched her sleeping for a moment, reflecting on their short affair. He would be moving out in a few hours and needed to get his head back in the game. Things were about to get a whole lot more serious.

14

T he village of Hu
        Approximately   10   miles   northwest   of
        Cafunfo

INLAND, far from the sea and trapped in a basin with little breeze, and the humidity was tortuous. King's shirt was soaked, and as he looked at the pool and its crystal-clear waters, tantalisingly inviting, he tried to imagine how the beauty and tranquillity would have been shattered when the Southside Boys had turned the scene into one of chaos and murder.

"Did you read much of Dickens?" Stewart asked, his eyes on the far shoreline.

"I haven't had the chance yet," he lied. King had chosen other pursuits, but he wasn't going to talk about that with Stewart.

Stewart grunted. "I stopped by your room last night. I'm guessing you were shacked up with the journalist..."

King shrugged. "Just finishing what we started," he replied lightly.

"Dog..." Stewart commented, then pointed to the far side of the pool. "See the area to the left of the large boulder?"

"Yes."

"We'll check that out first," he said. "There are paths adjacent, I imagine that is where they headed out of here."

"There'll be paths everywhere. People just walk from here in all directions."

"Can you think of another way to follow them?"

"No." King paused. "What personal effects were left by the hostages?"

"Towels and some clothing." Stewart paused. "To be fair, the locals probably snatched up anything of value. Why?"

King stepped off the rock and started down the track. "Shoes?"

"Not that I know of. There's nothing in the police report, but then again, the police just came out and looked at the lake, saw the Westerners were no longer here and contacted the embassy. Why do you ask?"

"I'm thinking hardened bush dwellers like the Southside Boys would realise that soft Western workers would make slow progress in the bush and jungle if they were walking barefoot. So, of course they would take all their possessions, but surely allowing them to wear their own shoes could only aid them."

"Yeah, you're assuming these twats have rational thought processes..." Stewart scoffed. "But I see where you're going. If we see tracks left by a Birkenstock sandal or wedges, or a classic men's brogue or Oxford, then we'll have our route. Regardless of how many flat flip-flop and barefoot tracks are among them. Good thinking."

"Can we find out what they were wearing the day they were abducted?"

"Nay, laddie. We're not here, remember?"

Tom and Piers had gone to secure the weapons from their contact. Jim was sourcing supplies and Reece was meeting with the pilot to discuss exfiltration and another helicopter. By the time Stewart and King returned to the village, they were hoping they would have the definitive route taken by the kidnappers and their hostages. Or at least, that was the plan.

King reached the boulder first. The pool was only a hundred metres wide and two-hundred metres long. The waterfall feeding it was over thirty-feet high, and the water-fall at the other end, feeding a branch of the splintered river below was a decent fifty-foot drop. King could see a few small fish in the depths, but as the locals had told them, it did indeed appear to be crocodile free. Ironic given that the Western delegation would have thought the pool to be safe, lulled into a false sense of security, when the deadliest predators of all had pounced and changed everything. Lucinda had used the phrase or acronym TIA back at the hotel swimming pool. TIA. This is Africa. A place where anything can happen, more often the unexpected, and certainly the unjust.

King scouted the ground. There were three paths and they spread out like a trident into the bush. King worked his way down the right fork for twenty metres or so. "I guess this path heads back towards Cafunfo," he said. "Or at least to a track or road that will get you there."

"Left will run down to the river and on towards the village of Hu," Stewart replied. "What a name," he commented. "I wonder what it means?"

"Perhaps the place is such a shithole they just started to

write down Hu... and couldn't be arsed to finish?" King said, returning to the bank and taking the centre fork. There were dozens of footprints, and many were completely flat like poor quality beach shop flip-flops, but there were also tracks that looked like vehicle tyre marks. King squat on his haunches, then looked up and said, "I think the locals make sandals out of old, worn tyres."

"Aye, they do, son," Stewart replied. "Got anything? This way is a bust, it just meanders down to the waterfall from the pool." He walked up to King, picked up a stick and prodded the flattened earth. "This looks promising," he said. "I'm guessing a men's size ten with a flat leather sole and a heel. No tread. Decent shoes, a hundred pounds plus a pair, with quality leather and stitching."

"That's remarkable," King replied. He had learned his tracking skills with Stewart on a course aided by the Royal Marines and their sniper training cadre on Dartmoor. Too close to Princetown and the prison for comfort. King looked at Stewart, aware that the agent beside him knew all there was to know about fieldcraft, while his own was still in its infancy. "How are you so sure?"

Stewart stood up and tossed the leather brogue onto the ground beside King's feet. "The poor bastard lost this..."

"Oh..." King felt foolish as he picked up the shoe and studied it. It was certainly a quality shoe, timeless. As Stewart had said, most likely over a hundred pounds a pair, but King supposed he was well off with his estimation. It wasn't from Clark's, which was the limit to King's footwear budget. He looked at the label inside. *Loake Shoemakers.*

"Nice item," said Stewart. "Better as a pair, though. It reminds me of the joke where Bruce is driving in the outback, and he sees an Aboriginal man standing on one leg wearing a flip-flop. He stops his ute and says: *G'day mate, you lost your thong?* And the Aboriginal replies proudly: *Nah mate, found one...*" Stewart paused, letting the punchline sink in. "The question is – did the poor bugger kick off his other brogue and set off barefoot, or did he hedge his bets and wear only one. Because if he did, we've got a sure-fire sign and an easy footprint to track..."

"I imagine if a man lost a shoe, knowing he was going to be heading off into the bush, he'd probably keep the other shoe on. Fifty percent less chance of stepping on thorns or scorpions, I suppose." King made his way down the track, picking out the left footprint made by the shoe every five or six feet or so. There were signs of other shoes. A trainer around a women's size five and a wedge-type sandal around a size six. The tracks were sporadic. Squashed down by either barefoot impressions from every size from a boys' three to men's twelve, or the sandals made from old car tyres. After four hundred metres, the track split again. Right would double back towards Cafunfo and left would avoid the river and Hu and head northwest. They figured that the further they travelled, the less likely it was that the villagers would use this path. They were rewarded after a further two-hundred metres as the path widened and the array of tracks were easier to read.

"OK, son. Let's get back to the village and get organised. We can be back on this trail in a couple of hours."

King nodded, cupping his eyes to watch a light aircraft bank and drop in altitude, its twin engines slowing and propellors changing in pitch.

"That'll be the press," Stewart commented flatly. "That prick Roger Siegfried was booking a flight after ours. Let's get organised and get the hell out of here before they get their bearings and work out what we're doing here."

15

Cafunfo was southeast of Hu, but the entire area had been growing as mining interests sought to extract diamonds from the ground, either legitimately for companies like *De Beers*, or independently using questionable ethics and occasionally slave labour. Hu now had a hotel, but King guessed that it was ambitious calling it a hotel. Hostel, perhaps. Boarding house, maybe. They had not checked in, but the hotel was the obvious place to use as a base, not least because the owner intended to serve them with food and bottled water whether they wanted it or not, and they could park out front and sort their kit in the shade of the outbuildings behind the hotel.

Tom and Piers had arrived back with the weaponry and Tom had thrown down a sheet and laid the weapons out on the ground. He had shooed away the local children and was now checking the weapons over and loading the magazines and unboxing the 7.62mm links for the GPMG. Jim was sorting basic rations and water. The water was bottled, bought in Cafunfo, and now decanted into canteens and camel packs, which were heavy-duty rubber bladders that were wrapped in canvas and sealed with snap-clips. The water was now so warm it was like drinking tea that had been left for ten minutes to cool. Even so, everyone drank down plenty from the pile of clear plastic bottles in the shade. Hydration was key to operating out here.

"The food is shit," Jim said in his Aussie twang as Stewart and King drew near. Both men took a bottle of water and drained them quickly.

"How so?" asked Stewart.

"Beans. And not the Heinz variety. I've just had a can and they're rock hard, three times the size as a regular baked bean and the sauce is piss-weak..." He shook his head. "I've got us plenty of dried biltong, tinned and dried fruit, and condensed milk. That's about as good as it gets." He paused. "I was going to get some bread, but we'll sweat into it, and it will be as humid as hell when the bush gives way to jungle."

"Well, we're not on a culinary weekend," Stewart commented tersely. "Boiled sweets and water will keep us going..." He looked up as a white minibus swept in over the dirt carpark and stopped in front of the hotel. "That's a problem," he said.

King watched as a Roger Siegfried got out, clearly discussing something with his guide. King recognised the photographer from the hotel pool. The guide turned around and talked to the driver. Their conversation was animated. King strained his neck looking for Lucinda, then relaxed as he watched her get out of the minibus. She was wearing khaki trousers and a loose-fitting white cotton shirt. She wore oversized sunglasses, and her hair was tied back tightly in a ponytail that exaggerated movement when she turned her head.

"I'll just be a minute," said King as he walked towards the minibus.

"King..." Stewart started to call after him but shrugged as King continued to walk over regardless. "Dammit..."

"Got a lot to learn, that one," Jim commented.

"And you've got to hurry up and get those ration packs finished!" Stewart snapped and headed for the hotel.

"You're in luck," said King. "I think the deluxe suite comes complete with hot and cold running cockroaches..."

Lucinda looked up and smiled, but her face hardened when Roger Siegfried dropped his bag beside her. He looked up at King, then over to Lucinda for an introduction. Or perhaps an explanation.

"Who's your friend, Lu?"

"Nobody important..." she said, then looked at King apologetically. "Sorry, that came out wrong," she blushed, taking off her sunglasses. "We met at the hotel..."

"Oh..." Siegfried had already lost interest in the stranger and caught hold of his bag. "Don't be long now, Lu..." He walked across to the hotel, no doubt after procuring a measure or two of whatever Stewart had gone inside to find.

"Sorry about that," she said. "I didn't mean..."

"Forget it," King replied. "About Siegfried's contact out here..."

"I can't divulge anything," she said quickly. "The old hack's keeping his cards close to his chest. He has an in, that's all I know. I've been offered a junior correspondent piece within his article. A sub-story. It's worth a great deal to my career."

King held up his hands in mock surrender. "I get it," he said. "No big deal. I'm out of here, anyway." He paused. "Look, I don't know where you're going, or whether your contact has anything to do with the people who took the delegation hostage, but all I know is that it is a tough and dangerous place, especially for a woman..."

"I've worked in the Congo before," she protested. "I covered war crimes and rape being used as a weapon..."

"I know," he shrugged. "I don't doubt you've seen great danger before, but..." He paused, taking a set of rosary beads out of his pocket. "These were my mother's," he said quietly. "Keep them with you, for luck."

"You don't strike me as a religious man," she said derisively.

"Well, we barely know each other," he reminded her. "I suppose I'm still figuring it all out. Religion, that is. Anyway, they've been lucky for me so far. Many of these Southside Boys were taken from their homes as children. Decent God-fearing families, and many of them Christian. Many were educated, however briefly, by nuns and missionaries. If they see you with those rosary beads, it may just trigger memories, compassion... I don't know what," he said. "But they could save your life in dark and desperate times. And that's not just a subliminal reminder to them that they once shared values, maybe you'll find some comfort, too."

Lucinda took them from him gently and passed them over her hand. The beads were well-worried and polished smooth. "But if they were your mother's..."

"Just hang on to them. We'll meet up again, I'm sure. You can give them back to me when we're someplace safer, and you can tell me whether they actually saved your life, or whether you just carried them around Africa for nothing," he smiled.

"Deal," she said with a smile. "I suppose, either way, I'll think about you."

King smiled. "Well, good luck," he said. But he didn't bother waiting for a hug or a kiss or an awkward reply. He turned on his heel and headed back to the rear of the hotel. He'd done all he could, and now he needed to leave. It was time to forget Lucinda and get his head in the game.

16

King watched the two South Africans and the Australian from the opposite bank of the pool. All three men wore a mix of khaki and camouflaged DPM (disruptive pattern material) and cradled their weapons loosely. They were travelling light and carried rations and water in small bergens on their shoulders and webbing pouches on their chest rigs were stuffed full of magazines, while bulky water canteens were attached to their webbing for easy use. Hydration was as important as ammunition in this heat, and the humidity meant they would be almost soaked through as they stepped into the bush, following the trail that both King and Stewart had highlighted.

King checked his watch. 14:00 hrs. Plenty of light until 19:00. By then, the three men would be in tune with their surroundings but would stop tracking and find an LUP (lying up place) as tracking in the darkness would be impossible. That gave the men five hours' start. Daybreak was 06:00 and by then, the men should be breakfasted and ready to move. They would keep moving and cross the border at a point known for its frequent crossing during the war by all sides. There were border patrols by the Angolan National Army and the DRPC Defence Force on the Congo side, but it was mainly road and track crossings that had fences and gated barriers. In the heart of the jungle and on the mountain ridges, people slipped over for all manner of reasons, and lately, it was the *Southside Boys of Da Congo* who were crossing with impunity and snatching Angolan women for rape rallies and slavery, as well as boys to indoctrinate into their ranks as soldiers. Assuming the three mercenaries could stay on the trail and follow the signs through the border crossing, then by the time they rested up for the second night, they should be in the ballpark of Southside Boys territory in the Congo. From then on, they would defecate in the plastic bags they were carrying and take extra care to avoid leaving traces. The Southside Boys would have roaming patrols and would engage anybody they saw in the vicinity.

"This throws up a curve ball," Stewart said behind him.

King turned around and nodded at his mentor as he approached. "It splits the troops," he agreed.

"We were never going in on foot," he said. "Leave that to the colonials." He grinned. "Once we have a bearing or two from them on the net, we'll counter using the chopper and approach in a pincer movement and recce the extraction point."

"No satellite photos yet?"

"No. London has cut all assistance."

"How do you deal with that?" asked King. "Given a job, then bugger all support."

Stewart shrugged. "I was in the Falklands War." He paused. "Only, I was there a month ahead of the assault force. Holed up in a hide, dug into the mountainside like you learned how to make on the Black Mountains..."

King nodded. He'd been shown by the SAS how to dig out a hole, use chicken wire and wood from crates to construct a roof and cover with turf and bracken. Lying prone with just a few inches of opening to view the enemy, there was just enough room to roll onto your side and shit in a bag, get a brew on with a mess tin and a solid fuel burner and eat cold rations. A spotting scope and rifle were beside him on the exercise, and the instructor had recommended having a grenade or two within handy reach if it all went south. King had spent a few nights making, testing, and sleeping in various hides. He couldn't imagine living in one for a month.

"It was so fucking cold that I couldn't wait to get out of mine at night and probe the enemy lines for intelligence. One night we bumped into a young Argie lad. Poor bastard was no more than eighteen and got the fright of his life when he saw us. He had an M16 and no spare ammo and a couple of grenades and a bayonet on his belt. He was shivering from the cold." Stewart paused as he turned and started walking back towards the village. King caught him up and walked beside him. "We couldn't snatch the lad. We were holed up on the mountainside just a few hundred yards from their camp and the taskforce was still two weeks off. We couldn't let him go, either. We were there to gather intel and the outcome of the war relied on what we knew. We couldn't afford to be compromised. A seasoned corporal stuck him in the throat with his bayonet and the problem was solved. We watched him dying on the ground and came up with a plan to make it look like he'd had an accident with his own grenade. Anyway, job done. We fragged the body and got back into our hide on the hillside. And that was when I realised that I was truly alone. No help would come if I fucked up, no help would get me out of any situation that befell me. It's been the same way ever since. When I went to work with MI6, I was already used to it. You see, in battle, the instant the first shot is fired, the plan changes. Nothing goes to plan. Not ever. You do your best, you try to fall back with a plan B or whatever, but in the end, you're on your own. You just keep your head down, and back up your team at any cost. Hopefully they'll always do the same for you. That way, you'll get through it."

King shrugged. "I guess that's me fucked if I need Jim and the South Africans to help me then."

"Aye, fucked royally, son. Just don't get yourself in a position where you need them. But make sure that you back them up to the hilt if they need you. Maybe you'll change their view of you."

"I won't hold my breath..."

"The battlefield holds many surprises."

King nodded. "I suppose..."

Stewart stopped walking and looked at him. "What's up?"

King looked back at the pool, not looking at the Scotsman or letting him see his eyes. "That thing with my sister," he answered. "I can see her life going down the pan, and there's nothing I can do about it."

"That was another life," Stewart replied. "You knew the score when you took the deal."

"I was serving a twenty stretch with no parole. I'd have agreed to anything..."

"But you're free."

"Free?"

"Walk if you want to."

"People don't walk from this line of work." He paused. "Some bastard like you would catch up with me one day..."

"Aye, well, you've got a point." Stewart paused. "But you don't know enough yet. You're not a threat security wise, but Mark Jeffries died on Dartmoor. There's no going back and if you threatened MI6 by causing a stir, then you will never be safe."

"I realise that," King replied. "So, what's your exit plan?"

"Meaning?" Stewart looked at him sternly. "I'm not going anywhere, son."

"Well, you're in your forties. You won't want to do this forever. So why should they just cut you lose?"

Stewart nodded. "I guess because as much as I am a risk knowing what I've done for queen and country, I can always remember those details. And that would cause a problem for my employers if say, I wrote down and recorded the details of my missions and stored them with a provincial solicitor to be released in the event of my untimely or suspicious death..."

"Really?"

Stewart turned and started towards the village. "It's called a security blanket, son," he said as King caught him up. "So, there you go. You know what it is. I'm not telling you to do this, by any means, in fact I'd deny it at any cost. But one would hate to become an untidy end in someone else's agenda..."

As they trudged back across the sun-baked earth and crossed the road to the hotel, Reece pulled up in a battered Toyota Landcruiser. It had been white once but was now so ingrained with red dust that the only traces of paint were around the doorhandles where careless fingers had streaked through the dirt.

"The bird's ready when we are," he announced. Like the

others he was dressed in khaki and DPMs. His boots were black British army issue and had seen better days. He wore a floppy boonie hat and King noticed it had the man's blood type etched on the side in permanent marker pen. "It's a Huey that has been in service with a Christian aid peace corps charity of some kind, because it's still painted white and sign-written."

"That'll stand out like a sore thumb," King commented.

Stewart shook his head. "Nay, lad. In fact, it's a good cover. There are charity helicopters flying around all over Africa and it will look less of a threat to these Southside wankers than a military bird flying low over their patch."

"That was my thinking," Reece said, but without a hint of malice.

King shrugged. "OK, I stand corrected."

Reece made nothing of it and said, "I've secured a Soviet era Mil Mi-17 for the extraction. The Cubans left it here during the late eighties. It's now a heavy-lift chopper being used by one of the diamond mines around here for getting digging equipment up and down the mountains. It's ours for the next week." He paused. "We contact the pilot on the satphone, and he'll leave immediately."

"What about the Huey? Is it just our infil, or do we have it for exfil, too?"

"He's all ours. As with the Mil, it's ours for the week." Reece paused. "Give me the satphone and I'll punch in the numbers." He took the phone from Stewart and entered the numbers. "There. Infil and Evac is the Huey, Evac Two is the Mil."

"Thanks," said Stewart taking the satphone off him and slipping it inside his jacket pocket. The unit was untraceable but came at a cost of several hundred pounds per minute to use but was worth every penny as it could get a signal anywhere on earth, piggy-backing satellites as they neared in orbit. He checked his watch and said, "The Huey will be here in an hour, let's make sure we're squared away and ready to go."

King watched a Land Rover Defender bounce over the rough ground that served as a road from Cafunfo to Hu. The man got out and stretched. He was white with tousled dark hair, six-one and around twelve stone. Lean and hard looking. King studied his stubbled face, decided the man was a predator. An alpha. He could feel his spine tingle and found himself unwittingly tensing his arms, adopting a broader stance as he neared. Like a gunslinger in the Wild West. He caught himself in time and relaxed his arms. It was the alpha male equivalent of dogs sniffing arseholes. He noticed that neither Stewart nor Reece had reacted in any way, and he reminded himself not to try too hard in this company. King took a breath. Tension was high. In an hour he would be aboard a helicopter looking for the mother of all fights. They passed the man by and walked around to the rear of the hotel. The weapons and kit had been stashed inside the Toyota that Reece had been using to make their travel arrangements back at Cafunfo.

"Get the vehicles parked away from view and be ready to move." Stewart paused, heading for the hotel. "And stash the keys under the wheel arches as arranged. We don't know who's coming back."

"That's fucking grim," said Reece quietly.

King realised this was the first time the man had spoken to him outside Stewart's hotel room back in Luanda during their initial briefing. The man was soft-spoken and there had been a hint of the sardonic about his tone. "Tell me about it," King replied.

Reece unlocked the vehicle and heaved out his kit. He

reached across the seat and pulled out King's webbing and handed it to him. "Don't worry about those South African arseholes... they're just dickheads by default. Life changed for people like them when Mandela became President. Now there's another black man in charge, I think they finally realise that their fun in the sun is at an end. The writing is on the wall for people like them."

"Part and parcel of living on this continent, I imagine."

"The Australian's just as bad, but he's a good man in the field... I've worked with him before." He smiled. "You don't look convinced..."

"I think I got off on the wrong foot with all of them and can't see myself gaining their trust now."

"Well, you can't go around breaking people's fingers just because they prod you in the chest and hope to remain friends." Reece smirked. "But a lot can happen when the bullets are flying. You'd be surprised who will be your friend out there."

King slipped on his camel pack, then put the webbing harness over the top. The camel pack carried two litres of water and enabled the wearer to drink it using a rubber straw that folded and clipped tightly to stop it leaking. King still carried two water bottles on his belt and webbing, though. The heat was searing, and the humidity reached out and touched you out here.

"I've got to get me one of those camel packs," said Reece. "How does it work in the field?"

"It's great," King replied, feeling a fraud as he'd never used one before. Until this mission he had tracked an IRA splinter group and some criminals in what had become a messy operation. He had halted the terrorists' objectives, rooted out a dirty MI6 agent, but lost an asset along with the money they had stolen. And then there was Beirut. He preferred not to even think about Beirut. King was a realist. He knew that Stewart had his doubts about his track record and that this mission was make or break. Unfair, given that nobody King trained with could beat him in unarmed combat disciplines or on the firing range, and despite his upbringing and physical presence, he had aced the theory and intelligence tests, rating a higher IQ than many of the data analysts and certainly more than any field agent had ever recorded. But you couldn't tell how a mission would go, and King's two solo operations had been the equivalent of walking into a casino, sitting down at a poker table and being dealt one shitty hand after another.

"Don't take their racism too personally," Reece said as he adjusted his webbing and checked his Browning pistol before securing it in a belt holster. "You said that you have a mixed-race brother. That must be tough hearing how they talk, but they're ingrained racists who grew up during apartheid. They don't know any better."

King nodded. Stewart had been right; King had already blown his legend with these people. Mark Jefferies had a mixed-race sibling, but Alex King was an only child. One mistake, one slip of the tongue and this man still remembered. "It's OK," King said. He holstered his own Browning rigged on the centre of his chest. Not only within handy reach, but it provided some protection to his heart and aorta. Enough to stop or deflect a bullet. Every little bit of protection helped. "I didn't expect Jim to be the same, though."

"He's an Aussie!" Reece laughed. "They're the bloody worst! The Aboriginals have been oppressed since Captain Cook. The Australian government carried out blanket oppression and ethnic humiliation policies for decades after the Second World War. It was just done quietly and away from the world's media. They made it almost impossible for Aboriginals to get work, herded them into remote communities, kept them below the poverty line. I guess it's getting better now, hell we're into a new millennium so it should be!" Reece looked past King and said, "I think that bird wants you..." King turned around and saw Lucinda hovering in the lee of the hotel. "You know her?"

King nodded and headed over.

"You're dressed for war," she commented.

"I'm dressed for the bush and the jungle."

"The combat knife and pistol would suggest otherwise."

"Dangerous country."

She smiled thinly. "Roger Siegfried has made contact. We meet with one of the Southside Boys' lieutenants tomorrow morning."

"Right."

"Oh, come on," Lucinda said sharply. "You're here to free the hostages. Don't bullshit me. Is that why you're hanging around here? Hoping to follow Roger's contact?"

"If it was that simple..."

"Take me with you," she said suddenly. "I'll cover the story. This way Siegfried can go fuck himself and I'll be there to report on the release of the hostages. It will make my career..."

King shrugged. "I can't do that."

"Please. Roger wants... more than I want to give him." She paused, her eyes moist and her expression pensive. "It seems there are no favours, no help in this game. I've got an in, a lead. I get to follow an old hand into the heart of the story, get the scraps from his table. But that has a price..."

"I'm sorry," said King. "Look, I'm just a grunt. I'm not in charge. It's not my decision to make."

"Please..."

"I'd hold back on sexual favours until you've got the story and are ready to print."

"You bastard…"

"What, he wants something else from you that doesn't include sex?"

"No," she spat back at him.

King shrugged. "The Southside Boys can't be so stupid as to take you to see the hostages. It's too dangerous, both for them and for you. It sounds like you'll get a story, but not the one you want."

"I can't do it like this," she said sadly. There were tears in her eyes and her bottom lip quivered ever so slightly. "I slept with you because I liked you. Felt attracted to you." She paused. "I thought Roger was giving me a hand up, but on the flight, he told me exactly what he expected from me."

"Then go back to Luanda." King paused as Stewart came out of the hotel with the alpha male he had noticed earlier. The two men shared a look, then Stewart headed back this way and the other man walked to his Land Rover. King looked back at Lucinda. "I'm sorry, I can't help…"

Lucinda turned around, then looked at Stewart and turned back to King briefly before marching up to Stewart and saying, "Take me with you. I will cover the rescue… discreetly, that is."

"Fuck off missy," Stewart said without hesitation. "That old hack Siegfried is looking for you." He paused, cracking a mirthless smile. "He's three sheets to the wind and half-way through a bottle of Scotch. If you've made a deal with him to get a story out of his bullshit meeting with the kidnappers, then I'd do it sooner rather than later. He has a reputation for a speedy delivery at the best of times, and a flaccid dick when he's had a few too many. Just close your eyes and think

of a third page substory. Hopefully it won't last long..."
Stewart walked on past and nodded for King to follow.

"You bastard!" Lucinda screamed at him. She looked
back at King tearfully and shook her head.

"I'm sorry, I've got to go," he said. "Forget the story. Fly
back to the city and re-evaluate. It's not worth it." He paused.
"And these Southside Boys won't show or tell you anything
worth printing. You'll end up being kidnapped yourself. You
and that old drunken hack." He watched as she walked back
to the hotel, wiping the tears from her cheek with her
sleeve. Roger Siegfried staggered out of the hotel, an empty
glass in his hand. He greeted Lucinda by wrapping an arm
around her shoulder and steering her inside. Lucinda
glanced back at King, then hesitantly climbed the steps, and
disappeared inside.

17

Despite the scarcity of technology in the Angolan defence force's arsenal, the pilot kept the Huey low. RPG's - or rocket propelled grenade launchers - were in use among the tribes fighting it out for supremacy in the region, but the pilot was skilled, and the craft was running low and fast. King appreciated the breeze – they all did – and with the helicopter travelling at around one-hundred miles per hour with both fuselage doors open, the air was cool and blissfully refreshing. The pilot was alone up front, and King, Reece and Stewart had all the room they needed in a bay that was able to carry twelve passengers. King had the GPMG resting across his legs, sixties rock music in his head as he imagined he was in a Vietnam war movie. Reece had the sniper rifle over his shoulder and cradled his 9mm Uzi as he watched the desolate ground below.

"Diamond mines have raped the countryside," Stewart said across the intercom. They all wore headphones with open mics to communicate and drown out the 1400 HP Lycoming engine and the rotor wash above them. "See over there?" Stewart pointed to vehicles and men working the ground, military style vehicles forming a perimeter. "They employ mercenaries and even have help from the Angolan army just keeping the employees safe from raids. They pay next to nothing for a fourteen-hour day of back-breaking work, just so *Kevin* can give *Sharon* an engagement ring because he got her up the duff in the back of his Vauxhall Astra..."

King watched the mine workers. They appeared to be digging along a seam of rock using just picks and spades. Men with automatic weapons watched them work and men with yellow flags and high-vis vests marked where the diamonds had been found. Within a minute of leaving the mine behind them, another was visible a mile to the east.

"Once they start work at the mines, the men and women can't leave for three months and work seven days a week," said Reece. "I worked security for one and was shocked at the conditions. It was practically slave labour. And these aren't even conflict diamonds since the civil war ended. Back then it was different. Especially for the poor bastards working for the commies. They were slaves in every sense. Sierra Leone is the worst place for this in the world right now. Every diamond that is cut has cost as many lives as carats." He paused. "I am told that De Beers is putting forward plans to mine near Luanda. They have indicated that it could be in the top five places in the world to mine for diamonds."

Stewart nodded in agreement. "Aye, lad. You can count on one thing in this fucked up world, and that's that wherever there are great riches to be found, there will always be poverty-stricken people to exploit in extracting it from the earth." Stewart nodded towards the port side of the helicopter. "The terrain is giving way to savannah. The hostages would have been taken past these mines, avoiding the security at all costs. The border is up ahead." As he told them, the helicopter banked hard to starboard and dropped in height. King felt his stomach rise towards his mouth. Stewart grinned and said, "We're going to go in low, between the mountains."

"Government forces up ahead," the pilot said through the intercom. His tone was tense, but he didn't sound to be panicking just yet.

The helicopter dropped lower and banked hard to port. Stewart vied to see out of the starboard door, but he was merely looking up at clear blue sky as the craft wound through its sharp turn.

"What strength?" Stewart asked, hanging onto his own harness as they all lifted out of their seats.

"A dozen vehicles. APCs and Land Rovers... shit!"

Nobody had to ask what the problem was as tracer rounds cut through the air, streaking past the open door and close to the rotors. As the helicopter levelled out, more tracer rounds streaked in front of the cockpit, then inevitably, cut back towards them as the soldier on the machine gun five hundred metres from them guided his rounds on target. King ducked, readying himself for the impact and when it came, a dozen or so .50 calibre bullets punched rather undramatically through the fuselage letting shafts of light in through the metal. He checked himself, realising the futility of his actions. Nobody walked away from a .50.

"Anyone hit?" Stewart shouted.

"All good," Reece said breezily.

King shook his head. "I'm OK..."

The helicopter rose and banked to starboard, closer to the soldiers, but that too was enough to ruin their aim and as the next barrage of tracer lit up the air, the pilot put the Huey into a dive and banked back the opposite way. Again, bullets hit the helicopter, but this time Reece grunted and said, "I'm hit…"

Stewart unfastened his harness and worked his way against the gravitational forces of the helicopter's manoeuvre. King looked on, then snapped to and unfastened his belt and pulled himself across the seat towards Reece.

"Keep your belts on!" The pilot shouted.

It was too late now, and both men had caught hold of Reece and Stewart had his hands behind the man's back, checking for the entrance wound, and thoroughly mystified that there was no dramatic exit wound the size of a tennis ball. He pushed Reece forwards, then unhitched the sniper rifle, the weapon falling to the cabin floor in two pieces. He smoothed his right hand over Reece's back, and the man winced.

"You're a lucky bastard!" Stewart shouted above the roar of the engine and rotors. "You've got some splinters and you'll soon have the mother of all bruises, but the bullet didn't go through…"

King fastened himself into the harness opposite Reece. He kicked and scraped his boot heel on the pieces of rifle between them, the squashed .50 bullet sliding on the deck. He bent down and retrieved it, then handed it to Reece. "Souvenir," he said. "They've got to be fifteen hundred metres back, and the fuselage and rifle stock slowed it down just enough!"

"We're all good," the pilot said. "Out of range and line of sight."

King looked out of the open doorway and noticed the mountainside. It was a similar view out of the other doorway. The .50 might well be good for three thousand metres, but it couldn't shoot around corners.

"Gentlemen, welcome to the Democratic Republic of the Congo..." the pilot announced.

King looked below them. The same Savannah, but ahead of them there were more trees. Beyond a thousand metres the trees thickened, and within a few minutes the hillside was green and lush, and the patches of Savannah were few, like remote islands waiting to be claimed by jungle. The hostages would have suffered covering this ground in the heat and sun, and once they entered the jungle, the humidity would have been stifling. His thoughts were interrupted by a stutter in the engine and change of pitch in the rotors. The helicopter dropped a few metres, but so quickly that they were lifted out of their seats and only held in place by their harnesses. The broken pieces of the sniper rifle lifted off the floor, then dropped back down. Almost instantly, the same thing happened, accompanied by a stutter and another change in pitch.

"We've got problems!" The pilot said but did not elaborate as he fought the control and the helicopter started to drop rapidly.

It all happened so suddenly, but King noted somewhat inevitably. The noise said it all. There simply wasn't the power to keep them in the air. With the loss in power, the pilot couldn't manoeuvre the craft back towards clear ground, and as he tried in vain to do so, the change in direction only compounded the stability and attitude of flight as they dropped in altitude and the trees rushed towards them. They never heard another word from the pilot – the man had his hands full, and it was obvious what was going to happen. And that was when it all slowed down. Time changed so perceptively that King was aware of his own heartbeat, his own inner voice telling him to brace for impact. The world in slow motion. Until he looked out of the open door-hatch, and he saw the tops of trees at eye level. He risked looking down and saw the ground rushing towards them – trees and bushes, rocks, long dried grass – and then nothing but blue, cloudless sky as the helicopter yawed around ninety degrees onto its side, and then tipped nose first into the ground. The sound of buckling metal and breaking glass upon snapping branches, the high-pitched whine of the rotors and the straining engine and the grunts of the pilot in his headphones as he fought to control the craft in vain drowned out King's thoughts. He realised he had been groaning, too. The effects of fighting G-forces and countering the helicopter's spin by gripping hold of the harness and straining to remain in his seat. And then came the sound of the rotors smashing into the ground and tilling the earth briefly before they disintegrated and flew in all directions like shrapnel from a mighty bomb.

King's ears were ringing, and he heard Stewart screaming for them to get out above the struggling engine's noise. The rotors were gone, but the tail rotor was still spinning. King could smell fuel. His senses curiously heightened by the experience. He was aware of the pilot screaming, although the intercom had stopped working, and of Reece struggling to get out of his harness. Stewart was already clambering out and had dropped heavily onto the ground. King was free and climbing out, but he stopped beside Reece, took out his K-Bar and sliced through the man's harness. Reece sprawled out and fell onto the dusty earth. The open hatch was embedded into the ground, so he followed King and climbed out through the starboard side and dropped out along the underbelly of the helicopter as fuel ignited and flames spread through the bay they had occupied just seconds before. Stewart had pulled on the emergency engine shutdown lever and the pilot could be heard screaming, desperately louder now that flames were licking at the rear of his seat.

King ran around the cockpit and started to kick at the plexiglass. The pilot was looking pleadingly at him, flames reaching his back and neck.

"My legs are broken!" He screamed, struggling with his harness.

King continued to kick at the plexiglass, which had now spiderwebbed but would not give completely. The man's screams were ear-splitting, and his face was contorted in agony as the flames engulfed him. King felt the heat against his own face, but he continued to kick in vain at the glass. The single gunshot rang out and the pilot slumped quietly in his seat. King turned around to see Stewart relaxing his aim on the Uzi.

"There wasn't any other choice," said Stewart. "He'd have burned up before we could get him out and like he said, his legs are busted..." Stewart turned and walked to the line of trees. The clearing was only twenty metres square, and the wreckage of the helicopter covered almost every part of it.

King shook his head despairingly. Reece was drinking water and checking what he had managed to keep of his kit. He was in pain and King would bet there was a gunstock shaped bruise across the man's back. Reece looked up at King and said, "He did the right thing." He paused. "Did the guy a favour..."

"Well, I'll be sure to extend you both the same favour if it's ever called for," King replied dismissively.

"Are you OK?" Stewart asked King, who simply shrugged and didn't answer. "What about you, Reece?"

Reece nodded. "Yeah, fine. Just bruised and shaken up." He shrugged. "You'd have to pay a pound for a ride like that at the fair..."

Behind them, rounds were cooking off in the fire. Stewart stepped into the trees and the other two followed. After twenty paces there were enough trees to stop errant bullets being a risk to them. Stewart checked his button compass and said, "This way is northeast. The colonials are heading on that bearing, so now our plan to head in on a pincer movement is down the pan, we'd better make our way towards them and rendezvous early." He looked at King and said, "I see you're not carrying the gimpy, and that little firework display means the seven-six-two ammo didn't make it out either..."

"In his defence, the sniper rifle was fucked, so we don't need the ammo anyway," said Reece.

"But a support weapon like the GPMG would have been invaluable."

"Well, you could have hung around and helped, boss," King replied. "I was a little busy seeing that Reece got out of his harness. Saved you another bullet, though..."

Stewart squared up to him and said, "Have you finished?"

"For fuck's sake!" Reece stood between them as a buffer and continued, "We know the bearing, and we know the objective. So, let's just tab out of here and get the bloody job done."

"Sounds good to me," King replied, not taking his eyes off Stewart's.

Stewart paused a beat, then said, "After you, Alex..."

King unslung his Uzi and said, "No boss, I insist. After you..."

Reece gave them both a shove and said, "For fuck's sake,

I'll take point. You two bitches can decide who follows next."
He took out his own compass and checked the heading,
then drew his machete and started out through the bush.

"Fuck it, he's got a point," said Stewart and followed him,
leaving King to bring up the rear.

King followed. He could smell the pilot's burning flesh.
It smelled like burnt roast pork. He wondered whether he'd
ever eat the pork and crackling at a Toby Carvery again.
There was also the acrid smell of melting plastic and electrical circuits which he imagined would carry on the wind.
Bullets still popped off, but less now that the fire had
worked its way through the helicopter and most of the
7.62mm had popped and banged and fizzed off into the air.
King thought about the unfortunate pilot and Stewart's
calm dispatch. Was it a mercy killing? Or was Stewart
simply a man who would not allow anything to get in the
way of achieving his objective? King knew the truth. He had
suspected as much over the past two years. And having
created a rift between himself and the other three men, he
realised that he could not afford to make any mistakes in
Stewart's eyes. He gripped his weapon firmly and studied
the jungle around him. Threats could come from anywhere
and, he reflected somewhat nervously, not just the men he
had been sent here to kill, but within his own team as well.

18

I t was the first time they had been allowed to leave the huts. Hot and humid though it was, the fresh air made them light-headed; the sunlight made them squint and almost at once a million flying insects swarmed them attracted by their sweat. Buckets of water had been given to them to sluice the fetid mess from the huts and when they had been shouted at and directed by both threats and the jab of a machete tip, what little water that was left was given to them to drink.

Fruit had been tipped onto the ground and they had all snatched up handfuls and squat down to devour their fill. Jane Hargreaves looked at her fellow captives. They had been reduced to animals in just a few days. She wasn't sure exactly how many days and nights had passed. Eight? Nine? She realised that she had forgotten. She had visibly lost weight – they all had – possibly ten or fifteen percent of their body weight already. Maybe more. She knew that she had not eaten at all yesterday. The day before had been a few chunks of hard bread, and before that there had been nothing. Posho or some other maize derivative had been given to them on the second day. She had passed the point of caring what food they had been given since then, just as long as it would fill her belly, but nothing had so far. The water given to them to drink was warm and thick and muddy, and they had barely a cup of the foul smelling and tasting stuff three times a day. Back in London, she drank a full two litres of mineral water throughout the day. More on gym days. Along with several espressos every morning and a glass or two of Pinot Grigio a few nights a week. The other hostages were suffering from the effects of dehydration, too. Muscle cramps, foul-smelling urine the colour of Guinness and a throbbing, persistent headache that made the days longer and denied them sleep throughout the night.

After they had eaten the rotting fruit, two boy soldiers carrying Kalashnikovs screamed at them to move and they were herded along by some of the older boys carrying machetes. They had all seen what the machetes could do to poor Brian Hanson and were all haunted by his death. They followed the boy soldiers to a small stream and were told to wash. Jane first drank her fill, as did everyone, and then sat in the flowing water and allowed it to wash between her legs as she cupped handfuls of the precious liquid and doused her hair and neck, then washed herself all over. The water was cooler than the stifling air, refreshing and revitalising.

Everybody's spirits were raised by the act of washing until two of the older boys pointed to her and told her to get up. Jane could hardly believe what was happening, and sat stock still, looking up at the youths. One of them pointed to the bank of the stream and motioned for her to lie down. She looked at the other hostages for support, but under-standably the other women cast their eyes downwards, grateful it had not been them who had been chosen, and the men seemed frozen to the spot, unable to move, unable to rise to the moment and be a hero, no doubt picturing the unassuming middle aged man who had been hacked to pieces because he had been unable to keep up wearing just one shoe.

One of the youths caught hold of her wrist and pulled her out of the stream. In any other situation it would have been ridiculous. The boy was no older than fourteen and Jane could have smacked him around his ear and sent him on his way. If he resisted, fought back in some way, she could have given him the benefit of her black belt and twelve years' experience in Judo, as well as her experience boxing on the heavy bag that formed the end of her regular gym routines. Even at five-seven and ten stone she trumped him in size and power. But the boys had machetes and guns and lust in their eyes. No help would be coming her way from the other hostages and nor could she blame them. Brian would always act as a reminder of the consequences in any potential action. The thought that the taking of Brian's life had merely served as a lesson suddenly sent a chill down her spine and made her feel sick through her stomach. One of the boys prodded her with the tip of his machete and as she looked back at him, she saw that he was highly aroused under his ragged shorts, and she nearly gagged in revulsion. The youth holding her pointed at the ground and when she didn't move, he hit her around the head with the flat of the machete blade and she cried out, the blade ringing like a tuning fork. He shoved her to the ground and one of the boys excitedly pulled at his shorts and caught hold of his member to bring himself to readiness. Jane closed her eyes, but she had crossed her legs and folded into the foetal position to protect herself and one of the youths kicked her, then flicked the safety down on the Kalashnikov in his hands and shouted at her in a mix of

French and Pidgin English. She knew what they wanted but couldn't find it in herself to willingly comply. The humiliation that it should happen in front of the other hostages – whether they watched or not, for she had seen how they had cast their eyes downward as if to be impervious to the horror and indignation of her ordeal – was all encompassing, and the fear that it would hurt and be a wholly degrading experience was almost secondary to her humiliation of such a public show. At the back of her mind, she prayed that she would not be infected with HIV or AIDS, or God knew what other horrors these odious youths carried. Rape had been a death sentence to thousands of women in the region and it had been encouraged on all sides during the Congo wars and the civil war in neighbouring Angola, and the rates of HIV infections and death through AIDS was higher in West Africa than anywhere else on the planet. Twenty-seven percent versus less than one percent for the rest of the world combined. Jane rolled onto her front, her instincts driving her towards survival. Fight or flight and she had no control over her actions. She could see the whites of the eyes of the four teenagers, and they were crazed and angry and out of control. One of them kicked her in the face and she stopped crawling and rolled onto her back, helped into place by one of the boys, who was holding his flaccid penis. The largest and most developed of the three laughed and told him to shake it to get it hard, but the boy was here through bravado and peer pressure and was not mature enough, so his friend took his place and spread her legs wide as he knelt on the ground and removed his tattered and stained shorts.

Gunfire erupted in the small clearing and several of the hostages fell onto their stomachs in the stream. There were screams and shrieks and the boys cowered as a large man pushed his way between them and spoke in rapid French. He held his Kalashnikov in his right hand. It was a folding stock model, and the curved magazine was in fact four magazines taped together with duct tape. There were gold studs hammered into the wooden fore-end of the rifle and rosary beads and a bunch of feathers hanging from the trigger guard. The boys were thoroughly and harshly admonished, one of them was kicked to the ground and spat upon, another was jabbed so hard in the ribs with the muzzle of the rifle that he fell into the stream and wept like a child. Which, despite the indoctrination and abuse and violent persona, he was.

"Get up!" The man ordered Jane. She did so and when she was on her feet, he looked down at her and said, "Did they have sex with you?"

"It's not sex," she said between tears of relief. She had held emotions together until the moment her ordeal had stopped, and now it was like an emotional floodgate had opened. "It's rape. And there's a huge difference..."

The man cut her short by slapping her across the cheek so hard that she fell backwards into the stream. "Enough!" He shouted, the boys cowering behind him. "I care not whether they fuck you..." He paused, staring Jane in the eyes as she struggled onto her knees. "... or rape you. Because for now, you are all worth something to me. But when you are not..." He smiled at anyone who was brave enough to look up at him. "... then my boy soldiers will do to you as they please..." He stared at them all, his eyes big and bright and with an intensity that only comes from drugs or sincere mental delusion. "My name is Julius Lombobo, and I am your fate and your consequence. I am your God, and you will bow to me..." The hostages cowered, but it was clearly not enough. He drew his machete from his belt and swiped it across the face of the man nearest him, opening his cheek with a four-inch gash, the sound of metal on bone as the blade caught his jawbone was clearly audible and the man shrieked and fell backwards into the stream. "You will bow to me!" Lombobo raged, then smiled gleefully as the hostages all bowed and remained bent over until he said, "Up! Up, my pretties. This is good. This is how you know who is in charge..."

Miles Preston, the unfortunate subject of the demonstration clutched his jaw, the four-inch gash bleeding profusely and the jaw clearly broken. He was a thirty-year old geologist and until now, Jane had thought him most likely to get through this ordeal. The man had told her that he ran marathons and was looking forward to running the Boston Marathon later in the year as he would miss the London Marathon because of this visit. He had a young wife and a two-year-old daughter, and unless he received medical attention, then he wouldn't be getting out of here.

"Mr Lombobo..." Jane said, aware that her voice sounded shaky. "Mr Lombobo, we are in no doubt as to your power and authority," she said, her voice gaining a little more authority, although she tried to sound subservient to the monster in front of them. "Our colleague needs medical attention... his jaw is broken... please will you show mercy and allow me to treat it? I will need some cloth and boiled water..." She watched the man's expression, which was impossible to read. "We are all worth more to you in good health..."

Julius Lombobo did not reply, but he snapped something in a flurry of French to one of the boys and the hostages were all dragged off their knees or prodded with machete tips or the muzzle of assault rifles and herded out of the jungle and back into the clearing. Lombobo led the way, then pushed and pulled each of the hostages towards the three huts. Jane found she was pushed towards a different hut than before, many of the hostages mixed up. They all waited at the steps of the huts as Lombobo strutted in front of them. Suddenly, he looked at Jane and asked, "What is your name?"

Name, rank, and serial number. That was what a soldier was required or expected to tell their interrogator. That was what the SAS instructors had told them on their escape and evasion course in the Black Mountains. The seventy-two-hour course was a compressed version, with survival training and orienteering thrown in before a six-hour simulated interrogation. A group of mainly desk-bound MI5 agents flailing around the Welsh countryside trying not to get hypothermia and learning how to tickle stream trout and light a fire. Well, she wasn't a soldier, and she had no official rank or serial number. She also recognised a mad man when she saw one. But Lombobo and his Southside Boys knew enough about the OPEC delegation and where to find them, so she couldn't treat the man as stupid. "Jane Hargreaves," she answered. "British government attaché."

Lombobo smiled as he pulled Miles out from the group of quivering hostages and held him in front of her. He looked at the hostages in turn, then drew his machete and swiped the man across his neck. Miles fell onto his knees, his throat sliced open and his blood spraying across the faces of the nearest hostages amid their gasps and screams. Lombobo hacked again, this time from the other side, like a woodsman felling a small tree with opposite blows with an axe. The head still did not sever completely, but Miles' eyes looked lifelessly upwards and Lombobo pushed the body onto the ground and a third strike sent the head rolling across the ground and blood pooled from the stump of neck flowing towards the hostages' feet like a pushing tide. Lombobo screamed at them all to get into the huts and some of the youths behind him fired shots into the air. Jane sprawled into the hut, people trampling over her, the screams filling the confines of the hut as everybody tried to get inside and as far from the open doorway as possible. Lombobo picked up the severed head and laughed as he tossed it inside the hut, and it rolled across the bamboo floor and knocked into Jane's legs. And then the door was slammed shut, bolted and darkness enveloped them all.

19

Roger Siegfried rode up front. The Russian driver was armed with a Steyr AUG rifle which was slotted into a couple of moon clips fixed to the centre console. Lucinda thought the man to be rugged looking and cut from the same cloth as King. A predator. Dangerous. She could see that the man had spent a great deal of time under the African sun. His skin was wind-burned and tanned, crow's feet at the corner of his eyes, but she imagined more from squinting against the sun than from age. He was acting as their driver, guide, and body-guard. Siegfried had secured the man's services for a few hundred dollars down payment and negotiated a deal that saw the man collect the bulk of his money only upon their safe return. This was Africa and it never paid to put too much trust in people. The man was called Dimitri and he spoke little, offered nothing more than one or two-word answers when he could and volunteered more in return.

Lucinda wished she had taken King's advice and made the return journey to Luanda. She had cheated on her husband a handful of times. Theirs had been a marriage few would understand, but it worked for them, and she loved him dearly. Certainly, he had given her reason to stray. But the man was at the top of his game in politics and few marriages survived that world intact, or at least unsullied. People did not realise the conceited and egotistical road they travelled, nor what it claimed from them along the way. There was no such thing as an honest politician and the sooner people realised that was indeed a trait that was needed to govern, and that they should not be held in such high esteem, then the less disappointed they would be in the system. Lucinda had known this from the outset of their relationship. She also knew that international journalism was the same. Maybe that was why the public soon lost interest when a reporter went after a politician for a yes/no answer because they hold the reporter or journalist to no higher account. There was an ever-growing expectation within the media to get the story out first, ahead of the rivals and often to the detriment of the truth, leaving those who did not read a newspaper *uninformed*, and those who did read a newspaper *mis-informed*.

"There's awards and prizes written all over this," Roger Siegfried said, turning around to Lucinda and Tom Rutland, his photographer.

Rutland smiled, his eyes a full second or two behind his lips. He was characteristically drunk, but that was probably his genius. The man was a functioning alcoholic, but not many photographers had won more photojournalism awards than Tom Rutland. "Great stuff, Rog. You find me the story, and I'll take the picture that saves you a thousand words, me old mucker!" He grinned at Lucinda next to him and said, "You're on the train to greatness, luvvie. Souls to be sold, next stop…"

Lucinda shuddered. It had been mercifully quick and

would no doubt be unmemorable as time wore on. But as she sat there, bouncing around in the back of the old Land Rover heading to the story, she imagined nothing short of a vagina transplant would make her feel good about herself again. She thought about King and his advice, and she wondered whether she would ever see him again. Subconsciously, she reached for the rosary beads he had given her and worried them between her thumb and forefinger. She glanced down at King's gift to her, and at least it took her mind off the grotesque image of Roger Siegfried on top of her, and the man she had fallen for in Luanda.

20

Reece led the way. He was on point, or stag. Naturally, as first to walk into an ambush, he was mindful of what lay ahead of him and set the pace accordingly. He worked smart, not hard. He used the animal trails, ever vigilant for trip wires or sticks that could be sprung as a trap. Either a carefully fashioned animal trap, or an IED (improvised explosive device) using a grenade or a mine. Landmines had been used by all sides in both the Congo and Angolan conflicts and there were charities east of here doing great work clearing them daily. His eyes were also checking for snakes. There were many venomous snakes from the Puffadder to the Black Mamba and a hundred varieties in between.

King was watching out for snakes, too. He knew that only a few species were deadly, but most bites would require antivenom and hospital treatment, and he couldn't help thinking about the fate of the pilot with his broken legs and terrible burns. Stewart had shown how much the mission had meant to him. It didn't bear thinking about being incapacitated and unable to finish the mission. King held back and checked his rear. There was movement in the trees. He filed off to his right, off the narrow trail made by animals and into the foliage. He shouldered the Uzi and kept the open sights on the trail. More movement. He tightened his finger on the trigger and waited. A chimpanzee crossed the path, walking upright, before dropping down onto all fours. King stepped back out and the ape looked at him, screwed up its face displaying a wickedly sharp set of teeth, then disappeared into the bush. King lowered the Uzi and kept the sights on the trail. There was no movement and no sounds. He backed up a few steps, then turned and stared right into Stewart's face.

"What's the problem?"

"Nothing," replied King, then added, "A chimpanzee."

"Vicious bastards," he replied. "We're in baboon and mandrill country, too. If we see a group of them, we waste them before they can attack us in a group. No hesitation." He paused. "Okay?"

King shrugged. "Of course."

"About the pilot..."

"Forget it."

"Not everything is what it seems." Stewart paused. "Somebody has sold us out." He checked behind him, then looked earnestly at King. "You're the only one I trust..."

21

A round her people sobbed and moaned quietly to themselves. Most prayed. Prayed for their safe return. Jane sat silently in the dark listening to their prayers. They were selfish wants, begging for singular salvation. Jane had not believed in God since she was a child and a degree in physics had given her too much information to debate the possibility of the divine. She had not prayed with her fellow captives, but each to their own. Instead, she was using all she had gleaned from the terrible events at the stream. Her work had taught her how to retain information. During her training with MI5, she had learned to count cards, to memorise scenes or events and recall the relevant information after a period filled with conversation or carrying out certain tasks. It was all about memory recall. And she had been brilliant at it. it was why she had been sent to Angola – to remember everything that transpired during the OPEC exploratory mission and report back to the MI5 and MI6 joint venture controller. She used the darkness of the hut to focus, tuning out the sobs and moans and prayers for safe return. At the stream, the sun had been high. But not directly above them. It was cantered approximately twenty degrees on a line away from the stream to the clearing of the camp. Julius Lombobo's watch was a large tasteless thing with a white strap, a huge gold face, and thick jewel-encrusted hands. A fifty-thousand-dollar piece on the Las Vegas strip or a market job bought for five dollars. Jane would bet on the latter. Perhaps the time was wrong if it had been a market job. Or perhaps the thing had stopped working long ago. But the time had read close to three o'clock, and she had no other choice than to take it as read. Ten minutes, or five minutes to the hour. She concentrated hard, imagined a compass, the position of the sun and the dials of the watch. Upon reaching the camp, she had registered that the huts that they were housed in ran on a lateral line from east to west. Which made the wall of the hut she was now leaning against, the wall furthest from the door, a pointer for due north. There were paths leading south and west. And she remembered entering the camp from the southerly path. Another path led east back to the stream. This would be the camp's natural water supply, and the width and smoothness of the path indicated that it was well used. She then worked out how many hours they had been walking, how many stops and breaks they had taken along the way. The thought ignited her memory of poor Brian and the way he had been hacked to pieces. All limbs brutally severed, unable to move as the machete came down and removed his head after several attempts. The way the animals had eaten his liver as a celebration of their own power and invincibility.

Jane stifled the rise of vomit in her throat. Her training kicking in. Retain fluids and calories. Don't waste a thing. Not even spit. The body only functioned for as long as it retained fluid. She closed her eyes and breathed steadily, calming herself as she tried to move past Brian's death, but it was in vain because the death of Miles was not just fresh in her mind, but she knew that she was entirely to blame for his slaughter. She had tried to help him of course, but her actions had not been solely altruistic – she had used the moment to try and establish a line of communication with her captors. A rapport that could not only lead to a bettering of their conditions, but hopefully lead to compassion and humanity. But that had not been the case, and she knew from that moment that there would be no chance of projecting Stockholm Syndrome upon their captors. She knew from that moment that they were as good as doomed. The Southside Boys would not ask for anything that could be quietly nor easily granted, and besides, 'Great Britain PLC' did not do deals with terrorists. The newly formed Angolan government would not be keen to grant access to foreign special forces and the rag-tag army of the DROC couldn't find coconuts in the Congo, let alone perform a hostage rescue. No, they were on their own. And now she had to formulate a plan for their escape.

22

They rested up in a shady glade, and ate hard rations – cold, no fire or Hexi-block solid fuel tablets to heat them on. King didn't bother with the beans, choosing instead to eat a few handfuls of nuts and dried fruit mix, and drink plenty of water from his camel pack. He didn't want a full stomach as he made his way through the dense vegetation, nor the comfort a meal would bring him. Comfort dragged at alertness and with a meal packed with sugar and fat and salt would come the inevitable sugar crash and tiredness a few hours later. Reece opted for a can of cold curry, eating it with a wooden spoon that had been trimmed down and threaded onto a leather cord he wore around his neck. He shrugged as King watched him remove it but didn't explain. The man simply wasn't going to be caught short. King suspected metal cutlery made unnecessary sound on mess tins, and the man had adapted. He watched him devour the last few mouthfuls, then lick the wooden spoon clean and hang it back around his neck, tucking it inside his shirt. Job done. King turned his eyes to Stewart who had simply taken a few swigs from his silver hipflask. Each to their own. King finished the handful of nuts and dried fruit, then took a few more sips of water from the rubber hose-come-straw of the camel pack. They had sat in a triangle and each man covered the area between the other two, thus giving them a three-hundred-and-sixty-degree watch.

"The numbers are off," said King quietly. "Now that the Huey is down. We needed both choppers for the extraction."

"The Mil will get the job done," Reece replied. "It will be tight, but we're not at any significant altitude to affect payload."

"It will be tight. And weight affects speed, so we'd better hope it's not a hot extraction," Steward said, with a shrug. "But I don't think the numbers will matter quite so much by the time we reach an LZ."

King thought about his comment but didn't say anything. The likelihood of reaching the landing zone with a full complement of hostages and their entire team was negligible. He'd suspected it, albeit somewhat pessimistically, but now Stewart had confirmed his suspicions. People would die.

"Right, let's crack on," said Stewart. He got up and slipped the hipflask back into his inside pocket. He checked the open breech of the Uzi for dirt and debris; pursed his lips gave the action a blow just to make sure. Some machineguns fired from a closed breech, while others fired from an open breech. Both had its merits, but you cut your coat to suit your cloth, and the simple mechanism of the Uzi, its lightness and ease of use as well as its impressive rate of fire without stoppages (jams) made up for its shortfalls.

King adjusted his kit and checked his Uzi. He hung back, preferring to have their six. Not because he wanted to be furthest from the contact, but merely that he was comfortable watching for threats to their rear. Many jungle ambushes relied upon the prey walking past an ambush, then being hit from behind. Reece was carrying a Heckler & Koch MP5, and he checked the safety before shouldering it and moving off. The H&K was an impressive weapon, but the safety catch could move to 'safe' if lightly knocked and the last thing you wanted in a contact with the enemy was a trigger that didn't say 'bang' when you expected it to.

As was standard operating procedure (SOP), the men spread out and walked around ten metres behind the man in front to cut down the chances of all of them being taken down by a single burst of machinegun fire. With every few steps, King made a mental note of nearby cover where he could claim sanctuary behind and possible escape routes through the heavy foliage. If they were hit, then he would know how far he would have to run to get out of the arc of fire and give himself time and composure to return fire. There was nothing to be gained from the 'spray and pray' technique of using a sub-machinegun. Used correctly, they were deadly accurate at a hundred metres and could give suppressive fire out to three-hundred metres. Used with wild abandon, they were useless at twenty feet.

Ahead of Stewart, Reece held up his left fist and crouched down. Stewart followed suit and King stepped off the path entirely, his eyes on the direction they had travelled from, his grip firm on the Uzi, its open sights filling the path. He glanced to his left, enough to see Stewart in his periphery. Beads of sweat built on King's brow, then trickled in rivulets tickling his neck and chest. He ignored the stinging of the sweat in his eyes, keeping them wide open and staring unblinkingly at the path. His heart hammered against his chest, and he worked on controlling his breathing. He hadn't been in contacts in this scenario before, but he had killed efficiently and without hesitation when tested. Like the time he had been up against IRA terrorists and London criminals, and last year in his ill-fated escape from Beirut, and again just two days earlier when both he and Stewart had been held up in Luanda. But this felt different somehow. And then he realised that he was not a professional soldier, and that he was close to battle.

King heard movement next to him and looked back as Stewart stepped closer to him.

"There are three tangos ahead. All armed with longs," Stewart informed him quietly. "Reece is waiting to see what happens next, but we think we should hit them and try to keep one of them alive for questioning."

"Are they a threat?" King asked. "Can we not just skirt around them?"

"They're armed. And they'll know the jungle like it's their backyard."

"It's a dangerous place. I imagine many people carry guns, especially after so many years of civil war." King paused, wiping some sweat from his brow. "They might not even be Southside Boys."

"And if they are, then we have a good source of intel."

"And if it's three blokes just making their way through the jungle?"

"Then, it's a bad day for them, I suppose." Stewart paused. "I want you in on it. I'll take the rear and cover you both. Work out with Reece who goes down."

"But..."

"But, fucking nothing!" Stewart hissed. "It's your job. Get it done."

King turned and made his way down the path. He came up slowly on Reece, who was now deeper into the foliage and aiming his MP5 at the three men. King crouched down beside him and frowned. "How old do you think they are?" he whispered.

"Old enough to carry AKs and not hesitate in using them on us."

King paused a beat, then said, "I get that..."

"I'll take the one on the right and you take the one on the left," said Reece. It made sense; King was on Reece's left and there was no sense crossing the arcs of fire. "Then we get up and rush the kid in the middle."

King was glad the man had said 'kid', for that was what they all were and there was nothing to be gained by pretending otherwise. King would hazard a guess at fourteen to sixteen. But like the man had said, they all carried either AK-74 or AK-47 assault rifles and wouldn't hesitate in using them. They were all dressed in shorts and dirty T-shirts. The boy in the middle was a full head shorter than his companions and wearing a bright red T-shirt. King aimed his Uzi at the person next to the smaller boy and took a deep breath. The 'target' was sixty metres from him. The path had entered a clearing and there was the sound of running water nearby. King guessed there was a stream or river behind the three youths. He blinked through the stinging sweat, allowed his finger to touch the trigger and rest still. Again, his own heartbeat thudded and the pulse in his ears meant he could hear little else. Another breath and he said, "Ready..."

"On one."

"Check."

"Three..."

King risked another breath. Willed his nerves to hold and his aim to be true.

"Two..."

The target in his sights had a second to live. He watched

him take the last casual and carefree breath he'd ever take, saw the last image of tranquillity in the man's eyes before there would only be fear, pain, and confusion. Or hopefully, immediate death.

"One..."

King fired three successive shots. He couldn't hear, but Reece had done the same. Reece's aim had not been as keen as King's and as the man stood up and charged forward alongside King, he suddenly stopped and took aim again, then sent another three shots into the boy, who had rolled onto his side and was screaming in agony and confusion. The boy stopped moving on the third shot and the screaming stopped with an eerie silence that was total in its finality. King had the boy in the red T-shirt in his sights. The boy had dropped his rifle in the confusion and turned and fled into the jungle. King hurdled the growth of lower fronds and branches and took off after the fleeing boy. Behind him, he heard Stewart shouting at Reece to check the other tango. King ran hard and fast and hurdled more branches. Thorns dug into his arms, some the size and thickness of fingers tapering to needle-sharp tips. There was no time to check for snakes, his boots trampling the ground and his eyes on the myriad of animal trails inter-secting one another. Ahead of him, he saw a flash of red and realised that it was the boy. King quickened his pace, then veered to his right and after ten more seconds of sprinting and hurdling, he had halved the boy's lead. King crashed through a bush that the boy ran around, and when he broke out the other side, he was just feet from the boy, and he risked a tackle. King cannoned into him, his shoulder smashing into the boy's hips and his left arm grip-ping around his legs in a textbook rugby tackle. The boy grunted and went down hard. King pushed the Uzi into the boy's face and with his left hand, he caught hold of his T-shirt and pulled him up. The cloth gave and the T-shirt ripped completely off him. King stared at the boy, the muzzle of the Uzi just inches from his face. The boy's eyes were white with terror, and then he cast his eyes to the ground and started to sob. King studied him closely and with a feeling of disgust. What had he done? The boy could not have been much older than nine or ten, and already King could see he had lived a harsh and tragic life. Scars criss-crossed his young skin and part of his ear was missing. To King's horror, he could see that several of the boy's fingers were missing, too. What had been the boy's fate to this point? And what would become of him after he answered Stewart's questions? If Stewart could shoot an injured pilot in his employ because he jeopardised their mission, then what would he do to an enemy boy soldier who he no longer had any use for?

"What is your name?"

The boy just looked at him. Not belligerently, just scared and confused.

"*Quel est votre nom?*" King tried again in French.

The boy hesitated then said, "*Je ne me souviens plus...*"

The boy could no longer remember. King frowned, then asked him why.

"*Je suis un chien soldat.*"

King allowed the boy's words to sink in. *I am a dog soldier...*

"*Un chien des Southside Boys...*" the boy added.

A dog of the Southside Boys...

King pulled the boy to his feet. He lowered the weapon but kept the business end on the boy. He asked him how he lost his fingers and how he got the scars.

"*Mes doigts se sont arrachés quand j'ai refusé d'aimer mes maîtres...*" The boy paused, tears welling in his eyes. *"J'ai été fouetté quand je n'ai pas appris..."*

King thought on the boy's answers. He was still learning French in the basement of MI6 using the DVD audio program and headphones. It was tedious and boring and if he had learned enough, then he had just heard that the boy's fingers were bitten off when he refused to serve his masters, and he was whipped with a cane when he did not learn properly.

King asked one more question.

"Je crois que j'ai neuf ans..."

The boy wasn't entirely sure, but he thought he was ten years old.

King stepped backwards and looked around him. The boy closed his eyes and slowly shook his head. Unthinkable that at just ten years of age, he suspected he was about to be shot. What had he seen in his short and tragic life to think such a thing? How much suffering had he endured or seen, or God forbid, bestowed upon others? King tapped him on the shoulder and the boy tentatively opened his eyes. King pointed to his right and said, *"Va par là et ne t'arrête pas..."*

The boy did not need telling twice and he took off in the direction King was pointing as if his feet were on fire. King trudged back through the jungle, eventually coming back just short of the clearing where Stewart and Reece were waiting. The bodies were no longer there. The two men had hidden them from view. Reece had one of the AK-74s slung on his shoulder. King saw that he had taped around the sling clips with some duct tape to stop any rattle. Stewart had favoured the AK-47 and had performed the same trick with the tape. That left the other AK-74 for King. He preferred the calibre anyway. Less power and recoil than the AK-47 and in theory more effective. The Soviets hadn't been an imaginative bunch naming their weapons. One was made in 1947 and the redesign had come along in 1974. King picked up the assault rifle and slung the Uzi over his shoulder. He would have preferred a more powerful weapon from the off, and now he had.

"Where's the fucking kid?" Stewart asked.

"Lost him."

"Then, what are you doing back here?"

King shrugged. "Couldn't stay out there all day. I didn't want to compromise the objective."

"We'll be fucked if they know we're coming," said Reece.

"Hey, I made a judgement call." He glared at him and said, "If you want to kill the little fucker so badly, then head that way..." He pushed past him and stood at the start of the trail northwards. "Are you both coming, or what?"

23

Dimitri kept the engine running and the Land Rover in reverse gear. It wasn't a suitable vehicle to perform an evasive 'J' turn, but reverse took them away from the truckload of men and their Kalashnikovs. His left hand gripped the pistol grip of the Steyr assault rifle. He may have been out-gunned, but he doubted he was out-classed, and he reckoned on taking out a few before they got their eye in. A swift reverse, an even swifter turn, and they would be heading back down the track and back towards Cafunfo.

Dimitri had it all planned out. But he was an experienced enough soldier to know his plan would go all to shit as soon as the first bullet was fired. He'd learned enough about battles in Afghanistan, and later in Chechnya when he fought with the Spetsnaz in the Russian army. Ramshackle civilians, ill-equipped and with poor tactics had almost brought the might of the Russian Federation to its knees. Russia had won, of course, but not without declaring just a third of the true Russian death toll and spending nine years fighting the ensuing insurgency and causing worldwide condemnation for war crimes and Chechen civilian casualties.

"What do we do?" Roger Siegfried asked, his eyes not leaving the men in the truck.

Dimitri shrugged. "You wanted to meet the Southside Boys," he replied. "Go meet them..."

Siegfried nodded to Lucinda. "Go on, honey. You want a story, too."

"Fuck off, Roger!" Lucinda said, looking at the man who had got out of the truck and now stood out in the open. "Jesus Christ, this seems such a stupid idea now..."

"I wouldn't recommend sending the woman," Dimitri commented. "No offence, Miss." He paused. "But you'd better make some sort of move before they do something irrational."

"*You're* our guard," Siegfried replied tersely. "*You* go."

Dimitri shook his head. "No, you need to discuss what you want from them. What else did your contact say?"

"He set the place and the time." Siegfried shrugged. "I thought he'd be here, too."

"And he's not?"

"No."

"Come on, Rog," Tom Rutland slurred. "It's not like we haven't done this a hundred times before. Remember Croatia?" He paused. "These arseholes haven't got anything on those fucking crazy Serbs."

"Right..." Siegfried nodded.

"Oh, fuck it," Rutland laughed. "I'll go and talk to the wankers and tell them what we want and how much we're willing to pay for the story." He paused as he opened the door. "I bet we can secure a deal with some trinkets and jewellery from Luanda market!" He closed the door after him and bent down beside the open window. "Not so different from when Livingstone, Speke and Burton did deals with the fuzzies. Not long down from the trees, but they certainly like shiny trinkets. These idiots will be the same..." He strode over confidently, although there was some whisky-induced swagger.

Dimitri watched intently. He could see the black man's face and he could read his expression. Although he could not see Tom Rutland's face, he could see from the man's body language that he was indeed relaxed and amiable. The two men spoke for five minutes, then Rutland patted the man on the shoulder and turned back towards them. He made it three steps before the other man pulled out a pistol and shot him in the back of the head. Rutland crumpled, but not before his face opened wide and his brains, blood and bone matter spurted into the air. His body fell forwards and lay twitching on the ground. Dimitri hadn't seen it coming. The gunman's expression had been calm and the action was so bizarre that for a moment the Russian had been caught napping. He slammed his foot down on the accelerator and the Land Rover shot backwards. Lucinda screamed and Roger Siegfried cursed a string of expletives. The only thing going for them was that the men in the rear of the truck had been caught napping, too. They shouldered their weapons, but not until Dimitri had swung the Land Rover into a suitable careful turn, and without drama, the Russian was working through the gears, the vehicle reaching fifty-miles-per-hour before the first shots were fired. Only there were many shots fired and before they could get out of the line of fire. The vehicle was being pummelled with bullets. Lucinda ducked down and sprawled on the rear seats. Bullets shattered the glass and rear door, and the spare wheel that was fixed on the rear door was torn up and bullets penetrated the steel and the rear seat rest. Roger Siegfried shouted, then moaned, then slumped in his seat. Another volley of gunfire and the reporter from The Times writhed in agony, then a bullet found the back of his head and the windscreen was painted crimson. The Land Rover struggled for stability and Dimitri lost control as both rear wheels were punctured and lost grip, inertia taking over and forcing the vehicle into a roll. Crushing metal on rocks and shattering glass sounded like gunfire.

Lucinda screamed and when the vehicle finally rested still, she was battered and bleeding and winded. She felt like retching, but she needed to get clear. Needed to get away. She crawled out, her hands catching in broken glass and gravel. Above her, the wheels were spinning, and it was only then that she realised that the Land Rover was on its roof. The fact the vehicle was upside down was almost impossible to compute. She could see the men running towards her, and she realised that if she could get a gun from the front of the vehicle, then she could try and hold them off. Or at least try. But then she realised that the Russian was her only hope. She turned and crawled back towards the Land Rover, desperate to get Dimitri out and beg him for his help. Perhaps together, they would stand a chance. Lucinda peered inside, but the space was taken up with Roger Siegfried's punctured and twisted body and the Russian was nowhere to be seen. Perhaps he had been thrown clear? She crawled around the front of the vehicle to the other side, but Dimitri wasn't there. She slumped helplessly, the first of the men making it to her, the muzzles of assault rifles in her face and shouts and screams in languages she didn't understand mixed with odd-sounding French and Pidgin English. She was terrified, but not about what had just happened. She was terrified of what was to come.

24

There were three pre-arranged rendezvous points using nothing more than coordinates on the map. The map showed the terrain and the elevation, but it did not show whether there were small settlements nearby. It was a punt at best. The first two rendezvous points were unmakeable. There was no point in even trying. The helicopter had gone down fifty miles short of their reconnaissance area. The plan had been to make their way in from the north, then meet up at the rendezvous points as the situation allowed. With no chance of making the first two coordinates, it was an all-out slog to reach the third. They hydrated regularly, ate on the march and shared point duty. Their comms would be essential for coordinating the raid and rescue but had little effectiveness in the dense jungle. The units would work within four miles line of sight, but in the dense terrain, that would be down to around three-hundred metres. Even so, Stewart tried to contact the others every fifteen minutes or so, hoping to get lucky.

King had refilled his camel pack twice from the myriad

of tiny streams intersecting the jungle, dropping two water purifying tablets into it, and allowing thirty minutes for it to kill the bacteria before drinking. It tasted like chlorinated swimming pool water, but it did the job. Animals had a nasty habit of heading for water when they were dying, and you never knew before drinking whether there was a dead antelope or goat upstream, half-eaten by maggots or ridden with Tsetse fly eggs and larvae. He checked his watch, then his compass. They were no longer on track to make the rendezvous. Stewart knew this, too. He put his own compass away and looked at King.

"An hour more at this pace," he said. "But I don't like walking into a rendezvous without scoping it out first."

"I hear you," panted Reece.

"Can you step up the pace?" Stewart asked King.

King shrugged. "I suppose so."

"I can if you need me to," said Reece. "I've got a bit left in the tank." He paused, still breathing heavily. "Not a lot, but I should be able to double my pace for twenty minutes."

Stewart looked at the two men, then shook his head and said, "No, King will go." King nodded. Stewart reached for his water canteen and by the time he had unscrewed the cap, King had disappeared into the jungle.

"Will he get there in time?"

Stewart nodded. "If anybody can, it's him." He drank thirstily, then clipped the canteen back onto his belt. "But hopefully as we draw near the comms will fall into range and we can contact the others."

"You didn't tell him we weren't going to make the third and last rendezvous," said Reece.

Stewart shrugged and replied, "He doesn't need that sort of pressure, but if he doesn't make it in time, we'll be running around this place like headless chickens and hoping we're in comms range and the units hold their batteries. After that, we're fucked." He paused and checked his weapon before starting off in the direction King had set off in. "Hopefully the colonials will have more luck than us..."

25

She had covered stories of war crimes, rape, and ethnic cleansing in the region, including the war with neighbouring Zaire, so she knew what happened when the United Nations soldiers were no longer around to offer a deterrent. The stories she had written for the broadsheets and magazines with sensational headlines and thought-provoking quotes seemed somewhat trite now that she was alone and in the centre of an unravelling story. Like many journalists she had written most of her stories from the comfort of hotel rooms using fact-finding excursions, interviews with the abused or eyewitnesses and information volunteered for a price. It was true that she had been to some of the scenes of the most harrowing crimes on the continent, but usually after the event and rarely during the conflicts. Her job was to mop up after the crimes and find the truth. Or at least, the bestselling version of the truth. But who would write her story? Who would write about the deaths of Roger Siegfried and Tom Rutland? And as she thought about how she was now the story, and not the person writing an account of what was happening, Lucinda felt helpless and alone. Resigned to her fate.

She was sitting cross-legged behind the truck. The man who had killed both Rutland and Siegfried held the same pistol aimed at her head with his right hand, and in his left, he held her own passport open, studying her details. Rutland's and Siegfried's passports were tucked into his pocket, and he had used a small digital camera to take pictures of both men's bodies. Lucinda suspected he was more than a drug-addled soldier of the Southside Boys, and perhaps handled their press and coverage. Indeed, if he was the man Siegfried had arranged to meet, her assumption made sense.

"This man *Seeg-a-freed* did not tell us you would be with them." He smiled mirthlessly. "I was under the impression that he was coming alone."

"Please, don't kill me..." she begged.

"He was meant to come alone. I did not like this man who spoke to me. I did not like the look of his driver, either." The man paused. "*Seeg-a-freed* was clearly not a man to be trusted."

"I'm sorry," she said, although she did not know what she was apologising for. "I did not know what had been arranged, Roger Siegfried said I could tag along and write my own story..." She trailed off as she remembered her thankfully brief time with the man, and the price she had paid to be in on the story she thought would be her biggest break to date. "But I can still write a story," she said, suddenly realising her value to him. After all, he *had* arranged to meet a journalist. "I can write the story you want told. The story you all deserve..."

He seemed to consider this for a moment. Right up until the moment a bullet smashed into his skull and lifted the top off his head like a car bonnet. Lucinda was sprayed with blood and bone splatter and the man dropped onto his knees, suddenly closer to her own height as she sat there. His eyes were lifeless, but still he remained kneeling. Time seemed to have frozen, but almost as if someone had wound the scene on with a fast-forward button, gunshots rang out and the truck was peppered with bullets. The men on board were caught in the hail of hot lead and copper and as Lucinda cast her eyes towards the vehicle, she saw men and boys cut down, and others struggling to return fire. Lucinda looked back at the man, but during her brief glance away, he had fallen onto his back, his feet underneath his back and his knees in the air; his arms spread wide.

She could hear the change in tone of the gunfire. The Kalashnikovs sounded louder, but with a less sharp report. There was a distinct pause in the gunfire that had taken down so many of the Southside Boys, and then it started up again. Three successive shots, then a pause, then three more. It continued like this for ten barrages, and the sharp smell of fuel as the truck's fuel tank was ruptured was replaced with burning rubber and oil and petrol. Lucinda realised that the fuel had been ignited by the muzzle flashes of the men firing from the truck bed and inevitably, many of the men were engulfed in flames as the vapour ignited.

Lucinda gasped as two men snatched her up, pulled her harshly off the ground and backed away into the jungle. They were firing their weapons using just one hand with the other hand gripping her tightly. Their weapons bounced wildly, and the bullets must have gone everywhere but towards the intended target. The truck was ablaze and there were the piercing and chilling screams from men burning alive. Lucinda felt the fizz of a bullet near her head as it sung past her, barely inches from impact. She felt herself turned around by rough hands, then as she managed to run under her own steam, she was guided and pushed into the jungle. Her eyes met another man's. He was crouched and firing past the truck. His eyes burned fiercely and she would have sworn that he was high on drugs by the expression and movements he made. And then he was dead. A bullet slamming into his right eye and blowing out the back of his head. He fell backwards and rested still. Lucinda was pushed past him and the two men forcing her away from the ambush screamed for her to keep moving and she ran for her life, away from the danger and into the unknown.

26

Dimitri had fled the crash almost before the Land Rover had stopped moving. Tactically, he knew that he did not have a chance unless he got clear of the vehicle and gained some distance from their attackers. The reporter was dead, and the woman was screaming inside the wreckage, so she was alive, but she would be dead if he remained there. They both would.

He had grabbed the Steyr and his webbing containing his knife, satphone, water bottle and spare magazines for both the assault rifle and his pistol. He used the wreckage of the Land Rover as cover, checked on the distance and view his attackers would have of him, then ran directly into the treeline. He could already hear the shouts of the men above the hammering of his own heartbeat and by the time he had flung himself into the foliage, he could hear them shouting instructions and taunts at the pretty female journalist.

Using the cover of the jungle, thick and lush just feet from the clearing, he had worked his way around in an anti-clockwise direction until he had a clear line of sight at the man who appeared to be interrogating the journalist, and the rest of the men who were either languishing beside the truck or had leapt back into the truck bed under the shade afforded them by the overhanging branches.

The Steyr was equipped with one of the best riflescopes in the business and unlike every other military weapon, was an integral part of the design. The rifle was a bullpup design, meaning that the magazine and working parts of the weapon were located at the rear and behind the shooter's cheek when fired. This made for a short, easily manoeuvrable weapon, but still allowed a longer barrel to be used which therefore gave the weapon unrivalled accuracy and increased the power and efficiency in ballistics of the 5.56mm ammunition. Dimitri was lying prone, well-concealed and thanks to the Swarovski x 1.5 sight, had a magnified field of fire at a distance of just under one-hundred metres. The term 'shooting fish in a barrel' had literally been coined for this scenario. And so, the ex-spetsnaz soldier had gone to work.

The man who had shot both journalists had a pistol aimed at the female journalist. Dimitri thought that made the man's intentions clear, and so he went down first. Dimitri had seen the pink mist of the headshot and had engaged his next two targets before the man had even hit the ground. He had worked his way through the men leaning and lying back against the truck first – the men inside the truck-bed with its wooden slatted sides were contained for now – and he had sent three rounds into the external fuel tank before working his way to the other men. By now the men had seen enough muzzle flashes from his position and he had bugged out. He ran deeper into the jungle, turned sharply, and put thirty good paces in before heading back to the treeline. From there, he had fired in well-disciplined bursts of three, each time rolling or crawling to conceal his position. He had put more rounds into the fuel tank, but he knew from his experience in the last days of the Soviet occupation of Afghanistan and his extended service in Chechnya that fuel seldom ignited from a bullet. However, he had seen muzzle flashes ignite the fumes many times, and the men in the bed of the lorry would hopefully take care of that aspect for him.

The Russian then put in his biggest tactical manoeuvre yet. He charged through the jungle putting fifty metres behind him, but when he dipped into the treeline to engage, the truck was already on fire and he could see the female journalist being bundled into the jungle by two of the Southside Boys, with another giving covering fire. By the time he had shouldered his weapon to use the magnification of the riflescope and shot the man who was returning threateningly accurate fire, they were gone.

27

They had been allowed out to empty the buckets used for defecation and to fill the bucket used for fresh water. Jane Hargreaves could see tiny larvae the size of poppy seeds in the water swimming erratically like the tadpoles she had collected as a child from the River Itchen in her native Hampshire, but she was too thirsty to care. Someone had rolled Miles' head out of the hut, and it rested in the earth two paces from the steps. The smell was putrid, and flies had massed around the eyes and mouth. Jane couldn't bear to look at it. Not only was it a reminder of the man who had once been alive and among them – a friend - but it also served as a warning that they had no control over their destiny and their own mortality was in the hands of the Southside Boys. Erratic and unpredictable hands at that.

They had been given two metal buckets of boiled rice to share between the huts. The rice was such a short grain and overcooked to the point it had become a porridge-like sludge. Naturally it had not been seasoned, but anything was better than posho. When she had burned herself trying to tip out the rice one of the men had tossed her a metal spoon. The implement was ridiculously small for the task, but she scooped it out nonetheless and the guard sauntered off to talk to another man. Jane got the rice out into the assortment of metal mess tins, chipped porcelain plates and halved coconut shells. The hostages ate hungrily, their filthy fingers scraping the rice into their mouths before greedily licking the bowls or plates. It was by far and away their largest meal to date and as soon as the food settled in their stomachs, most of them doubled over in pain.

"Drink as much water as you can," said Jane, scooping water out of the filthy bucket with her own coconut shell and drinking it down quickly. "It will help to aid digestion. Our stomachs are working overtime..."

Many of her fellow hostages heeded her advice, but some were already squatting to defecate, such was the effect of the heavy stodge in their guts. There was no dignity in their lives now.

One of the guards yelled at them, barking out orders in pidgin English and French. They scurried into the huts and the doors closed behind them, a void of darkness enveloping them, save for the glint of light as the metal spoon in Jane's hand glinted in the tiny shafts of light penetrating the straw and hardened mud walls.

28

King had made the rendezvous point with minutes to spare. It had been a good call on Stewart's part, but that was only to be expected. The man had fought in the Falklands and in covert contacts the world over ever since. His experience was unrivalled on all sides of the Cold War and the current state of play between East and West that sometimes seemed a hell of a lot more active than it had ever been.

King was breathing hard as he stared at the two bodies on the ground. He looked back at Jim and Tom. Tom was subdued, but Jim didn't appear to care either way. The Australian had no connection with the man outside of this contract and it was clear that he was just a hired gun.

"The idiot hesitated," said Jim, as if justifying his demeanour. "And now he's dead."

"He was a good man, bro," Tom said gruffly. "A good man to have with you when you need it most."

"Unless he refuses to shoot a kid..." Jim said before spitting a flob of spit and snot near the two corpses. "Now we're a man down when we need him the most."

King stared at Piers' body. The man had taken a round to the throat and judging by the quantity of blood on his clothing, he had bled out quickly. His features looked pale and gaunt, as if loosing so much blood changed the shape and mass of the man's body. Which King supposed it had.

"Jim settled it," Tom explained, nodding towards the boy's body. "Serves the little cunt right..."

King saw that the body was riddled with bullet holes. The boy's eyes were open, and his mouth was agape. Flies had already found their way inside. But it wasn't the sight of the boy's dead eyes, the flies or the blood that turned King's stomach and made him fight the urge to retch. It was something else. It was the feeling of regret.

"Fucking poor operational security," Stewart commented as both he and Reece broke cover and stepped into the clearing. "If we'd been Southside Boys, we'd have cut you all to ribbons..." He paused, staring at the two bodies. "Jim, get to the other side of the clearing and set up a firing position." He turned to Tom and asked, "What the fuck's happened here then?"

"The boy stepped out of the jungle with two others. The other two ran for it, but that little fucker raised his AK. Piers hesitated and got himself slotted." Tom paused. "He was a good man. My friend. He didn't deserve to go out like that."

"And yet that's ultimately our fate. Fighting men can't avoid it forever," replied Stewart. He unfastened his water bottle and drained half of it in large gulps. He tipped the rest over his face and rubbed the sweat and insects away before saying, "And I'd rather that than die in my fucking slippers in front of the TV..."

"Jim fired down on the kid. He went batshit crazy. The other two didn't get far, either. They're lying dead in the jungle about a hundred metres west of here."

"He got them both?"

"Yes."

"Proof?" he asked, glancing at King, then back at the South African.

"He's got the right ear off each." Tom looked at King, who was frowning. "Jim's old school." He shrugged. "Anyway, we've all been paid for ears or fingers in the past..."

Stewart nodded. He didn't condone the practise, but mercenaries were a different breed. They worked solely for money, and you cut your coat to suit your cloth. "OK. Well, get the man's effects and tidy him up. We can't take him with us. You can say a few words if you like." He turned to King and said, "I want a word."

King followed Stewart to the other side of the clearing. He already knew what was in store. As he followed Stewart, he eased off the safety catch on his weapon, and checked to make sure nothing would snag. He was in a dirty little war that would never be recorded, so he would make sure he did not become expendable.

"That little shit just killed one of us," he said. "Don't bullshit me. It's the same little bastard who you chased into the jungle." Stewart stared at King intently, reading his protégé's expression. "Only, you didn't lose him. You let him go." King shrugged and nodded, but he said nothing. Excuses weren't going to help Piers now. "So, he hooked up with some of his friends and ended up killing Piers."

King shrugged. "I'm sorry. I didn't think it would pan out like that."

"Why did you let him go?" Stewart asked earnestly.

"Why do you think?"

"Because he was just a kid?"

"Yes."

"Well, let me tell you that they're not," Stewart growled.

"These boy soldiers are brainwashed and lethal. They are taught to rape and torture and kill and as you can see by Piers' fucking body, they won't hesitate to do either."

"I get it," King replied curtly.

"Does it bother you that you fucked up and a man is dead?"

"Of course!" King snapped.

Stewart looked behind him, noticed that Reece and Tom were watching them. "Be ready to move in five!" he shouted at them, before turning back to King. "If those guys find out that you lied about killing that little bastard, and that he lived long enough to kill Piers, then you're toast. They'll burn you the first opportunity they get."

"Then they'd better not find out." King pushed past Stewart and returned to the bodies. He crouched down and took the spare magazines out of Piers' webbing and stacked them beside his body. The man had carried an Uzi also, so King helped himself to three magazines and left the rest for Stewart and Tom. "Did he have anyone at home?" King asked Tom. "A partner or kids?"

"Kids all over from what I gather," he replied sullenly. "There was a woman in Durban that he sometimes spoke about."

King opened the man's tunic and could see a notebook. He took it out and flicked through it. Addresses and phone numbers. King was about to pocket it when Stewart snatched it from him.

"No condolence letters home to loved ones on this job," he said. "The man knew the risks." He tucked the notebook back in place and ordered Tom to frag the body.

"But..."

"No buts," Stewart said coldly. He cast his eyes down at Piers' body and started to pray, "Our Father who art in heaven, hallowed be thy name. Thy kingdom come. Thy will be done on earth as it is in heaven. Give us this day our daily bread, and forgive us our trespasses, as we forgive those who trespass against us, and lead us not into temptation, but deliver us from evil. For thine is the kingdom and the power, and the glory, forever and ever. Amen." He paused, allowing the stark finality to settle in the silence. "Stand easy soldier, your duty is done..." He looked at Tom and said, "Frag him and let's get going."

Stewart swiped the magazines and headed for the edge of the clearing. When he turned around, Jim, Reece and King were following, and Tom was pulling the ring out of a fragmentation grenade. As the men got clear, Tom knelt, eased up Piers' shoulder and released the spring-loaded striker lever, before pushing the grenade under the body. In one fluid motion he rolled up to his feet and walked quickly away. You never ran. Running led to tripping. After four seconds Tom was clear, and the grenade exploded and did its job. Piers was unrecognisable, and the notebook had been turned to charred confetti.

"Move out," Stewart said tersely. "Let's get this job done and get the fuck out of here..."

29

Dusk was falling. The gloom inside the hut was darkening, the shafts of light penetrating the worn mud and straw walls that had once shone white and yellow had deepened to gold and red and was threatening to fade completely any moment. Jane had turned her back on her fellow hostages, although the hut was too dark for most people to notice, and she had worked at the wall with the metal spoon. The mud was dry and dense, not unlike old and crumbling concrete, and the straw bound the mortar in pace, difficult to break with the makeshift blade of the spoon. But she worked hard at it, estimating it to have taken an hour to create a hole the size of a tennis ball. Nobody asked what she was doing, everybody was in their own personal hell of heat, stress, and fear.

An indeterminable time later – perhaps an hour, perhaps four or five - and she had a hole large enough to squeeze through. Her hands were bloody, and she was drenched in sweat. Her thirst had been quenched by the bucket of larvae-infested water, and somewhat interestingly voices murmured in the darkness that she was drinking too much. An unfair share of their supply. Those same voices though, did not tell her to stop her excavating. The constant chipping away of baked mud, the sound of it crumbling onto the wooden floor. It was obvious what she was doing, and yet all that had been voiced was concern for their own water supply. It did not take long for the veneer of civilisation to peel and break and splinter.

Jane now had to weigh up her options. The hole was big enough for her slight frame, but many of the hostages would struggle to get through. Dawn was not far off and the risk that the hole would be discovered was great, especially as it was clear that many of the Southside Boys defecated and urinated around the side of the huts. And then there was the other two huts. There was no guarantee that they would be able to get them out. Jane suspected that many of the occupants of her own hut were so terrified that they would not risk escaping because of the consequences of being recaptured. They would all remember the images of Brian and Miles being cut down with machetes for the rest of their days. No, Jane had the training, and she had the will to survive. And if she was captured, then at least she would have died fighting for her freedom, and not like some fatted veal calf in a stall.

She had earlier noted the direction of the rising and setting sun, the time on Lombobo's tasteless wristwatch and the direction from which they had been marched into the camp. The points all added up to a compass and she was well-read on the region – enough to know that the village of Latistra would be to the northwest. There was a temporary UNICEF aid camp there and an airstrip used by Oxfam twenty miles further north. She estimated it would be ten miles to Latistra. Perhaps twenty. But that meant the jungle would thin to plains. To the northeast were the diamond fields. There would be people there, but nobody that would help her. Still classed as conflict, or blood diamonds, they were extracted from the ground using slave labour. There was more reason to avoid such an area than to seek help there. And that left Angola to the southwest, south, and southeast.

She started to squeeze out through the hole, wondering how many of her fellow hostages would follow her out into the darkness. Dawn wasn't far off and the best chance she had of escape was to put distance between herself and the camp in the darkness. A dangerous thing to do but better than her fate if she remained. And this way, she had the smallest of chances to get help for the others. The jungle was full of thorns and scorpions, spiders, and snakes – big cats, too. In fact, everything that inhabited the plains made its way into the jungle for shade and food and water. So, she knew that when she stepped out into the jungle, she was stepping into her place within the food chain. But she figured that was several links further up the chain than where she was now.

Her first breath of freedom was malodorous, putrid. Rather than digging a latrine away from the camp, the guards had used the area directly outside the rear of the huts as a toilet. Flies and other winged insects made the piles of excrement look like a living, breathing entity and as Jane pushed and scraped her way out, the mass of insects shifted and buzzed around her face, pitching near her eyes and nose and mouth. Disgusted, she wriggled a hand clear and swiped at them, and by the time she squeezed her torso out, she was covered in the creatures. She could not hear her fellow hostages make any attempt to follow her, but she imagined they remained resolutely silent in the gloom. Frozen in fear and regret that they too had not escaped when they had the chance. Perhaps others would follow. But as she dropped onto the ground, her shins scraping raw on the dried mud, twigs, and straw of the hut's wall, she already knew that nobody would follow. Perhaps they had faith in the British Government to negotiate their freedom. Perhaps they had no faith in their abilities to survive in the wild of the jungle. Jane did not know, and nor did she care. She was out and on her own, and her own survival was down to her. She had taken control of her destiny.

30

"No sign?" Stewart whispered.

"None."

"But there's Southside Boys around. We slotted two and you killed three." He didn't look at the man as he said this, he did not want to show any sign of a tell. He had not said that the boy who had killed Piers and been shot up by Jim was the same person. That would lead to too many questions for King.

"So, now we still don't know where the hostages are being held, but the enemy will be aware something's wrong." Tom paused, taking a sip of water from his canteen. "These lads had been sent out to patrol. When they don't come back, their commanders will get worried. They may even move the hostages."

Stewart checked his watch. Another hour until dawn. Until then, they would remain on lay-up. King was asleep, having chopped some ferns to make a makeshift mattress in a depression in the soil. He was completely out of view. Jim had chosen to lay nearby, his back to the other two men. He had rolled over as he had started to snore. Reece should have been asleep, but he had woken twenty minutes before and was getting a brew on for a cup of tea. It was a simple case of burning a solid fuel tablet in a mess tin and placing a tin cup with water and a teabag on top. The Londoner had tipped a sugar sachet and dried milk in as well. It would look and taste more like a tea soup. Normally Stewart would have denied luxuries over hard routine, but they had let off enough rounds and the grenade would have announced their presence if the camp was nearby. A cup of tea wasn't going to jeopardise the mission, although he conceded that had probably happened before darkness had fallen. He was glad this was a deniable operation – he was beginning to think it wasn't going to look good on his CV.

"We're close," Reece said quietly. "Topography wise, they'll need their camp to be near a water source. We're elevated at present. If we find a gradient, we'll find water. And when we do, it will be a case of working up or down stream."

Tom nodded. "Makes sense. Or about as much sense as anything else does out here. I'll go with that." He paused thoughtfully, peeling at the tape around his finger. He flexed it a few times, the ligaments were starting to tighten up and allow movement. "I just want to get this done now."

"Aye, we all do, lad," Stewart commented flatly.

King eased out of his sleeping pit and rubbed his face. "Got enough brew for two?" he asked, looking at Reece's smouldering mess tin.

Reece shrugged. "Sure. I think it will taste like shit anyway..." He poured half the brown liquid into another mess tin and held it out for him.

King grinned and took hold of the handle. He sipped some of the steaming liquid and pulled a face then said, "I've had worse, I suppose." He drank it down, blowing on it and swirling the tin to distribute the heat. "Cheers," he said, handing the empty tin back to him.

"Give Jim a nudge," Stewart said to King. "We might as well get ready to move out."

King crawled over and shook the Australian's leg. The man swung his arm wide, the blade of his knife scything through the air. King blocked the attack away and moved back to create distance should the man counter, and he drew his Browning before the man could do anything to retaliate. King kept the pistol close to his chest so that the blade would not reach his own hand. As standoffs went, King was holding all the cards.

"Don't ever do that..." the Australian growled, but King suspected it was to refrain from losing face. His attack missed and he had no chance of a follow-up. "Next time, maybe you'll get cut."

"Next time, maybe I'll shoot you in the face," King replied gruffly. "Anyway, drop your cock and pull your socks, we're moving out."

They all urinated and refilled with water, checked their weapons' safeties, and muzzles for debris, reapplied camo cream to their faces and checked themselves and their kit for three and the five S's. Sound, shine, and smell. Silhouette (or shadow) and shape would be down to them on the move. There was no glimpse of light on the horizon to be found, just the sense that the jungle gloom had become less consuming. Dawn had broken and they headed out with Reece leading on stag or point. Jim followed twenty paces behind, then Tom after that. King followed Stewart, keeping their rear covered.

"Comms check," Stewart said quietly into his throat mic.

"Got you, boss," King replied.

"Roger that," said Jim.

"Have that," Reece replied.

"Got you," Tom answered.

"Switch off until we either find the camp, we have a contact or one of us becomes separated." Stewart flicked off his comms unit and took a sip from his hipflask. He screwed the lid back on and slipped it into his left breast pocket. It was his habit to keep it there after he had heard tales of soldiers saved in the First World War when they had been shot and their hipflask had been enough to deflect a bullet from their heart.

King was down to the last of his dried fruit and nut mix. He shovelled in the handful and chewed, savouring the natural sugars and the taste. Whether it was the oppressive heat or the dank smell of rotting vegetation, or the simple fact that he was ravenous, he noticed that the modest mix had so much flavour. But then again, all his senses felt heightened. He heard every sound, saw the slightest movements from colourful birds and insects, and one time sensed the presence of a coiled snake at the edge of the animal run they had travelled along. He felt in tune with his surroundings, at ease in the hostile environment.

And that was when he realised that they were being followed.

King waited until the path rounded a thick concentration of thorny trees with thorns the size and length of bear claws, only with hypodermic tips. Naturally, Reece had led them around, where the path continued through. Whatever had made the trail would had to have been no more than a metre tall. A warthog or a small gazelle. Maybe even a troop of chimps. Reece made the right call and their progress slowed as they skirted the trees then made their way back onto the narrow trail. King darted off to his left, grunted as he annoyingly speared his arm on several of the wicked thorns, then crouched low, deep within the bracken. He raised the Uzi, his finger tentatively closing in on the trigger. In his periphery, he saw Stewart disappear into the foliage. He knew the Scotsman would notice his absence before long, then double back for him. King just hoped he could put down the threat before Stewart wandered into the arcs of fire. As was the protocol, he switched on his mic and waited for the others to come on to the net.

Sweat dripped from his brow, stinging his eyes. He blinked the salt away and refocused on the trail. His hands were wet with sweat, yet his mouth was as dry as desert sand. He licked his lips, the salt of his perspiration stinging his tongue. He was tempted to reach for the tube of his camel pack but resisted. He could not risk the slightest movement. King could hear the faint sound of boots treading cautiously on the trail, of sticks breaking and being trampled into the soft earth, of thorns catching on clothing and the branch springing back as whoever was following them pressed onwards.

King blinked the sweat away again, then got a start when he opened his eyes to see the man crouching, his weapon aimed at him. Both men saw each other in their sights. King's heart raced. To fire was to risk being shot, but to hesitate would surely mean death.

"Put the gun down, we've got you covered..." Stewart's brusk Scottish voice echoed around them. "King, don't fire..."

King frowned. His sights did not waver and nor did the man's in front of him.

"Dimitri, it's Peter Stewart. We appear to have stumbled into each other's plans. Now, be a good boy and put the weapon down carefully. Then we can have a talk. I've got trigger happy mercs with me, and they haven't taken well to my man here. So, no great loss there. They'll nail you though, and they don't really care much if he lives or dies."

Great, thought King. He needed to ease the tension, so he stood up carefully and steadily and lowered the Uzi, but he kept the muzzle in line with the man's body and his finger was still touching the trigger. "I'm going to lower my weapon," said King. "Do us all a favour and lower yours, too."

The Russian shrugged. There was little he could do. He knew he was good enough to take out a couple of them, but he did not have eyes on the other two men, and he knew how many had stumbled upon his trail, corrupting the tracks he had been stoically reading and following. Better to live to fight another day. He slowly and tentatively lowered the Steyr, but he kept his hand on the grip and his finger hovering over the trigger. "I didn't expect to see you again," he said to Stewart.

King recognised the man as whom he'd seen talking to Stewart at the hotel back in Hu, near Cafunfo. He had recognised him as a killer, and now that he had seen him operating in the field, he knew he was an extremely dangerous man indeed.

"Gentlemen, this is Dimitri. Former Spetsnaz and now a bodyguard and private soldier." Stewart paused. "Put your weapons down, lads. Dimitri got screwed over royally in Afghanistan and Chechnya and has helped me with information from time to time, as well as being a safe pair of hands on some of the firm's more deniable operations." Stewart walked over and patted the Russian on his shoulder. "And what brings you down to the woods today?"

The Russian shrugged. "Those journalists got themselves either killed or snatched..."

"Who?" King asked quickly, his heart racing as he thought about Lucinda.

"The two men were both killed. The woman was taken into the jungle."

"Lucinda?"

"Yes."

"And you're on their trail?" Stewart asked hopefully.

"I was. You guys have muddied it. In fact, I think they veered off a way back."

"Southside Boys?" King asked. "Lucinda was tagging along with that dick, Roger Siegfried. He had a meeting planned."

Stewart looked at King. "You never told me that." He looked back at Dimitri. "So, find the woman, find the hostages."

"Not in my case." The Russian grinned. "Find the woman, get the rest of my fee." He paused. "Siegfried's paper put up the fee. Half upfront, half upon return. If I get the woman back, well, then it shows due diligence on my part."

"Classy," said King.

"That's the job I'm in," the Russian glared at him. "Give yourself a dozen years and wait and see what your career prospects are like when British Intelligence has had enough of you." He paused, looking at the three mercenaries. "We've all been there, in one way or another." Tom and Jim smirked. Reece remained impassive. "Just another swinging dick in another secret war, or bodyguard to someone who doesn't deserve protecting. Mark my words and wait and see..."

King said nothing, but he held the man's stare and the Russian looked away first. He put down the Uzi and unbuttoned his tunic. Stewart frowned as King pulled out a small

206 A P BATEMAN

control unit. "Lucinda told me what she was going to do. I tried to convince her to return to Luanda." He paused. "I didn't tell you because I didn't want you to use her. But when she made it clear she was adamant about going, I gave her something for good luck. This is a receiver for the Type B personal tracker. Lucinda is carrying the Type B tracker in a set of rosary beads. The large, centre bead is hollow and as it is open at both ends to enable it to be threaded onto the string of beads, it will send a clear signal." He glanced at his Rolex. "There will be about another six hours of battery life left. But if what our Russian friend says is correct, they can't be anywhere near that far away."

"Where the hell did you get that?" Stewart frowned.

"Beirut. It helped me in a tight pinch," he replied dismissively. "I didn't give it back to the quartermaster." King paused, looking intently at Stewart. "Like you said, find the woman, find the hostages..."

31

The camp was in the centre of a large clearing within the jungle, and as Reece predicted, was located lower down the gradient beside a stream. King had concealed himself on higher ground and as he watched the camp and the many Southside Boys either doing chores or lounging about in the shade, he wished they had the GPMG and the sniper rifle at their disposal. He tried to remember how long it had been since they had crashed, and the helicopter and their equipment had gone up in flames. He knew that the expression on the pilot's face as he had started to burn would remain with him forever. It seemed like so long ago, but it had been just two days. King was exhausted and hungry. He was low on water, too.

Stewart was a hundred metres to King's right, and Reece was a hundred metres to his left. Jim, Tom, and Dimitri were spread out accordingly and as King checked his watch for the tenth time that minute, he finally backed away and pulled back to the rendezvous point. Dimitri was already there. King nodded and the Russian gave a sort of half nod.

That was as good as it was going to get. Jim and Tom pushed through the bush and Stewart followed a minute later.

"Where's Reece?" Stewart asked, but the men merely shrugged.

"We need more firepower," said Tom edgily.

Jim nodded. "Agreed. Piers screwed the pooch when he decided machine pistols would do the job. The wanker."

"Fuck you!" Tom snapped, squaring up to the Australian.

"Stand down!" Stewart got between them. "For fuck's sake. The fight's out there, not amongst ourselves."

"Well, we need water, and quick," said King, to de-escalate the situation. "I'm completely out."

"Well, I wouldn't fill your camel pack downstream of that place," Stewart commented flatly. "It'll be full of turds and god only knows what else. The animals are shitting everywhere."

"Take the village and we can get water from their own supply," said Jim, turning his eyes away from Jim. "I saw plenty of bowsers. Hopefully they haven't taken a dump in those," he grinned.

Reece pushed through the foliage and said, "Sorry, I got lost..."

Stewart nodded, then said, "Dimitri, you're the sniper. I know it's not got a great magnification, but it's better than we have, and you've got the firepower, and can engage targets at a greater range than we can. Jim and Tom, you're on the middle hut. Reece, you take the hut to the east. It's smaller and I imagine there will be less hostages inside. King, you and I will take the hut to the west." He paused. "But first, we take down as many of the enemy as possible. I'll decide when it's time to storm the huts. Listen out on the comms or keep an eye on me."

"And if you don't make it, mate?" Jim asked casually.

Stewart shrugged. "Then, I guess you'll know when to go. When it's a lot less congested down there and you can get the hostages out without them walking into the crossfire."

"Then tab out southwest?" Reece asked.

"Exactly," replied Stewart. "Five miles of jungle and the chopper meets us at the prearranged landing zone on the edge of the plain, on top of the hill."

"Would it not be better to land on the plain? The hill seems to make more work for us." Tom paused. "That's quite a hike at the best of times, but the hostages will be running on empty. I imagine we'll meet resistance once the Southside Boys inevitably regroup."

"It gives the pilot a chance to see us, and it gives us chance to see him. The pilot also suggested if we're overloaded, he can use the hill for a rolling lift."

Tom nodded. The other men didn't have any questions, so Stewart stood up and said, "Right, let's get them out and get the fuck out of this shit pit."

32

Julius Lombobo's eyes gleamed white, highlighting his almost jet-black pupils. Many of the men around him had yellowed whites from malaria, but the Southside Boy's leader had been lucky. He had told the people that he met that it was God's will that he should be immune to the world's largest killer, and that he did God's bidding in return for his immunity. He used the lyrics of his carefully selected rap-music and his deluded preaching to 'speak' God's words. And God had told him to build a nation and rule it with impunity. Violence was his way of purifying ethnicity, and rape was his way to spread the seed of the chosen race. He had smoked a lot of weed and chewed a lot of khat in his twenty-seven years. He had used cocaine and heroin, too. He could not remember when God had first spoken to him, but it was a safe bet that it wasn't before he had become an addled-brained drug addict.

Lombobo looked at the man in front of him and told him to lead the way. Boy soldiers were examining the hole in the rear of the western hut. Lombobo did not even glance at it as he ordered the door to be opened and the prisoners to be marched outside. They lined up one by one. Fearful and broken. Lombobo looked at them all in turn, his fist gripping the handle of his machete so tightly, that the veins popped up on top of his knuckles.

"Where is she?"

Nobody answered.

He swiped the machete through the air and said, "I will ask only once more." He looked at them all in turn, the whites of his eyes both large and intimidating. "Where is the woman?"

"She... she went before first light..." a woman answered meekly.

Lombobo walked up to her as she cowered in front of him. "And you did not think to tell us?" He spun the machete in front of her. The sharpened blade glinted in the sunlight. "You have seen how we expect you to behave. And what happens when you do not..."

"We... were... scared," she managed to stammer.

Lombobo stared at her, then cast his eyes over the other hostages. "I will take a head for this," he announced casually. "But I will leave you all to decide who among you will *volunteer*..."

Many of the Southside Boys had congregated in the clearing. If there was blood to be shed, nobody wanted to miss it.

The hostages looked at each other frantically. Each person looked fearful and desperate. There was nothing civilised or honourable about their behaviour, and as one man was pointed to twice, the rest sensed their chance, survival instincts kicking in, and the man was clearly singled out repeatedly. The man in question was a middle-aged OPEC executive who until seconds ago, would have thought himself popular and amenable to all. He had thrown generous barbeques and drinks beside the pool, with many of the people standing here beside him in attendance, at his lodge in Namibia. The man looked around him, his fellow hostages' fingers pointed, their eyes not meeting his own. Julius Lombobo stepped forward and pulled him out in front of the line. He pushed the man down onto his knees and said, "You will see what happens when you deceive me. You will see what happens when one of you tries to escape..." Lombobo slowly and deliberately raised the machete, eyes wide and glaring white. He gritted his oversized teeth, large and white and straight. Together with the eyes, it made him look maniacal and enraged, deranged. He hesitated, then his entire body tensed, and he started to swing the machete downwards. The bullet clipped his shoulder, and he dropped the machete and clasped the wound with his left hand. And then the gunfire erupted, and chaos ensued.

DIMITRI CURSED. He had thought the shot had been good. One hundred metres, x 1.5 magnification and centre mass. He resighted, but the man had dropped the machete and ducked, then darted behind the hut. Dimitri searched for another target and took down a boy soldier about to fire upon the hostages. The boy went down, and Dimitri thought nothing more of it. Some batches of ammunition produced 'flyers', or Dimitri may well have jerked his shot. Either way, his accuracy had been good the second time and he moved between targets, noting how many men were falling to the onslaught of automatic gunfire from the other five men. Inevitably, if not predictably, the hostages ran for safety, but in doing so they cut through the arcs of fire and two went down. Neither seemed to be suffering life threatening injuries and they both crawled for cover, clutching their wounded limbs. He surveyed the scene below and realised that the other men were now going for the huts. Dimitri did not have a communication unit, so was reliant on watching the scene to guess the state of play. He still needed to provide covering fire for them, but he also realised that he needed to get closer to narrow the arcs of fire and have more fluidity in his movements. He headed to a fallen tree, twenty metres closer to the clearing. The height was still enough to command a good dominance of the battlefield and he rested the rifle and fired three shots in quick succession at three individual targets. The men went down convincingly, and Dimitri started firing at the fleeing enemy, who were now heading into the jungle without looking back.

They had rounded up the hostages and positioned them on their knees with their hands on their heads. Standard operating procedure when recovering hostages, just to ensure everybody was who they said they were. There were three hostages unaccounted for. Stewart knew that one of them was the woman from MI5. He cursed and did not hide his annoyance as he paced along the line checking the faces with the photographs on the single sheet of laminated paper. Not only had her absence endangered their escape, but she was one of three on his list that should not, at any cost, be left in a position to compromise Her Majesty's Government. He simply could not leave her here, but he also needed to make the rendezvous with the helicopter at the landing zone.

Stewart looked over at King. He was with the one hostage that had been allowed to stand and leave the group. Lucinda Davenport had hugged King closely and didn't look like she was going to let him go anytime soon. She still carried the rosary beads and subconsciously smoothed them with her finger and thumb. Stewart wondered whether she'd ever know they concealed the tracking device that had undoubtedly saved her. He watched them hug again, and she kissed King's neck. He responded and she smiled. Stewart checked his watch and shouted for King to join him. King nodded and guided Lucinda over to Reece, who was checking the satphone.

When King joined him, he said, "The general consensus is that Jane Hargreaves escaped through the wall of the hut an hour before dawn. It is likely she will be heading north to the village of Latistra. She will know enough about the geography of the region to make that her best bet. She's trained as an MI5 field agent, although she works in analytics. So, she knows how to move cross-country and will not be running around like a headless chicken." He paused. "I want you to track her and bring her to the LZ."

"Yes, boss," King replied.

"And King, you remember our talk in the hotel room, right?" King frowned, then nodded, suddenly catching the man's drift. "Do what needs to be done," Stewart said coldly. "And if you're caught, the government will deny all knowledge of you, and there certainly won't be a rescue or negotiation. Any questions?"

"No."

"Then why are you still fucking here?"

King turned on his heel and filled his camel pack at a nearby bowser. He dropped a couple of purifying tablets in and gave the pack a shake before putting it back on and adjusting his webbing. He checked the Uzi's open breech for debris, checked the safety and headed for the back of the hut. *Jane Hargreaves must have been a determined woman,* he thought. The sides of the hut were hard and dry and not far off the strength of concrete. King rubbed his hand over the dry and crumbling mortar, then looked at his fingers. Blood.

A fair amount of it, too. So, Jane Hargreaves was bleeding, her skin rubbed raw or lacerated by pushing through the hole. Now he had something to look for that would be unique to her. Combine that with the tread, footprints or indentations that should still be fresh and uncorrupted, and he had her signature. When he worked his way along her trail, she would leave more unique signatures, and tracking her would become progressively easier as he recognised her signs.

Behind him, gunfire rang out. He ducked instinctively, then pressed on. He had his own job to do, and he couldn't waste time. He doubted he would make the landing zone if it took him longer than four hours to find Jane Hargreaves, and that was if she had managed to remain on a northerly heading. If indeed she was heading for the village of Latistra and its landing strip and Western charity workers. And if she wasn't, then King knew he would be unlikely to find her, and certainly unlikely to make the landing zone. He thought about what Stewart had said and wondered whether he could kill Jane Hargreaves rather than allow her to be captured. He had an image of her, and the other two intelligence officers indelibly imprinted on his mind. If the scenario was called for, she would have to be a target like any other. He shook the thought away. It wouldn't come to that. He would not allow it.

King studied the ground. There were multiple footprints. But he could discount many. Jane Hargreaves was five-feet-seven and an estimated ten stone. That would typically put her foot size as a five to a seven. Many of the prints were barefoot. King had asked the hostages and although most hadn't noticed, the consensus was that Jane had been wearing sandals. One of the female hostages had said they were a slight wedge. King scoured the ground and found the tread that was most likely. It was doubtful that anybody else had used the path after Jane, so it was the most prominent footprint, although that still didn't make it easy to spot all the time. He then looked about the foliage and saw blood on a leaf. He estimated it to be shoulder height for the woman and that seemed about right – the widest point of her body would have been where the hardened mud had cut and scraped her skin.

The jungle floor was a myriad of trails, cutting through short leafy vegetation. Hundreds of creatures intersected the trails, all on their own route and all with their own plan. This gave the people inhabiting the jungle – notably the Southside Boys, as they had driven out any jungle dwelling tribes in the region – a choice of where to walk, without stepping off paths and increasing their chances of stepping on snakes coiled and waiting for small creatures to pass. Thorny bushes and stinging plants like Northern Hemisphere nettles, only with ten times the toxicity in their leafy stingers, grew everywhere, as did coconut palms and ferns, bracken and several hundred species of trees that bore nuts and flowers and fruits. Some were edible, while others were lethally poisonous. King's jungle experience was limited. He had been attached to an infantry regiment and trained for two weeks in Belize in jungle warfare and survival techniques, but he did not recognise the plants and trees around him. All he knew was that he was starving, and his energy levels were low and would only get progressively worse until he ate something substantial. He unclipped the tube on his camel pack and drank thirstily. It tasted like swimming pool water, and King just hoped it hadn't been pissed in as much as his local swimming baths.

King trudged on, ever mindful that the area could be flooded with Southside Boys who had fled the camp. When it had been clear that their numbers were being decimated, the men and boy soldiers had scattered. Chances are they would regroup at their own pre-arranged rendezvous sites. As he continued through the jungle, keeping on top of the footprints he had singled out as Jane's, he realised how little ammunition he had and that the chances of an engagement with the enemy was likely. He cursed at not equipping himself with a Kalashnikov from the many scattered around the camp beside the fallen. King shook his head at the thought. He wasn't a soldier. He had trained with the SAS for the endurance and to break him, and he had accompanied various regiments on Salisbury Plain on training exercises, but the bulk of his training had been range-based with Stewart and the Special Operations Unit. He was a field agent, and his skillset was gathering intelligence and surveillance. He had been forced to kill in the course of this work, and in doing so the SOU had flagged him as a potential assassin. King was yet to receive a dedicated assassination mission, or 'contract' as they were referred to. But he guessed he had hit the ground running with this mission with orders to kill three of his country's own intelligence officers if they could not be extracted safely. As far as King was concerned, the contract would only be successful if he did *not* kill the primary targets.

There was movement ahead of him. King ducked down and edged into cover. Great thorns lacerated the side of his face, one dangerously close to his eye. He rested still, daring not to move. The movement was steady and coming straight towards him. King carefully eased the thorn that was near his eyeball aside. His hands wrapped around the Uzi's grip firmly, although they were damp and sweaty, and he would have given anything to have been able to wipe them. He eased the weapon up to his right eye, the open sights surveying the ground in front of him. The foliage parted and King was mere grams from the weapon's unbelievably heavy seven-pound trigger pull. The warthog charged towards him, apparently oblivious to his presence, then veered at the last second and charged on through the bush. King got up, his heart pounding and a flutter of relief inside his stomach. Almost at once, there were shouts and he saw why the warthog had been running away. Three black men carrying Kalashnikovs stared at him, two of them starting to raise their rifles. King brought his weapon to bear far more quickly than his opponents and fired. The man to his right sprawled backwards. King was already moving the weapon and fired again, but the burst went wide. He resighted, mindful that both men's weapons were levelling out. He fired again, but instead of a short burst which would usually send a dozen rounds towards the target in a six-hundred round per minute burst, the weapon fired two rounds then nothing else happened. There wasn't the 'click-click-click' seen in the movies, the weapon's trigger simply did not respond, and King knew that a spent shell casing or a misfed live round had blocked the breech. He discarded the weapon and darted to his left as he drew the Browning pistol. He could see that one of the men had been hit, but he had not gone down and was aiming his weapon at King using just one hand. The clatter of a Kalashnikov on full-auto filled the quiet air, and King watched the wounded man's aim get progressively higher as the weapon rode up in his hand, the recoil too much for a one-handed grip. King fired three shots at the other man. He wasn't injured and he had yet to fire his weapon. The calculating part of King's brain told him that the man was less than a second from firing and when he did, he would undoubtedly have more ammunition and a better aim than the wounded man who was operating solely on instinct. The man went down, and King threw himself on his stomach to present himself as a smaller target and fired three more rounds at the wounded fighter. All three men were out of view from his prone position, his field of view cut short by grasses and ferns. King rolled three body widths to his right and up against the thorny tree for cover. He got up slowly, resting on his left knee. One of the men was moving and King fired two more shots. The man rested still. King stood up slowly, looked all around him and crossed over the open ground so he could come up on the bodies from another angle. He watched for movement, noted where their weapons had fallen. As he approached, he could see that they were all dead. He picked up one of the AK-74 rifles and checked it over. Two of them had carried the same weapon and ammunition, but one had an AK-47. King preferred the later model, although the world still seemed to call them AK-47s, even though no recognised state or country had equipped their military with one for more than twenty years. The AK-47 had transcended the inanimate and gained a soul, if not a personality. It appeared on the flags of some nations, on T-shirts with revolutionaries, in rap-music and other forms of popular culture and was often misquoted by the press and world media to be seen in the hands of soldiers and terrorists alike and was estimated to be owned by one in twelve people around the globe. It was to assault rifles what *Biro* was to ballpoint pens and *Hoover* was to vacuum cleaners. But King preferred the lighter weight of the AK-74's ammunition, its greater velocity and lack of over-penetration. And so did its makers. That's why the Soviets had changed it in 1974.

King checked over the magazines and stashed them in the pouches on his webbing. He kept his last magazine for the Uzi because he could empty out the ammunition and use it in the Browning. He did just that, replenishing the pistol's magazine with six 9mm rounds. He slammed the magazine in place, then spun around and aimed. The sights levelled on the centre of Jane Hargreaves' forehead, less than ten feet away from him.

"Are *you* my rescuer?" she asked, apparently undaunted at the weapon aimed at her face. "I suppose I'm in the shit if you're not…"

King thought about the answer should the scenario change. Rescuer or executioner. He'd have to see how things panned out. "Yes, I am," he said quietly. The woman had been through hell, and he had smelled her before he had heard her, but he was still taken with how beautiful she was in the flesh. "I'm King."

"Jane." She paused. "You can lower your weapon now, soldier."

He holstered the Browning and unslung the Kalashnikov from his shoulder, then checked his Rolex. It was secured to his wrist with a green NATO strap instead of its usual chunky stainless-steel bracelet. King thought it a more sensible choice for the Jungle where sound and conceal-ment were everything. "We don't have much time," he told her. "We have a helicopter rendezvous and if we double back to the camp, we're likely to miss it." He paused, unclip-ping the tube on his camel pack, and offering it to her. "Drink?" She walked right up to him and took the tube and drank thirstily. King looked at the abrasions on her arm. The blood had dried. He could clean the wound for her and patch it up, but time was precious. It didn't look like it was septic. Not yet at least. His priority was to get her to the LZ. "Besides, the camp will likely be full of Southside Boys returning to regroup."

Jane pulled back from the drinking tube and wiped her

mouth. "They're everywhere," she said. "I kept almost bumping into men going between the two camps. I've been walking around for hours."

"Two camps?" King asked incredulously.

She nodded. "The camp where they held us was tiny. The bulk of Lombobo's men are at the second camp. Not the boy soldiers, his *infantry*. It's more like a garrison. Adult males, all equipped with rifles. They have some trucks and motorcycles, plenty of water and stores."

"Shit..." King shook his head. "Show me."

She scoffed at the notion, then her face fell when she saw his expression. "You're kidding, right?"

King stared at her, his eyes cold and grey. Like a wolfs, or a dog you'd never want to pat on the head. "No," he replied. "I need to see it now..."

34

There was madness in MI6's methods. The operation was deniable, so there was no paper trail, no requests for re-tasking a satellite for surveillance and no logs on the computer system. Instead, Stewart had been briefed by two senior officers and left to get on with it. So, in treating the operation in such a way, they now risked complete failure. Had Stewart been given a complete intelligence report and satellite photographs of the area, he would never have made the calls he had been forced to make. He may never have accepted the assignment, which King now thought was an overriding factor in MI6's decision. King shifted on his belly, pulled a leafy branch out of the way, and craned his neck to see the far side of the camp. He estimated close to a hundred men. Julius Lombobo was in the middle of the camp, seated on the bonnet of a pickup truck with forty men gathered closely around him, while the bulk of his troops were readying themselves loading magazines from Soviet era wooden ammunition crates. King couldn't hear what the man was saying, but he recognised a troop-rousing speech when he saw it in motion. There was a track in and out of each end of the camp. Narrow, but suitable for a pickup. Lombobo was having his shoulder stitched by a young man. He was a hundred and fifty metres away. An easy shot with the Kalashnikov, but their escape would be impossible. The Southside Boys would surely catch up with them, especially if the track ran towards the route to the rendezvous point and they could use the truck to head them off.

"You've seen it. Now, let's get going to the rendezvous point." Jane whispered as she leaned closer to King. "I want to get out of here."

"They're getting ready to move."

"So?"

"So, they'll try to head off my team and the hostages."

"But they won't know where to go."

King sighed as he watched one of Lombobo's men sidle up to him with a folded map and began to unfold it on the bonnet of the truck. Lombobo was pointing and the man seemed to be agreeing with him. "They'll know how quickly the hostages will make progress through the jungle," King replied, his voice barely above a whisper. "And they'll know the best possible places for a helicopter to land. They also have enough men to head for multiple points to hedge their bets."

"Forgive me if I'm being a bit dense, but you seem to be inferring that you should do something about it. Rather than getting me to the bloody helicopter."

King thought about Stewart's orders, the contract placed on the three intelligence officers if escape was not an option. He glanced at her, barely able to conjure the thought of killing her, but he wasn't out of this yet. And nor was she. He closed his eyes for a moment, as if shutting down one of his senses would allow him to work through the thought process more easily. When he opened them again, he did not look at her. Instead, he handed her his compass and told her the heading she should take. He then gave her the Browning, knowing it was the weapon all agents trained with on the foreign posting weapon handling course. "Stick to the trails as much as you can and watch out for snakes..."

"That's it?"

"That's all I've got."

"Well, how far is it?"

"Five miles. Where the jungle thins out and meets the plains."

She nodded, checking the safety on the left-hand side of the frame of the Browning. "We'd be better sticking together."

King rolled back and slowly got to his knees. "Just get to the helicopter..."

35

King had spotted the fuel dump and knew that it was his best bet. To reach it, he needed to skirt the camp from the cover of the thicker part of the jungle. That created a distance of over half a mile and when he finally edged closer to the clearing, he realised that he had over-cooked it and need to adjust. He had come in past the fuel dump, so edged back into the thicker growth and when he emerged, he could see the rear of the pickup and the back of Julius Lombobo as he instructed his men. King couldn't make out what the man was saying because of the noise of the rallied troops drowned out the man's voice, and the French he spoke was unlike any other King had heard. The accent was strange and interspersed with a tribal vocabulary and pidgin English.

King edged closer to the stacked fuel drums. Beside them, three trail bikes with off-road tyres and long suspension forks were propped up on stands. King thought about taking one of them, but simply starting one of those machines could prove problematic and he had no idea whether they were fuelled or not. One problem starting one of the motorcycles and he could be riddled with bullets before he even got it into gear. An awning of canvas had been affixed over the fuel on four wooden poles to provide shade from the sun but leave the sides open. The canvas wafted in the breeze like a slack sail. He ducked as he heard gunfire. He almost opened fire on the crowd but realised just in time that they were the start of celebratory gunshots. The group were chanting, too. King used the noise and distraction to his advantage, and he drew his Ka-Bar knife and thrust it through one of the steel fuel drums. Fuel gushed over his hand and poured onto the ground. King slammed the knife into the other drums, again and again, the hardened blade making short work of the drums, the fuel pouring onto the soft earth. King looked at the fuel soaking into the ground. It wasn't going to be enough. He looked at the crowd, the truck and Lombobo giving his sermon to the masses. King took out his Zippo lighter and readied it in his hand as he replaced the knife to its sheath. He then took a deep breath, as much to steady his nerves as to ready his lungs for the inevitable sprint ahead of him and powered a kick into the fuel drums. Two of them toppled and rolled, and after a second kick, another was following the first two. Men already stopped their chanting and Lombobo turned around and stared. King backed away, then struck the wheel of the lighter and tossed it gently into the centre of the fuel dump. He turned to run as he both saw and heard the ignition and was blown clean off his feet as the petrol flamed with a 'whump'. Diesel ignited too, normally slower to combust, the volatile petrol helped it along and a mushroom cloud of smoke and heat bellowed high into the air.

King was already scrambling to his feet and sprinting as fast as he could. Behind him the burning fuel drums met

the truck and the flames caught up with the fuel and vapour
and the truck, the motorcycles and a dozen or more men
went up in flames. Lombobo had dived off the bonnet of the
truck and staggered to safety. All the time, the fuel ignited,
and men were caught in the vapour and then the inevitable
flames followed. Screams pierced the jungle and monkeys
and birds screeched and took flight. All the time, King ran
for safety and survival. More explosions thumped and
echoed as the unpunctured drums boiled in the heat and
spilled fuel onto the flames when they split open. Like
brandy in a flambé dish, the liquid ignited more fiercely
when heated and the explosions increased in severity and
devastation. King could not see the damage, nor the ensuing
carnage, but he knew that it was bad. Or at least, bad for
them; good for him. He had no idea, but the dozen or so
casualties had massed to three times that number and the
chaos which followed had bought him some time. He shuddered to think of the horror those men had experienced in
death, but this was all about his own survival and he would
never put a price on that. It was either him or them.

Ahead of him, Jane stepped out from a cluster of trees,
the Browning in her hand, held unthreateningly towards the
ground. "Jesus! You're mad!" she exclaimed.

"I thought you'd gone!" King snapped at her.

"I was scared out here on my own!" she replied. "Besides,
it's better we stick together." She looked at King, then
glanced past him, raised the pistol, and fired four shots.

King turned and watched as the man staggered and fell
to the ground. He was just fifty metres from him. "Shit, I
thought that would buy us some time," he said, snatching a
breath. "Come on!" He grabbed her arm as he dashed past
her. "I've destroyed one of their trucks and their motorbikes,

and thinned out their numbers, but they obviously know where we are!"

"I saw the truck go up," Jane panted. "I couldn't see if you got that bastard Lombobo, though."

King darted to the left and Jane almost tripped as she followed. "My compass," he said. "Give it to me." He snatched it off her, grateful that she had returned and that he could use the compass to check his course. He didn't know what he had been thinking, but it was clear he couldn't check the sun and measure its direction of travel while he was running for his life. "Thanks," he said between breaths. "And thanks for back there... damned good shooting."

"Right," she replied. "But it feels different to paper targets..."

"But better to be alive, right?"

King didn't listen for her answer. The bullets fizzed past his ear, and he pushed Jane to the ground as he dived for cover. Jane sprawled and rolled and landed heavily on her back. King turned and fired. He was not short of targets. Four men were running, their weapons firing and muzzles flashing. In the few short seconds that it took King to dispatch two of them, the other two men had closed the gap from fifty metres to twenty. King fired again, but as the man went down and he adjusted his aim from his prone position, the angle was all wrong to shoot and he rolled over and got to his knees as the man bore down on him. King swiped the rifle across the man's kneecap and brought it back just as swiftly to knock the man's rifle aside. The man's head rocked, and a crimson mist puffed out the back at the same moment as the gunshot rang out. King turned and saw Jane lowering the Browning. He didn't thank her, but his face said how grateful he was as he caught hold of her as they started to run.

The jungle thinned out and they crossed a rocky stream. King checked their rear when they scrambled up a muddy slope and into denser foliage. There was nobody behind them when he stopped and checked, but they were leaving a body trail and easy tracks for the enemy to follow. It was only a matter of time before they caught up with them again. King took the Uzi magazine out of his webbing and unloaded a handful of bullets. He passed them to Jane and said, "Reload as you go, I'll keep a lookout." They walked briskly and King kept checking their rear. When Jane had reloaded the Browning, he unclipped the hose on his camel pack and drank down some of the sickly water. He offered some to Jane, but she shook her head. "It's not an option. Hydrate now or pay for it later."

She shrugged, relenting and sipped some water down. "God, that's grim," she said, wrinkling her nose. "I need a bloody gin and tonic." She paused. "And a shower and a roast chicken dinner, oh and a comfortable bed with crisp cotton sheets."

King nodded. "That all sounds pretty bloody good to me," he said. "Table for two at the best hotel back in Luanda?"

Jane laughed, but King sensed it was just adrenalin. Fear manifested itself in many ways and coping skills differed from person to person. As they trudged on, she said, "Definitely up for the gin and tonic and dinner."

King chuckled. "Don't worry, the bed would only be for sleep, I've never been so bloody knackered!"

"Charming!" she replied. "But God, I could sleep forever..."

Gunfire erupted behind them, and they darted for cover.

King could not see the muzzle flashes, but leaf debris fluttered down and after the next burst of fire branches snapped and dropped and bullets fizzed above their heads. "They're strafing the riverbank and the cover above," said King. "They shoot up the area, then cross over where they would otherwise be exposed." He stood up and pushed Jane forwards. "There's too many guns to take on for us not to have a strategic advantage. We don't have the high ground, or any barricade cover."

Jane did not reply, but she increased her pace, and it was clear she was both fit and determined to survive. King checked the compass and veered around a cluster of trees. The jungle was becoming denser again. He could picture the map he had studied back in Luanda and Hu. To the north it continued for three hundred miles, but just a few miles to the south and east and the terrain turned to plains. Partly because of logging and deforestation for mining and farming, and partly because of environmental changes in the climate. Droughts to the southeast had dried-up entire rivers and starved the jungle of water. As a result, the jungle was steadily shrinking.

King studied the terrain, checked the compass, and pressed on their southeast heading. They had been putting in a terrific pace and were just a mile from the edge of the jungle and less than two miles from the LZ. He noted that they had continuously headed to their left between compass checks. The old adage about walking in circles was certainly true. In the Northern Hemisphere the Earth's rotation made people veer to their left when covering sufficient distances. He had heard stories of snipers and marksmen taking the Earth's gravitational pull and rotation into account for extremely long shots. The opposite was true in the Southern Hemisphere.

The jungle thinned once more. Thick tree stumps indicated that the largest trees had been felled for timber some years previous. King pushed Jane onwards, directing her on the heading. Ahead of them, Stewart stepped out from cover, his Uzi aimed at them. He lowered his weapon and cracked a thin smile. "Fuck me, you made it..."

"Barely," King rasped. "Short version... The Southside Boys had a larger base camp away from where they held the hostages."

"And?"

"Think fucking *Zulu*. Do you want to be Stanley Baker or Michael Caine?"

"Shit." Stewart looked behind him, then back at King. "How far behind you?"

"Close."

As if to confirm his evaluation, bullets fizzed past them as gunfire rang out a hundred metres away. King pushed Jane down and spun round to return fire. Stewart had already opened up with his Uzi, cutting two men down with a burst of fire, and King was aiming at specific targets with the Kalashnikov on single fire. He fired two rapid shots, or 'double taps' at every target. Jane returned fire with the Browning but at a hundred metres in the heat of battle at a moving enemy, she had no effect on the enemy's attack.

"Withdraw!" screamed Stewart. King knew what the man meant, but also knew that the Scotsman would never utter the word 'retreat'. They edged back through the cover and met Jim and Tom coming to give them support. "Get back!" Stewart yelled at the two men. "Back towards the hostages! There are boulders for cover over there, and higher ground!" Reece appeared, his face ashen. He took in everyone's expression, got the gist, and turned and ran back the way he'd come.

When they reached the hostages, they found Reece had already roused them to their feet and Dimitri was checking his compass. Reece was speaking into the satphone when Stewart shouted to him. "What are you doing?"

"Checking on the chopper's ETA..."

"And?"

"An hour," he replied. "We need to hold them off until then!"

"Impossible!" Stewart snapped. He looked at Jim and said, "Get back there and put some rounds on them while we work this shit out!"

"Boss," Jim nodded and looked at King and his AK-74. "Swap?"

King nodded and handed the man his rifle and the last remaining magazines. Ninety rounds in total. It was the right tool for the job and there was no sense in trying to keep the weapon for himself. He took Jim's MP5 and the spare magazine. He'd been short changed but needs must. King looked at Lucinda. Their eyes met, but they both saw the uncertainty on the others face. He looked back at Stewart and said, "Send one man with the hostages to the LZ."

"And the rest?" the Scotsman growled.

King looked at him coldly. He had never felt so close to death, so accepting of his fate. He suddenly realised with some amusement that he was no longer scared. "We buy them time," King replied. "By going hunting..."

King watched as Stewart drained his hipflask, savouring the whisky as it burned down his throat, igniting his senses and making his cheeks flush. He had drunk it down as though it would be the last time, and in the ephemeral moment it had taken, as each man had checked their kit and discarded anything they would not need for a fight, he looked as though he had taken great pleasure from it, and that all was right in this world. He gave the flask a little shake, seemed pleased that there was another mouthful left and twisted the cap back on.

Reece and Jim were using single shots only and firing at anything that moved. They were receiving a huge amount of gunfire in return, but both men moved freely and fired at a different position with every shot. It couldn't last for long, though, and they would soon expend their ammunition at this rate. Tom was draining his water bottle thirstily, and King was taking on as much water as he could with his camel pack. It was going to get tough, they needed to be hydrated. King was low on ammunition and had flicked the selector on the MP5 to single shot. He watched Stewart take out a small silver snuff box, but the white powder he pinched and sniffed into each nostril wasn't pulped tobacco. King caught Stewart's eye, but he looked away as he put his drinking tube away.

"Marching powder," Stewart said by way of explanation. His eyes were wide, and he was already looking buzzed. "And if I take a bullet, maybe I won't give a shit..."

King went forwards and called Jim and Reece back. The two men scrambled down the slope, bullets sailing above their heads. "We're heading out now, keeping a heading of northwest to buy time. The hostages are enroute southeast."

"What if we don't make the fucking chopper?" Jim drawled, his Australian accent rising on the last two words.

"We'll make the chopper," said Reece. "It makes sense. Someone needs to tail back, give them something to shoot at as well as follow."

Jim looked at King and said, "I guess that's a job for you, rookie..." He held out the AK-74 and said, "I'll swap back now, there's only a few rounds left." King said nothing, but his stare bore into the man, and he couldn't hold it. King wasn't going into battle with just a few rounds, so he turned and caught up with Stewart and Tom, who were already heading out away from the hostages. Reece and Jim ran past King and Jim laughed. "You're on the tail end of this shit show now, you Pommie wanker!"

King turned and checked their rear. There were two boy soldiers at the top of the bank. They darted back into the bush and King spared them a volley to conserve ammunition. He would have likely missed at that range and needed every bullet to count. He jogged onwards, the short column of men fifty metres ahead of him. He caught movement out of his periphery and was bringing the MP5 to bear when he realised that it was Jane Hargreaves running hard, the Browning in her hand.

"They're crazy, but they're not stupid," she said breathily as she caught up. "Let them see me and they may well buy it. Otherwise, unless they see a hostage, they'll smell a rat."

"Shit, that's a good call," King replied, and with that he caught hold of her arm and stopped. Almost at once, bullets pinged off the ground in front of them. There were a dozen men heading their way. King snatched her back and pushed her ahead of him as they ran. "That ought to do it..."

"You bastard!"

"It was your idea!"

Ahead of them, Stewart was standing in the middle of the trail. Reece was on the satphone, and Tom and Jim were covering either side of the trail. "What the hell is she doing here?" Stewart snapped at King.

"I'm as surprised as you, but she's here and we haven't got time to discuss this!" He turned and covered the trail. When the Southside Boys charged into view King, Jim and Tom unloaded on them and they were cut down before they could return fire. He caught hold of Jane's arm and took off ahead of the others. "Let them have the rear for a while," he said.

"How much further," she asked as she ran alongside him.

"Fifteen minutes or so," he replied. "Then we break northeast and then southeast to close the circle."

Gunfire broke out again behind them, and King pulled Jane down on top of him as he dived for cover. They landed heavily, but King let go of her and rolled onto his stomach and brought his weapon up to aim. Reece had engaged with two men who had broken cover almost flanking them. Tom and Stewart were firing at men further back along the trail.

Stewart backed up towards them and said, "Get moving!" He changed magazines and started running. "Another two hundred metres and we start to turn the circle!"

"That's too soon!" King protested. "We need to put in more distance, or we'll just lead them back to the hostages!"

"Well, you're not in fucking charge, son. So just bloody well do it!"

37

L ucinda had fallen for the dozenth time. The route was a well-trodden path, but tree roots undulated the soft earth, and the path was narrow and edged with thorns the size and sharpness of sewing needles. She wasn't the only person to fall, and it was clear that the rest of the hostages were struggling. They were all thirsty and at a small stream, Dimitri waited while they fell into the water and drank their fill. Lucinda drank, too. She had not suffered as the hostages had, but she had never been more thirsty, hungry, or tired. She had watched the woman talk with the Russian, then run back the way they had come. The journalist in her wanted to know why. Wanted the story. But she lacked the courage or will to run towards danger. She had seen enough death and suffering, feared for her life and now had a brief glimpse of her own salvation. They had been told that the helicopter was on its way, and she would make damned sure that she was on it.

As the jungle thinned, the paths and trails widened. The air became a little easier to breathe as the dank humidity was left behind and after thirty minutes, the landscape had changed to grassy plains and sporadic baobab trees. Ahead of them, a large hill loomed. The Russian stopped and took out his compass, told everyone to get down in the grass and remain quiet. Lucinda did as the man said. She had passed the point of wanting to know more, wanting to learn the story. She wanted to get on board that helicopter and she wanted to see her husband again. The more she thought about the life waiting for her in England, her husband, their home – the more she wanted to live to see it all again and never set foot in Africa again.

38

The air was already easier to breathe, despite the ferocious heat. The jungle had been steaming. Hot, dank, and wet. The clearing towards the river gave way from jungle to thinned out trees and scrub within two hundred metres. After that, the plain consisted of grasses, some patches grazed short by everything on the safari tourist's herbivore list in the more hospitable and amenable African countries. When they had entered the plain, antelope and zebra had bolted as if chased by lions. With the herbivores taking to their heels, the plain in front of them now looked ominously sparse and devoid of life compared to the jungle. But they knew that the predators would be in the long grasses, masters of camouflage. Watching. Waiting.

The river was wide and shallow. They had crossed without drama, but King could see crocodiles further downstream and the thought that they had crossed the water without seeing them made his stomach flutter and his heart race.

"Here they come..." Tom said. "Movement on the fringe of the forest at eleven and two o'clock..."

"Have that," Stewart confirmed.

They had an elevated position and three hundred metres to play with. Tactically, they could hold greater numbers from the high ground. Practically, the MP5 and Uzi submachineguns put them somewhat behind the curve. They were well within range of the enemy's AK-47s and AK-74s, but they were woefully under gunned. Stewart quietly cursed Piers and his weapons contact, and their lack of intelligence regarding the way jungle – ideal terrain for the short, 9mm weapons – gave way to great swathes of plains that required assault or battle rifles.

"We're fucked," said Reece quietly. The ex-SAS soldier pointed along the fringe. "Twenty or more x-rays at ten o'clock, another twenty at one o'clock. That makes around seventy combatants at my estimation..." He paused, allowing his statement to settle. "We need to bug out. Now."

"No, we need to stop them here," said King. "Otherwise, they'll overwhelm us and get to the hostages."

"No one is listening to you, rookie," Jim hissed at him. "Reece is right. If we bug out, we may find a better position to fight from."

"And chance getting overrun and the hostages snatched back?" King shook his head. "The evacuation is in process, and we don't know what the terrain is like in front of us, but we have distance and elevation here. If we don't try and stop them now, we could be overrun at the exfiltration point. This is the best option. Possibly the only option."

"They're out of bloody range on the veld!" Tom snapped, his voice guttural and his accent laced with Afrikaans.

"They are," King agreed tersely. "But at the river they will

be just about close enough." He paused, watching the crocodiles lower down from their own crossing point. He scanned
along the bank, saw several more a hundred metres further
up. It was a miracle they had crossed unscathed. Perhaps their
crossing had woken the beasts and now they had the scent of
food. With any luck, the Southside Boys wouldn't be so lucky.
"We hit them as they cross. Wait until the first of them are
almost across, perhaps even let a few cross over all the way,
then we hit them on the far bank. We can get our rounds to
about fifty metres past the far bank. If they retreat, then so be
it. We bug out. But if they try to cross, slow them down and let
those crocs do their worse. Once there's casualties and confusion, we can pick them off. Or at least thin them out a bit..."

The men looked at King for a moment, then Stewart
said, "Aye, lad, that's the shit right there." He turned to the
other men and said, "You heard him! Spread out, check your
range and wait for orders."

King shouldered the submachinegun and took in the
sight. The enemy had broken cover and were testing the
open ground with the youngest of their ranks. The boy
soldiers walked tentatively, cradling their Kalashnikov
rifles, heavy and cumbersome in their hands and barely
shorter than the boys were tall. "It's two hundred and
seven paces from the near riverbank to our position," King
said quietly. "I paced it out. The river is forty paces wide.
Fifty metres after that is our maximum range. But as you
know, range and accuracy are two entirely different
matters."

Stewart smiled as he glanced across at King and looked
at the fear on the other men's faces. Jane mirrored their
expressions. By contrast, King looked calm, determined, and
ready for a fight. Stewart expected no less. He had trained
the man well and even among these experienced soldiers of

fortune, it showed. Nobody else had paced out the range and made mental notes of the terrain.

"The cluster of boulders halfway between them and us is an issue," King informed them. "We can't afford to let them get behind it and take cover. I'll get down there and use it, it will give me a better chance of accuracy as well. I'll fire first, then I'll leave it up to you."

King slid through the grass, but Jane caught his arm. "Wait," she said. "It's too dangerous to go down there."

King shook his head. "I know what I'm doing," he replied earnestly, then cracked a smile as he said, "Stay close to Stewart. He's a complete bastard, but he'll see you right." He pressed on and half slid, half crawled down the slope to the cluster of four boulders. He moved stealthily and knew he had remained unseen when he came up on the first boulder without hearing any gunfire. He got into a crouch and eased the weapon between the two boulders. The enemy now seemed frighteningly close and the first of the fighters had reached the riverbank. He watched as the first soldiers picked their way down the muddy bank and started to cross. King could see the crocodiles starting to cruise lazily downstream. Just their nostrils above the surface and the occasional glimpse of tail. The first six boys had already made it across and were making their way towards the rocks. Behind them, the numbers had swelled and there were as many men standing way over six feet tall among the diminutive figures of the boy soldiers. The numbers grew and as the tenth or eleventh man crossed over the river, there were twenty or more reaching the halfway point. King took a deep breath, then eased out and sent a burst of fire into the men and boys in the water. The commotion started at once, with bullets sailing down over his head as the rest of his team opened fire, and the enemy returning undisciplined fire into the hillside. King caught sight of the first of the crocodiles taking one of the men, and then more came from downstream. There were shouts and screams as the men were snatched and taken under the waist deep water, and the water frothed red as the crocodiles entered their death rolls to rip the limbs from their prey and drown them in the frenzied attack. The enemy fired into the water, some bullets hitting their own men and some hitting the giant beasts, some of the creatures fifteen feet or more in length. Men and boys ran forward, retreated, or simple stayed still and fired chaotically. All the time, disciplined volleys of gunfire came from the hilltop and the bullets found their mark. King fired again, changed to a new magazine, and picked at the targets nearest him to avoid becoming over-whelmed. When he changed to his third magazine, he aimed for the furthest soldiers, making good use of his closer proximity.

Inevitably, the soldiers on the far bank retreated. Lacking both cover and the resolve to enter the frothing, crimson-coloured water, they made for the safety of the jungle and took themselves out of range. King realised that he would be cut down if he attempted to climb back up the slope, so he reloaded his weapon and broke from cover, working his way around the hill. He glanced to his right, saw a steady convoy of crocodiles heading upstream and the inevitable bodies floating towards them. The water frothed and great tails whipped out of the water as the beasts rolled with the bodies. King shuddered at the thought but kept his head in the game as he gained sufficient distance and started to climb.

"Tom's down and Reece has fucked off!" Peter Stewart shouted breathily as he pulled King the rest of the way to the crest of the hill and over the ridge to relative safety.

"Jim's heading on direct coordinates to the LZ to warn Dimitri and the hostages."

"What do you mean, Reece has fucked off?"

"He's gone. Deserted." Stewart reloaded magazines, checked his kit then started off down the hillside. "We opened up on them, and when I backed up and reloaded, Reece was no longer there."

Jane was crouched in the longer grass, holding Tom's Uzi. King noted that she held it confidently. But then again, the woman was competent with the Browning and when all was said and done, a gun was a gun and all military weapons had been designed to be easy to use. Firearms needed a loading source, a charging or cocking mechanism, a safety mechanism, a trigger, and sights. Jane seemed to have grabbed the basics and as if to confirm this, she fired a few rounds at movement in the grass on top of the hill.

"And Tom is dead?" King asked, turning his eyes to the hilltop.

"Outright."

"Shit."

"The bullet hole..." Jane said. "It looked as if it came from behind..."

"What?" King asked incredulously.

"A small hole at the back of the head, a larger hole in the forehead," she shrugged. "Reece was behind and to the right. And Jim was in completely the wrong place for it to have been him. He was way off to the left and slightly forward of Tom."

Stewart shook his head, then cursed a string of colourful expletives. "We've got to get going," he stated flatly between breaths. "I reckon we nailed thirty of the fuckers. Between us and the crocodiles, that is."

"Would have nailed more if we had the right weapons!" King retorted.

"And if your aunty had a dick, she'd be your uncle," Stewart replied. "It is what it is. We have to get on with it."

"It doesn't make sense, Reece bugging out. He has a good record." King paused as they trudged on through the brush. "So, what are we thinking? He shot Tom on purpose, or he fucked up, had an ND, and panicked when he saw what he'd done?"

"Who can say," Stewart replied. "I didn't get a chance to check the body," he replied somewhat dubiously. "And who knows what someone is thinking in battle? But the man was too experienced to have a negligent discharge." Stewart paused as he snatched a breath and climbed up a ledge that looked like a fissure that had torn through the earth. "Good work, by the way. That was a great ambush. We've hurt them badly and gained some time to make the LZ."

King didn't reply. Coming from Stewart, that was the highest praise indeed. He glanced at the fissure which went on for a hundred metres or more in both directions. The spoil face of the fissure was dry and as he scrambled up, he slipped back down, clawing at the earth. He cursed, having dug the submachinegun's muzzle into the dirt and he upended it, tapping the barrel to free the clod. It didn't work, so he swiped a smooth, opaque stone out of the bank and used it to tap the dirt out. He let Jane go up ahead of him while he tried to clear the obstruction.

"Come on, man!" Stewart said from the top. King went to toss the stone but stopped when Stewart asked what he was doing. King frowned. "That's a fucking diamond, lad!" Stewart paused, then said, "Here, let me take a look..."

King was about to hand him the dull, smooth but lustre-less stone that was around the size of the top section of his index finger, but several bullets slammed into the bank, as the sound of automatic gunfire erupted on the hill behind them. King dropped the stone but swiped it up as he crawled his way up the fissure. Stewart had lost all interest in the stone and engaged the enemy with short bursts of automatic fire. King rolled over the top of the fissure and down the other side. When he got up, he tracked a burst of gunfire up the hillside and two men fell and rolled down. Stewart accounted for another two – one wounded and clawing his way back to the crest of the hill, and the other sliding down the grassy hill on his back, his limbs still and lifeless.

"On me! On me!" Jim called out. He was fifty metres ahead of them and twenty metres to their left, and he had been afforded the luxury of a mighty Baobab tree, that looked to have fallen in a lightning strike, for cover. Jim fired above their heads as they ran towards him. "I've been hit, fellas. I've bloody well been hit..." He said as they all scurried behind the large tree trunk for cover. "It's bad. I didn't feel it until I made it down the hill and my leg suddenly stopped working..."

"King, keep us covered while I take a look," Stewart instructed him. "You can help me," he said to Jane tersely.

King nodded and using the tree trunk as a handy rest, he switched the weapon to 'single fire' and started to engage the enemy. The men fell one by one, and King counted them off as he fired. The 9mm rounds weren't stopping the enemy soldiers outright, but he could see them fall and some rested ominously still, while others clawed their way back up the slope having tasted hot lead and copper. But a bullet was a bullet, and the wounded were highly unlikely to continue to pursue them, let alone fight.

At the hill's summit, King watched a large man holding a

machete in his right hand and what he suddenly realised
was Tom's head in his left. Julius Lombobo had made it out
from the burning hell of the second camp. The leader of the
Southside Boys pounded the fist that was holding the
machete against his chest and chanted something distinctly
tribal. The other men around him joined in and their voices
carried tunefully on the breeze. King aimed high and fired.
The round went nowhere near him. He adjusted his aim by
dead reckon and fired again but the man ducked his head
and continued to chant. "Fuck!" King swore. "I might as well
have a bloody air rifle!" He fired another single shot, but the
round wasn't close enough for the man to duck from the
whizz of a close call. He turned to Stewart and Jane and
asked, "How is he?"

Stewart stood up. "Morphine and a pad and bandage
have sorted the pain and the bleeding for now, but the
bullet has shattered his femur and it's still inside." He drew
his Browning pistol, his face telling King all he needed to
know.

"Fuck that, boss. I'll carry the bastard," said King, his
adrenalin flowing and his eyes wide with endorphins, the
buzz of the moment. He quickly reloaded. "Last magazine,"
he said, then caught hold of Jim by his lapels and hoisted
him to a standing position, before tipping him over his
shoulder in a classic fireman's lift. The man grunted in pain.
"That bastard on top of the hill is taunting us," King
complained once he had gotten the man balanced over his
shoulder.

"Aye, lad. But it doesn't mean nothing unless we let it."
Stewart led the way, his Uzi slung over his shoulder with the
GPS in his hand as he checked the route that they were
taking with the coordinates. He trudged ahead, King
following with Jim's dead weight on his shoulder. Stewart

pocketed the GPS and took hold of his weapon. He had taped a button compass to the weapon's frame and so could check their direction of travel regularly without stopping. "Two miles to the LZ."

"Piece of piss," King said sardonically. He glanced across at Stewart and frowned. "Problem? You don't sound too sure."

"Reece has the damned satphone. I got him to alert the chopper pilot while you got all heroic and went back down the hill."

"Shit..."

Stewart nodded but did not reply. The comment simply hung in the air with all the inevitability it entailed.

Jane jogged alongside King, the Uzi in her hands. She was breathing heavily, but her pace was good, and he could tell she was fit. "I never really thanked you," she said.

"Don't mention it," King said.

"It's just, that I wanted to thank you for finding me."

"We haven't escaped yet."

"I know," she replied. "But something tells me we might not make it home."

"We will."

She nodded, but she did not look convinced.

"Are you dating anyone?" King asked.

"What?"

"Keep your traps shut and run!" Stewart snarled from in front.

"Don't worry about him, he's all heart really," said King. "Are you dating anyone?"

"Well, yes, I am," she replied.

King chuckled. "Just my luck. You can't even buy me a drink."

"I could do that," she smiled.

"Well, it's a date."

"No, not a date, it's a drink."

King shifted Jim's weight over his shoulder, found better balance and increased his pace. The man groaned again, but it was difficult to tell whether it was from the pain, or the euphoric high he was experiencing from the morphine ampule Stewart had slammed into the man's thigh. "Well, once you've been submitted to my sparkling repartee over a couple of *Babychams*, you'll change your mind."

"Really?" she managed a smile, clearly fearful for her life, but making the best of it all the same.

"Maybe. But once you've seen me dance, it'll seal the deal."

"Because you're so good?"

King shook his head. "No. Because I'm so bad. You owe it to womankind not to let me inflict my moves on anybody else. You'll feel compelled to take one for the sisterhood and get me off the dating market."

Jane laughed. "If we ever get out of this, then I promise to consider it at least."

"You two finished?" Stewart stopped in front of them, checking the GPS. "Less than a mile to go. But I can hear gunfire up ahead. You two would too, if you'd shut your mouths."

39

He had made good progress. The hostages were the right side of frightened to take orders and press on, but not so panicked as to give up all hope and sink into despair or flee like startled deer. The point of rescue was often the moment hostages would relax, imagine they were safe and that it was a done deal. It was when they thought they were truly free that they were in the greatest danger. Dimitri treated them like cattle – pushing them forwards, shouting for them to remain alert and motivating them with the experience of what that fifteen years in the Soviet and Russian Federation military had given him.

The first burst of gunfire peppered through the hostages and two of them fell to the ground clutching their injuries. One of the women fell, poleaxed. The bullet had hit her in the head and switched off the lights. Dimitri returned fire but the second burst of enemy gunfire dug up the ground around him and he rolled frantically to avoid the track of bullets. When he got back up, the hostages were fleeing in all directions.

"Get back here!" he shouted. "Get back! Get down and

take cover!" He looked up as Reece broke cover and ran
towards him. Dimitri lowered his weapon and beckoned
him towards him, but saw the man raise his own weapon
far too late. He caught a bullet in his shoulder and spun
like a top. He fell but had kept his hand on the rifle and he
sat up and fired single shots with just one hand. They had
the desired effect and the man turned and bolted, diving
for cover as the rounds drew near. Dimitri struggled to
reload the weapon using just one hand, but he got it done.
When he searched for the target, running, and panicking
hostages were in his line of fire. He struggled to get up and
get to a more suitable and tactical firing position. In the
distance he could hear a helicopter. A torquey model, a
heavy craft with a thunderous engine and large rotors. He
would have bet everything he owned on it being a Soviet
era Mil, and when he saw it in the distance, his suspicions
were confirmed. He looked back at the man who had shot
him, but he was in the distance and just running over the
ridge of the hill. The helicopter banked and lowered and
appeared to follow the man. He turned back to the
hostages, but they had scattered like sheep pursued by an
errant dog. Dimitri looked at his shoulder. The wound was
bleeding, but he had not lost feeling in his shoulder and as
he checked more thoroughly, he could see and feel that he
had not lost movement. The trickle down his side told him
the bullet had gone through, but he would have to staunch
the bleeding and infection was already a given. Dimitri put
down the rifle and unclipped the medi-pack from his
webbing. He took out the dressings he would need, then
looked up to see Stewart, the woman from MI5 and King
carrying one of the other men. He dropped the dressings
and picked up the rifle. He had no idea what had just transpired, but he took aim, nonetheless. The brash and craggy-

looking Scotsman was in his sights. He adjusted for the man's pace, then fired.

The bullet impacted in the earth half a metre from Stewart's foot. He froze, already looking to the direction of the shooter. He could see Dimitri aiming, and he knew he would not return fire before the man could get off another round from his super accurate Steyr AUG rifle. He held up a hand to halt King, who was beginning to struggle under Jim's weight. "What gives, Dimitri?" Stewart hollered.

"I could ask you the same question!" Dimitri shouted back. "Your man just shot me!"

"We have a problem!" Stewart shouted back, then glanced up at the sound of the helicopter's engine pitch changing the other side of the hill. "And if you don't let me get after him to that chopper, we'll have a hell of a lot of a bigger one!"

Dimitri slowly lowered his rifle and Stewart took off up the hillside. He ran hard and fast and was undoubtedly helped by the cocaine in his system. The marching powder was doing its job, but he'd have a hell of a crash soon. Homeostasis would be a bitch if the Southside Boys were still on their tail for much longer. Stewart reached the top of the hill and looked down on the blades of the helicopter as it rose off the ground from where it had landed in a depression in the grassland. He raised the Uzi and saw Reece sitting in the rear bay. Reece saw him and shrugged, then looked away. The helicopter gained height and started its turn. Stewart fired a burst at the fuselage and the bullets sparked off the toughened underbelly. An assault rifle may well have fared better but the 9mm rounds were ineffective against the steel. He aimed at the cockpit and emptied the magazine at the pilot's window. The plexiglass was punctured and cracked like a spider's web, but the helicopter continued its turn unimpeded. Stewart could see Reece sit back comfortably in his seat as the aircraft banked and climbed and was soon a spec on the distant horizon as Stewart watched their only means of escape head east towards Zaire.

40

King tore open the medi-pack and started to get the dressings out. Jane was cutting Jim's trousers with the scissors on a Leatherman. King looked up as Stewart squatted down beside them. "Jim took a bullet."

"I know," Stewart replied.

"No, another while I was carrying him," said King. He eased Jim over onto his side and placed a dressing under the bullet wound between the man's shoulder blades. He looked back at Stewart, frowned, and shook his head. The Australian didn't see the exchange of looks between the two men. "I don't think he felt it because of the morphine," he added.

"Wouldn't the force of the bullet have thrown you forwards?" asked Jane.

"It doesn't work like that, luv," Stewart replied. "I've seen dead bodies strafed with machinegun fire and they didn't move at all..."

"I'll take your word for it," she said, not hiding her

disdain for the sights he had seen and no doubt, the life he had led.

"I don't need a half-arsed patch up job, Pommie..." Jim slurred, the loss of blood affecting his cognitive reasoning, as much as the morphine. He raised an unsteady hand and beckoned King closer. King bent forwards and Jim rasped, "Sorry we got off on the wrong foot, mate. You're a hell of a bloke to have carried me this far..." He coughed and spluttered, then continued, his eyes fading, "Thank you..."

King watched the life leave the man's eyes, the body sagging with its last breath. He stood up and pulled the map out from his breast pocket. "It's just you and me now, boss," he said to Stewart. "Dimitri, get going southeast to the border and towards the diamond mines. He dug out a leather pouch and handed it to the Russian. "You too, boss," he said, then watched Stewart do the same. "There's fifty gold sovereigns there. Worth a hundred and fifty quid each. Use them to pay or bribe your way to safety." He looked at Jane. "I want you to go with the hostages and cover the rear. Don't let anyone fall behind and shoot anybody who tries to stop you." He walked over to Lucinda, and she stood up and smiled meekly. "Are you OK?" he asked.

"I'm still alive..." She paused. "Who's your girlfriend?"

"A safe pair of hands," he replied. "And do what she says, because she has a gun." He heard Stewart calling him to get going.

King kissed Lucinda on the cheek, but she turned her head so that their lips brushed together. She smiled and pulled away and King turned and walked after Stewart. He wouldn't look back. The best soldiers never did. King remembered an old man on his estate telling him so. The man had fought in World War Two and often told King anecdotes, but never about battles and only ever stories like having stew, with peaches for pudding served together in his helmet, while American GIs had steaks, ice cream and Coca Cola at the camp next door. But the man never spoke about what he had done, and he never looked back as he moved through Europe to victory. King now knew what the old man had meant. He vowed never to look at the carnage in his wake, and he sure as hell wasn't going to tell another soul what he had seen or done. And he wouldn't look back at a loved one, just take the memory of them with him as he moved forwards.

King picked up the Uzi Jim had been using and Stewart handed King a full magazine for it and a handful of rounds to Jane. Jim's body lay where he had died, but Stewart had closed the man's eyes. He had scavenged the body for kit and had the man's Browning in his hand and had managed to fill a second Uzi magazine for himself. "We need some pick-ups pretty damned quick," he said. "We'll lure them out and kill them close. Once we've got longs instead of these submachineguns, our job will be easier."

King nodded. "There's an island of thick jungle south-west of us. On the map it looks like ten-thousand acres or so. I imagine it is dense but made up of trees too thin for the loggers to be interested in. It may just be the place we can end this."

"You're both crazy," Jane said quietly.

"They'll catch us up before we reach the border," Stewart snapped. He shrugged. "King, you were right. We should have pressed on further, given Dimitri a longer lead with the hostages."

"It doesn't matter," said King. "What's done is done." He was cut short by gunfire and turned to see four men sliding down the embankment. "Looks like we're on..." He picked up the AK-74 with its few bullets remaining and took careful aim. As he fired, Dimitri joined him and picked off the man on the left. King had the man on the right and one of the men left standing charged at them screaming, while his companion turned and crawled up the bank. He fell and rested still after Dimitri hit him dead centre between his shoulder blades. King missed the running man with three shots, and as he returned fire, they all threw themselves onto their stomachs, bullets whizzing over their heads. Stewart cut the man down with fifty feet to spare. He darted forwards and picked up the man's weapon.

"Damn it!" Stewart scowled. "He's not got any spare mags!"

"It's a start," said King as he tossed the empty AK-74 on the ground. He turned and looked at Jane. "Stay safe," he said.

She smiled. "And you."

King started running towards the ridge. He picked up the dead man's Kalashnikov and slung his Uzi over his shoulder on its sling. He didn't look back, but as he trudged up the incline to the body resting still in the sandy earth, he found himself hoping that she would be alright, with little thought to the rest of the hostages. There was something about the woman that made him feel something other than lust. A connection he could not explain, nor wanted to dissect. He was just pleased the connection was there because he had never experienced the feeling before.

"Fuck me, we're out in the boonies with Christ knows how many of the enemy coming for us, with no helicopter extraction and little hope of survival, and you've got your choice of two women, both holding a fucking candle for you..." Stewart laughed. "Not a bad way to go out, lad."

"I'm not going out today," said King. "And nor are you, boss."

Stewart grinned. "Aye, I like your attitude." He paused, his expression suddenly serious as he got back to the job at hand. "They've got plenty of bodies. And they're sacrificing them to keep us under pressure. That's why they are sending them out with a dime a dozen Kalashnikov, but not much in the way of precious ammo."

"Trust me, I know. I've seen the numbers."

They both eased onto their bellies and tentatively edged over the ridge. King stared into the eyes of a man, less than three feet from him. The man's eyes widened in surprise and King lashed out and plunged a finger deep into the man's right eye socket. The man hollered in agony and surprise, but it gave King time to draw his knife and he caught hold of the man's T-shirt with his left hand and lashed out with the knife in his right. The man pulled backwards, and the T-shirt ripped and pulled over his head. King wriggled forwards, still on his belly, but his feet missed any purchase on the sandy earth behind him, and he was left hanging onto the man's shirt. King dropped the knife and drew his Browning. He fired once and the man slumped forwards. King tossed the T-shirt over the mess to the back of the man's head. He looked for Stewart, but the Scotsman was in his own fight and was on his knees and fighting for control of another man's rifle. King couldn't get a clear shot at his torso or head, but he could see the man's legs well enough, so he fired, and the man's knee shattered and as he slumped, Stewart snatched the man's rifle away from him and King fired and hit the man in the chest.

"We're fucking in it now, son!" Stewart shouted. He turned the man's rifle around and started firing down the slope. "Fucking dozens of them!"

King picked up the AK and started to fire. They had interrupted the Southside Boys' attempt at swarming them, and they had reversed the element of surprise. The men were crawling up the slope on their bellies and made easy pickings for the two men with their advantage of holding the high ground. But it couldn't last forever. Men scattered at the bottom of the slope and found cover and distance and soon, the rounds were coming in with ever increasing accuracy and both men darted back over the ridge.

"We have to show them we're heading southwest to the jungle," King said.

"What do you suggest?"

"I'll run along the ridge. You cover me."

Stewart shook his head. "It won't do you any good, there's forty or more guns down there!"

King didn't wait for him. He scrambled back up the hill and started to sprint along the ridge. Bullets sailed over his head and around his feet and Stewart cursed and clambered up, nestled into the ground as close as he could and started to return fire. After thirty seconds, he glanced to his left and saw King leaping back over the ridge. Stewart got up and ran, changing magazines on the move. He dodged back over the ridge and used the incline to traverse at speed. When he reached the bottom, he was just fifty metres behind King, and they ran together towards the treeline ahead of them. Bullets eventually drew near them, but their pursuers knew that they could either keep firing at rapidly gaining targets with every shot becoming more ineffective, or they could join the chase and hope to close the gap. Gradually, the gunshots subsided and both men knew that they were being pursued. They just hoped that they could make the cover of the jungle island in time.

41

King didn't wait for the man to stop groaning or moving, his legs twitching irritably as death slowly took hold. He wasn't going anywhere, and the rifle he had been struggling to get hold of was out of reach. Any last-ditch attempt to avenge his brothers or his own imminent death wasn't going to happen, no matter how much the man would want it. King wiped the blood off the blade of the knife on the man's shoulder, before sheathing it and picking up the FN rifle. The rifle was heavy and hot from the contact. King checked the magazine and breech then bent down and pulled two more magazines from the dying man's bandolier. The FN packed a punch in its full-fat 7.62x51mm. Heavy and cumbersome, the magazines were heavy, too. But the rifle tended to be a one shot, one kill weapon and he checked that the front and rear sights were square and undamaged before shouldering the rifle. Ahead of him there was movement in the brush. The man beside him let out a moan, and King pressed his hand over the man's mouth, pinching his nose with his thumb and forefinger, keeping the weapon aimed at the brush. The man barely struggled and was gone inside a minute. King removed his hand from the man's face and wrapped it around the fore end of the heavy rifle, glad to take some of the weight off his right hand and shoulder.

The jungle glade was hot and humid, dank, and dark. The sunlight broke through the fronds in the canopy in multiple beams, like spotlights on the stage. A foot appeared in one of those spotlights. It was followed by a leg and an arm and part of the body. Dark skin, beads of sweat glistening in the light. The figure froze. Twenty metres from King and unaware that he was standing in the middle of the peep-sight of the SLR. His face still out of view. King waited. A shoulder emerged from the darkness, illuminated in bright sunlight. The man's vest was brown and torn and had probably been white once. King slowly and steadily took a knee, his entire form in the shadows. The man's face clipped the light. Black and dripping with perspiration. The whites of his eyes, big and bright. King's finger tightened on the trigger. There would be others for sure. Directly behind him. King had a choice. Take down the man in front of him or wait and see how many more stepped out of the brush and into the killing ground in front of him. King got his answer as another figure stepped closer to the first, and a boy soldier ducked around the second man. Ten years old if he was a day, carrying the AK-47 on a sling around his neck because the weapon was almost longer than he was tall. King kept his aim steady. The presence of the boy didn't change a thing. He'd seen enough to know that the boy soldiers, the 'infantry' of the Southside Boys had been trained to be fearsome, fearless killers. Snatched from their homes then beaten and abused, made dependant on mind-altering khat, indoctrinated into an existence of pure violence, and turned into soldiers before they even reached puberty. King did not want to kill a child, but he'd seen what had happened when a grown man had hesitated, and dead was dead in his book.

He would not make the same mistake.

Behind the backs of the men in front of him several shouts drew their attention. King had known the enemy would lack discipline, but he supposed what they lacked in tactical skills, they made up for in numbers and a complete and utter fearlessness, and the khat that made them feel invincible. The mind-altering state had certainly meant that the dead man behind him had put up a fearsome fight and had been butchered by King's blade before the inevitable loss of blood made even the invincible stop functioning. King was glad he now had the SLR in his hand. The FN, or the LiAi as it had been known in British military service was certainly a more reassuring option than the 9mm Uzi he had ditched after running out of ammunition. Three of the Southside Boys had taken at least six rounds a piece before they had stopped moving.

The three hostiles were all looking behind them now, waiting for something. Another shout and the foliage beside them parted and two more men stepped out from cover and into the glade.

"So, what the fuck are we waiting for?" came the whisper. Not even a whisper, a barely audible hum.

King's heart raced as he realised that he hadn't heard the Scotsman creep up on him. He kept his aim, like he had known his mentor had been there all along. "More of them to show up," he replied in a low murmur.

"That FN is semi-auto only and the barrel is almost long enough to poke them with from here." Peter Stewart paused. "Too many more of them and your odds are lowering with

every single swinging dick inviting themselves to the
party..."

"The range lessons are over," replied King, as he lowered
the rifle. He reached for the grenade attached to his belt and
eased out the ring pin with his thumb. "Don't worry, old
man. There'll be enough meat left for you..."

There was no quiet way to release the lever, and it
sprang off its half hinge and clattered into the foliage. The
lead man looked over, his wide eyes white in the beams of
light parted by the fronds like a child's kaleidoscope. King
silently counted, but Stewart blew their position when he
dived for cover. King threw the grenade and followed
Stewart into the brush, rolling around so he could lie prone
with his rifle facing towards the enemy as he buried his face
into the dirt and covered his head with his left hand. The
concussive thud of the grenade was felt through their bodies
– in the hollow of their chests and in their guts - and shrapnel, plant debris and body parts rained down around the
glade. There were screams and groans, a child's scream
turning into a sob. Stewart was up and pushing through the
brush, his Uzi held out in front of him in his right hand, and
he had characteristically drawn his knife and had it firmly
clenched, blade downwards, in his left hand. King followed,
taking Stewart's beaten path out into the clearing. The boy
was sitting on his backside and was clearly dazed and
confused by the concussive blast that had robbed him of
both his legs. Stewart put a bullet into the boy's forehead
without hesitation and King guessed that the action both
gave the child a swift end and paid a debt for one of their
own. But even though their losses had been great, King felt
no better for it, no sense of vengeance or justice for the
bullet he put into the next man, nor the one after that.

Stewart was charging through the clearing and King

couldn't help thinking, for the second time on this mission, that his instructor and mentor taught the theories of close quarter battle procedures but forgot almost everything in the actual firefight. However, he still had one procedure down, and King could see that unless he quickened his own pace, the tough forty-something Scotsman would be leaving him behind again. To remain static in a close quarter battle was almost certainly to die, and Stewart was like a whirlwind, darting this way and that. He crouched and leapt, ducked, and dived and alternated the speed at which he cut through the men in front of him.

King could see that the man had taken down three more men in a volley of gunfire and with downward stabbing motions and slashes left and right with the Ka-Bar US Marine Corps knife until they had stopped moving. King fired at the men as they engaged, each shot aimed at the centre of the torso and taking a man to the jungle floor. Stewart buried his knife deep between a struggling man's shoulder blades, dropped onto one knee and changed magazines as the man fell to his knees. King watched Stewart heave himself up using the embedded knife as a handle, then tugged it free and resumed his charge into the enemy as the man he had just killed fell forwards onto his stomach.

King took a knee and reloaded the heavy rifle, then remained in his position and fired at a group of three men. When he looked up, Stewart was no longer there and the enemy were massing to the edge of the glade, torn between fighting, and fleeing into the cover of the jungle. King cursed Stewart and got moving again. There were twenty men ahead of him, many of them boy soldiers. He was in it now. To show mercy was to die. He had been told of the things he would see in this profession, and until he had landed in Angola, he had killed just one man in his time with MI6. That man had been a rogue agent, and he had been trying to kill King at the time. He had killed before, two men in a bar fight, and that had started a chain of events that started his path with MI6 and ultimately saw him about to die in a jungle at the hands of boy soldiers high on khat and with a bloodlust in their eyes.

King dived onto his stomach, taking cover behind a dying man as he changed the magazine in the FN rifle. He was aware of his movements being painfully slow, the enemy advancing, their aim getting closer with every shot fired until dirt flicked up into his face as the bullets drew dangerously near to him. Several bullets hit the wounded man that he was taking cover behind, and he groaned and lurched then went still. King got the rifle up to his shoulder and rolled several times, much as a child would down a meadow hillside, then stopped himself when he was ten feet away from the body and on the edge of the glade. He started to fire at them, picking just the closest person to him, or the man who seemed most in control of his weapon. Gunfire erupted from behind them, and Stewart appeared from the edge of the jungle some twenty-five metres from where King had last seen him. In jungle warfare, Stewart had taught what he had casually called the 'peek-a-boo' technique and was using it to good effect. He disappeared again, and after a few seconds, he emerged ten metres to the right, now flanking the men after he had sprayed them with gunfire from behind. King rolled into the thick foliage, scrambled to his feet, and ran as fast as he could through the brush to mimic Stewart's tried and tested technique. He almost stumbled into a boy of ten or eleven years, crawling through the brush. King shouldered the rifle and the boy looked up at him, his eyes fearful and his hands held up in front of his face as if they could offer protection to a 7.62mm bullet. Futile, but hopeful. King could see that the boy had lost his weapon. He must have come close to Stewart too because there was a six-inch gash running from one side of his forehead to the opposite side of his chin, just missing his eye but making up for it by putting a lateral cross over his mouth. His lips were hanging loose, and blood had turned his dirty T-shirt red. King cursed himself for hesitating. He had shown a young boy soldier mercy just two days before. Allowed him to run, scared and defeated. But at what cost? Your mistakes shape your future. King had made a costly mistake and one of their team had died. Stewart had primed them all to show no mercy, give no quarter. And the old bastard had been right all along. King had thought him wrong to play God, but there really was no other safe option. Without further hesitation he squeezed the trigger and moved on. The nightmares, drink and darkness would surely take hold of him now. He would become just like the tough Scotsman who had trained him. He had gone down the road from which there was no return, no salvation.

King pounded on, his mind in a fog, not even sure if the fight was worth the cost. He worked his way to his right, and eventually came out into the glade slightly behind the line of men, mindful to stay out of Stewart's arc of fire. King fired the weapon for all he was worth, bracing his weight behind the mighty recoil and aiming at each man through the peep-sights. The melee lasted a few seconds and when every man was down, King could see Stewart reloading at the edge of the clearing and drawing his pistol. King changed over to his last magazine and tried to ignore the Scotsman as he worked his way through the clearing giving a bullet to the heads of both men and boys with his 9mm Browning pistol, regardless of whether they were moving and breathing, or lying quite still.

King was fighting for breath, his chest heaving. He felt unsteady on his feet and sucked in lungful after lungful of precious, dank air. He hadn't eaten in two days and the effect was taking its toll.

"You're forgetting to breathe in the contact," Stewart observed. "When you were boxing, I bet you didn't hold your breath..."

King nodded. He had done, and his trainer had always nagged at him, telling him he couldn't always win in the first round and that breathing kept the fight in you to last the distance. He had put King up against hardened distance fighters to teach him the lesson or swapped over sparring partners after each round until he had got the message. Out here, he had done the same thing and high on adrenalin, he had probably only taken a couple of breaths throughout the entire battle.

"Hydrate," Stewart snapped, but King noted that the man was drinking from his own hipflask and water and glucose was the last thing he'd find in there.

King sipped from his own camel pack. Water was plentiful in the jungle, and he'd soon find some more water and drop a few purifiers into it for a sickly cocktail of sterilised mud, water, and dead parasites. He sealed the drinking tube, his eyes on the bullet hole in the child's forehead. He looked at the boy's legless corpse, knowing that it was the grenade that had done for the boy what Stewart had finished. Without any warning, King retched and vomited next to the child's body.

"That's a fucking waste of good water, lad," the Scotsman called out harshly. King wiped his mouth with the back of his hand and spat on the ground. "Must be the adrenalin, son."

"I think so," King lied.

"Aye..." Stewart shrugged. "The little bastard would think nothing of slicing off your own dick and shoving it down your throat, so don't waste your tears... or the contents of your stomach... on him."

King looked away from the body of the boy and watched as Stewart took his second swig of whisky. "There'll be more of them coming soon," he said.

"I'm counting on it," the Scotsman replied. "The more the better. Let them come after us while Dimitri heads south. We need to buy them some time."

King looked around the clearing. The bodies were strewn in a grotesque display of angles. Of splayed limbs, broken skulls and the ground had soaked red, the penetrating light through the canopy highlighting the macabre scene that he knew he would see as a snapshot in twenty years' time. If indeed, he was lucky to live that long. But after following the crazy Scotsman, he seriously doubted that. He did not want to count the bodies, better he didn't know. Early on, Stewart had told him never to put a number on it. That had not been possible before this mission. He knew the numbers. Both before his service and since he had signed his life away. He could have counted his death toll on one hand, and still have a couple of digits spare. And two of those souls had been unintentional. A stupid argument fuelled by alcohol and ego. But now? After just one week, he had no idea how many people he had sent to their graves. And he knew he wasn't out of this yet.

Stewart picked up an AK-47 and ejected the empty magazine, tossing it onto one of the bodies. He started checking through the dead and soon had four fully loaded magazines shoved into the pockets of his bandolier and had decided to ditch the UZI machine-pistol for the rifle. King found the body of a man who had been carrying an FN SLR and started helping himself to ammunition and magazines. He already knew the weapon worked, so he wasn't bothered about the veritable display of hardware strewn before him. He looked down at the teen's body. The SLR rifle in his hand had earned the moniker, 'The right arm of the free world...' But not for this guy. His world had not been free. His fight had not been just, and had not lasted long, either.

Both men froze as they heard shouts further down the trail. Stewart was already ducking into the brush, and King followed suit, stepping backwards, and disappearing from the glade when he was less than a foot into the foliage. Perspiration stung his eyes and he ignored it, as well as the biting flies that were after his sweat, and crawling insects that were working their way between the top of his boot and where his combat trouser leg had become untucked. King took a deep breath to steady his nerves as he shouldered the rifle and readied himself for the second wave.

42

"**F**ate whispers to the warrior, 'You cannot withstand the storm...' And the warrior whispers back, 'I am the storm...'"

"What the fuck was that?" King whispered.

"Someone once said it to me when they thought I needed it," Stewart replied.

"I like it," said King. He kept his aim on the advancing man. Two hundred metres across the clearing. The place where they would live or die. There was no more retreating, no infinite supply of ammunition. No more energy. It was to be here. Victory or defeat. "Seems fitting..."

"King," Stewart whispered. "Do you believe in fate?"

"I guess so."

"And fate? No one alive has ever escaped it, neither brave man nor coward, I tell you - it's born with us the day that we are born..." Stewart said whispered. "It's not my quote, it's from Homer's The Iliad, but I believe it. If we were meant to get out of this, then we will. And once you realise that, then you're not scared anymore. It's what makes a good solider great, and in knowing this and acting accordingly, you have a better chance of being the last man standing."

King said nothing. There were twenty men now, each of them starting to cross the clearing tentatively. They had another few paces to go before King and Stewart either lived or died. Two paces. One. And then one of the men stepped on the fishing line with the fifty-pound breaking strain, attached to two grenades. King ducked as the debris hit them and the clearing billowed with smoke. They kept their heads down, as the second line detached when King pulled it and swung into the clearing behind the scattering men, weighted with two full AK-47 magazines and another two grenades, their pins already pulled and detonating at head level a few seconds after the levers sprung off into the air. In thousandths of a second, the magazines ripped apart and sixty bullets and the tinny metal of the magazines acted as shrapnel, some of the bullets detonating and firing into the carnage. King was up and charging forwards, the heavy FN rifle in his hands as he fired at anything that moved. Stewart caught up with King and fired bursts into the smoke, bodies falling and screaming in the chaos.

The smoke started to clear, and boy soldiers ran back into the denser part of the jungle, while the adults either tried to fight or begged for mercy but were shown no quarter. King saw the once imposing figure of Julius Lombobo, now cowering on his hands and knees as he struggled to make sense of the situation. King aimed and squeezed the trigger, but the rifle dry clicked on an empty chamber. He cursed, saw the light in Lombobo's eyes as the man realised that he had a second chance and reached for his machete on the ground. King spun the rifle in his hands, caught hold of the scorching barrel and swung it like a club. Lombobo smashed the machete into the butt stock and King dropped the rifle, the palms of his hands burned from the hot metal. The blade flashed backwards and forwards in front of his face, and King backed away instinctively. Lombobo lunged and King blocked the flat of the blade with his right forearm bringing the machete across the man's body, he lunched forwards and caught hold of Lombobo's wrist with his left hand and moved his arms apart. The machete twisted and Lombobo released his grip. King drove the point into the man's stomach, then hammered his right hand repeatedly onto the end of the handle as he barged forwards. The machete drove deeper in three successive hits until it buried itself to the hilt and Lombobo fell onto his back, the blade pinning him to the ground. He looked up at King, blood seeping from his mouth. He tried to say something. Perhaps it would be an eloquent speech, or perhaps one filled with hate, but King wasn't listening. He drew his Browning and shot him in the forehead, then turned to see Stewart sitting in the middle of the clearing, clutching a bullet wound to his leg, with bodies all around him and nobody left to fight.

43

R AF Brize Norton, England

THE HOSTAGES HAD BEEN MET by the foreign office representatives and the Hercules C130 that had brought them all back from Angola was taxiing further up the apron towards the second set of hangars. There were hotels being put on for them, and reunions with families and loved ones, and representatives from OPEC. As well as doctors and psychologists to examine them and talk to, and counselling sessions for the weeks and months ahead. But not for King. He had caught Lucinda's arm as she had declined the minibus to the hospitality suite and the waiting buffet and debrief. But it would seem that Lucinda Davenport had been granted special dispensation from the circus awaiting the other hostages. Her husband had seen to that. Prominent cabinet members and multi-millionaire CEOs were able to pull strings like that.

King and Stewart had caught up with Dimitri and the hostages at the border with Angola. Stewart had taken a bullet to the leg which had shattered the man's femur. King had staunched the bleeding and bandaged most of his leg and carried Stewart over his shoulder for almost ten miles. Less than halfway into their journey the Scotsman had begged King to shoot him. A few miles after that, he had *ordered* King to shoot him. By the time King had caught up with Dimitri and the hostages, Stewart was unconscious. They had crossed over the border and avoided an Angolan defence force patrol for political reasons and used most of the gold sovereigns – standard MI6 issue in clandestine foreign operations – to buy safe passage in the form of hiring three Toyota pickup trucks and their drivers to drive them down to Cafunfo, where Stewart and the wounded hostages had been given medical attention by a highly competent local doctor in a surprisingly well equipped medical centre consisting of just three rooms. King had arranged for flights to Luanda and a night in a hotel before being met by an RAF Hercules at the airport the next afternoon.

King watched Lucinda walk towards her husband, then turned and walked away. She wasn't his to watch. Her husband was still standing by the steps to his private jet. He suspected the man would know that the two of them had slept together, but still he remained beside the aircraft. King couldn't imagine what kind of man would do that. Anyway, Lucinda had made her choice and that was that.

"Wait!" Lucinda shouted and ran to him. King turned around and she rushed into him, hugging him close. She smelled good. A heavily scented shampoo. Jasmine perhaps. He wasn't the best judge at such details. He felt her firm breasts press into him. No doubt there, he was a good judge of that. "I love my husband, Alex," she said tearfully. "I don't expect you to understand our relationship. Lord knows, sometimes I don't understand it myself. But You and I, Alex? We wouldn't work. You're a special man, but your world is a million miles from mine."

"You were happy when our worlds converged," he replied. "And you were pleased to see me when it meant saving you."

She wiped a tear away, glancing at her husband before saying, "That's not fair, and you know it." She paused, the words sticking in her throat. "Please look back on us fondly because it happened, rather than sadly because it ended, or indeed, bitterly because I chose my husband over a fling..." And with that, she hugged him even closer, then broke away and walked back to her husband and the waiting airplane. The night was dark and only the lights from the windows of the airplane and the airfield apron illuminated her. King watched as they walked up the stairs together, her husband's hand on her shoulder as they paused at the top and dipped their heads and stepped inside. The steps raised and the door closed, and the tiny jet started taxiing immediately.

"She belongs in another world to you, lad," Stewart said quietly. "A politician's wife. A wealthy businessman using politics to further his empire. Her world is silk cocktail dresses and bottles of champagne that would cost you a week's salary. Forget the bitch. You did your job. She'll forget all about you by next week. Just make sure you do the same." He nodded towards Jane Hargreaves standing next to Charles Forrester beside a non-descript saloon car. "That's a mighty fine woman over there," he said.

King nodded. "Tough as hell, too."

"She likes you, lad."

"Really? How can you tell?"

Stewart smiled. "It's in her eyes," he replied. "They twinkle when you're near her. Look closely enough into them and you'll see your own wedding day in those eyes. Your unborn children, too."

"Fuck me. I never had you down for a soppy twat, boss..."

Stewart laughed as Forrester led his agent away to the waiting car. Stewart's ambulance had arrived, and two RAF paramedics were wheeling a gurney out for the Scotsman, who was holding himself up unsteadily with the aid of a pair of crutches. The Angolan doctor had done a terrific job, but Stewart was off for x-rays and a medical assessment before being discharged. "Mark my words, son. If you meet up with that lass again, there'll be wedding bells soon afterwards..."

King smiled. Who knew what the future held? He doubted the Scotsman was right about Jane Hargreaves and the feelings he perceived her to have about him, but he would have to admit to himself that there wouldn't be many women to compare her to. Tough, resourceful, intelligent, and beautiful. King shrugged off the thought almost immediately. Lucinda had seemed to possess those qualities, too. And as he watched her husband's private jet taxi onto the runway and heard its engines build in pitch, he decided that he was done with women for a while. He watched as the jet reached take-off speed and lifted off the runway taking Lucinda out of his life. When he turned back, Forrester's car had stopped on the apron and Jane Hargreaves was standing twenty feet from him. Stewart was being wheeled to the ambulance, and King realised there were no more vehicles waiting for him.

"I thought you might need a ride somewhere," she said. "Maybe get that drink?"

King smiled. Lucinda, her husband, and his five-million-pound private jet were already three miles away. With every mile she travelled, Lucinda was further into his past and an ever more distant memory. "Sure," he replied. "I'd like that."

S ix months later,
Macedonia

THE MOUNTAIN AIR was cold at this time of year, where autumn was giving way to winter, and especially this early in the morning. Sunrise was still a couple of hours away. King adjusted the collar of his wool-lined leather bomber jacket and cupped his hands, puffing warm air onto them before he rubbed them vigorously and stamped his feet against the cold. Peter Stewart grinned as he put on the pair of thick leather gloves the Macedonian solider had given him. He looked up as the senior officer walked confidently across the yard and halted a few paces away. Either side of him, an enlisted man stood with their AK-74 rifles cradled in their gloved hands.

"You have the... er, paperwork?" the officer asked.

"Indeed," Stewart replied. He handed the man the envelope containing ten-thousand pounds sterling in twenty and fifty-pound notes. "It's all there," he added, looking the man in the eye.

The officer neither opened nor counted the money and after feeling the weight for a moment, slipped it quickly inside his great coat. "Your friend should keep better company," he said in a somewhat off-handed manner. The NLA are a bunch of dogs. The men he was captured with will be shot tomorrow."

Stewart nodded. The Albanian National Liberation Army were formed from veterans of the Kosovo war and had attacked various targets in Macedonia a month earlier. Not satisfied with the recent peace deals throughout the whole of the Balkans, they sought to gain ground in Macedonia where there were many Albanian settlements and a growing Albanian population, thus fracturing the country and starting an Albanian state within Macedonia free from Albanian or Macedonian rule. Only it wasn't just Kosovo veterans fighting here. Mercenaries from all over the world plied their trade for cash. And that was why both King and Stewart were at such a remote mountain military post before the 'crack of sparrow fart', as Stewart would say, on a cold morning in December.

"I hear you," Stewart replied. "And he'll be our problem now, not yours."

"He is an important man, no?" the officer said quietly, the merest sliver of a grin forming. "Maybe I should have asked for more money?"

"Do you play heads and tails?" King asked.

"What?"

"Coin flips," said King. "Heads you get to keep this gold sovereign worth about a hundred and fifty quid. That's a nice little bonus."

The man smiled. "And tails?"

King took out the gold coin and rolled it over his knuckles. He got the coin ready to toss and said, "Tails, you stick to the deal we made like a real man and don't start quibbling about the fucking price like a bitch..."

The two guards tensed, and the officer frowned. "You are a brave man."

King shrugged and tossed the coin. The gold coin glimmered in the darkness, lit only by the arc lights a hundred metres away. He caught it and said, "Call..."

"Heads, of course."

King looked, then smiled and stepped closer with the coin. "Looks like I'll be keeping this, and you won't be bitching about our deal." He slipped the coin back into his pocket and said, "Now, take us to the prisoner."

The officer scowled and turned on his heel. He snapped something at the guards and marched away briskly. One of the guards said, "We will show you."

King followed and Stewart fell in behind. He walked more slowly than usual. The healing process had been a long slog and he had only just got rid of the cane he had progressed to from the set of crutches. He had been told the leg would ache on cold days, and this was as cold as he had felt since leaving Africa. The surgeon had been correct – it ached with a dull throb that reminded Stewart that he was no longer a fit man.

"You don't fuck about, do you?" he said quietly as he caught up with King.

"A deal's a deal," King replied.

"Always."

"Which is why this can't stand."

"Agreed."

They walked across the icy yard and at a concrete hut that looked like a storage depot, one of the guards worked the bolt, while the other stood back with his rifle and covered them, as much as he covered the open door.

King peered inside and as if to answer his concerns, one of the guards flicked on a switch and the inside of the hut flickered into bright, white light.

"Leave us," Stewart said to the guards, and they looked at each other, shrugged then one of them handed King a set of keys and they both stepped outside, but kept their weapons trained on the open doorway.

There were five men in total. They wore hoods and were each chained to a ring on the wall. It became apparent that this was a former cattle shed and that the military installation would have once been a working farm. The men wore worn and faded camouflage fatigues. Soviet issue from long bygone days. King stepped forward and pulled off the hood from the man on the right. He was familiar with the man's size and build, but mostly it was the boots. British army issue. Worn but well looked after.

Reece blinked up at him, then he cast his eyes to Stewart. He sagged and looked at the floor. King put the hood back on him and undid the handcuffs with the key that one of the guards had given him. He refastened them behind the man's back, then worked the key off the loop and pocketed it.

"I..."

"Save it for the court martial," King cut him off.

"But I'm no longer with the armed forces."

"Shame, that. I guess it's down to us, then."

"Where are we going?" Reece asked gruffly.

King pulled him out of the hut, then man-handled him roughly across the yard. "Where the hell do you think?"

"Look, it wasn't personal..."

"Shut up!" King snapped.

They reached the hired Toyota Landcruiser and headed back down the mountain road. King drove and Peter Stewart rode in the back alongside Reece. The Macedonian army had secured the area from Albanian militia, and both he and King had only come under fire at the pass on the other side of the valley. But they would not be returning by that route. King swung off the main mountain pass and took the rutted track to the east. They rounded the eastern side of the mountain and were met by a terrific sliver of gold from the breaking dawn. The sun still wasn't up, but the light had been switched on for another day.

"I already said that it wasn't personal." Reece paused. "It was purely business."

"Aye, lad. And I've just spent six months learning to walk without a stick," Stewart said. "And there are the bodies of three brave men in the Congo, who might've lived to see another day."

"Hardly saints," Reece replied.

"None of us are," said King.

"Dimitri said you killed a hostage, too," said Stewart. "When you tried to kill him and ran for the chopper."

Reece shrugged. "Shame. It wasn't my plan."

"But, if the hostages were all recaptured, then that would have been, OK?" King asked.

"That *was* the plan."

"So, you sold us out. For what?"

Reece shook his head. "For Christ's sake! Take off this bloody hood and I'll tell you!"

Stewart snatched off the hood and tossed it behind him into the boot space. "Better?"

"Much. Have you got any water?"

"No."

"Where are you taking me?"

"You'll see soon enough." Stewart patted his leg. "Seven-six-two-millimetre. Broke my femur and if it wasn't for King here, I'd have bled out and been left for dead like those three unfortunate bastards."

King stopped the vehicle and switched off the engine. Ahead of them, the sun had started to nudge above the distant horizon. The light was golden. King turned in his seat, now able to see the man's features in the dawn light. "South Africa still doesn't have a mining concern in Angola," he said. "But I'm guessing if the hostages didn't make it out, OPEC and Britain would have stalled, and South Africa would have been given the drilling rights."

"*You're* guessing?" Reece scoffed, then broke into a laugh. "Who are you kidding? Your *analysts* worked that out. *You're* just the hired help!"

Stewart smiled. "The mission was a success. As Wellington said of Waterloo, *it was a damn near run thing. The nearest-run thing you ever saw...*" Stewart paused. "But like the out-numbered Wellington, we succeeded despite the odds. And as far as London is concerned, we got the job done. Acceptable hostage losses. They didn't get to know the details; didn't care. They don't know who in our team died or who lived. And they especially don't know that someone betrayed us."

"It must have been shit in Iraq," said King. "Making a judgement call, then that call costing the lives of every man in your unit. Except for yourself, that is. Can't have been easy. I've been to Hereford a few times, done a lot of training there with the regiment. It's a small town. I hear you were shunned. In the NCO's mess, the bar, at the local shops." He paused. "And then there's the survivor's guilt. But I suppose you don't really suffer from that, do you?"

"I..."

"I don't imagine he knows what survivor's guilt is," Stewart said coldly. "The way you sold us all out got us thinking. Maybe the doomed mission in Iraq wasn't what everyone thought it was. Maybe the sole survivor of that operation had something to hide."

"Was it really your team who wanted to kill the goat herder?" King asked coldly. "Or was it you? Not only would you have waltzed back into Hereford all righteous and high and mighty, but you would have sullied the names of good men. The wives and girlfriends and families of your dead colleagues who suspected that your story wasn't true. Of course, they couldn't prove it, and nor could the head brass. But they all knew. That was why you resigned in the end. Nobody bought your bullshit story. Except on paper, at least."

Reece didn't reply. He simply stared straight ahead, avoiding eye contact with both men, an obstinate sneer to his lips. Stewart opened his door and got out. He stretched and walked around the other side, opened the door, and caught hold of Reece's shoulder.

"Out you get."

"Where are we going?" Reece replied as he got out of the vehicle, half under his own steam, half pulled out by Stewart.

King got out and held the Makarov pistol by his side, the muzzle pointed at the ground. Reece saw the weapon then looked up at King pleadingly.

"No, don't..."

Stewart pushed the man forwards and King stepped to one side, raising the weapon just enough to let Reece know where the bullet would go if he tried anything. Not that he would get far, his hands tethered behind his back and the loose stone surface treacherous underfoot in the morning frost.

"Your South African oil contacts had a line with the Southside Boys," King stated flatly. "That's how they coerced the waiter Bartolomeu to show the gunman to my room. Did you know I was going to be a target?"

Reece shrugged. "It wasn't personal..."

"Like hell it wasn't," King growled. "So, were all the team to be hit, or was it just me?"

"You must have tickets on yourself, pal," Reece replied. He shrugged like it was too late to deny anything and said, "Everyone was to be hit. I went to lay low, but those stupid bastards fucked it up. They sent one man while the other two had themselves a rape rally at the waiter's flat."

"So, you cleaned house?" Stewart asked.

"Yes."

"You killed the man's wife and two daughters?" King asked, bemused.

"I didn't want to. But a white man in Luanda killing two black men. I wouldn't have gone far when the wife and kids inevitably talked." Reece shrugged. "And it was a hell of a lot of money."

"So, that was you driving out of there like a bat out of hell, just after we arrived?" Stewart asked.

"I suppose. I didn't see you, but I knew it would be close."

"Cold," said King.

Reece sneered. "It's early days for you, rookie. But you'll cross the line one day." King did not reply, but he tightened his grip on the man as they walked across a loose section of rock. "Look, we can still do a deal." Reece suddenly pleaded. "I have funds put aside. Close to a million pounds!"

"That figures," said Stewart. "Blood bounty money. What

the Ministry of Defence pays for civilian casualties in times of war."

"What?" King asked, stepping aside, and keeping the weapon on their prisoner.

Stewart nodded sagely. "You see, in Iraq when a rocket overshoots a target and wipes out a family having their dinner, or one of our soldiers gets a little scared and trigger-happy and shoots an innocent farmer riding on his motor-bike or a donkey, along comes an officer of the British army and pays out approximately three thousand pounds per death. If negotiations get tough, they are authorised to go to almost four thousand. That's it. No further recourse, no lawsuits, compensation paid. So, a man loses his two daughters, his son and his wife and ends up with a cash payment of around twelve grand. *Sign on the dotted line, and we won't see you in court later...* The true value of a life calculated and signed off in Whitehall." Stewart shrugged. "Only I did some checking, and a unit going around making these payments was hit in the same area as your team. The officer and adjutant and their three bodyguards were all killed. The money was never recovered. Just over a million pounds should have been accounted for."

Reece's shoulders sagged and he breathed out a long, sullen breath. "We didn't hit them," he said. "But we saw and heard something going down and by the time we got down there they were all dead. We engaged the enemy, but they didn't have a chance. They were all gathered around the case of money." He paused. "It was all over in a matter of seconds."

"And you all had different ideas about how it would get reported," King stated flatly. "The thieves' charter."

Reece nodded. Stewart pushed him onwards and after a dozen paces, they had reached the edge of a precipice. Reece went leaden, his legs starting to sag. Stewart kept the man upright.

"Yes," Reece managed.

"And you killed them," said Stewart.

Reece sighed, shook his head, then took a deep breath. He had tears in his eyes and the look of belligerence and indifference upon his face earlier had given way to something else. King would later think of it as a look of relief.

"We retreated back to our hide and our objective. We called it in," he said. "But we had the money with us. Some of the boys were joking about divvying it up, buying a car when they got home, or paying off the mortgage. It was a laugh. But then it all turned so serious. A couple of the lads wanted to keep it, the rest said that it wasn't even an option. It all got so heated and during the argument one of the lads had an ND."

"He discharged his weapon?" Stewart said incredulously.

"It really *was* a negligent discharge," Reece insisted. "But it all went batshit crazy. The guys serious about handing the money in thought it was a mutiny and returned fire and when it all went quiet, I was the last man standing. It was over almost as soon as it had begun. I don't even think we were all serious about keeping it. It was just a lot of bullshit banter that got out of hand. The bloke who had the ND shot one of the *opposition* in the gut. He didn't mean to, but the rest was reactionary. Highly trained soldiers suddenly amid a close quarters battle, fighting for their lives."

"But you kept the money," said King. He looked at Stewart and said, "What about the autopsies? Surely the five-point-five-six-millimetre bullets would have shown up?"

"We'd captured some weapons. Thought having them would help our cover if we were seen carrying Kalashnikovs.

We still carried our own sidearms under our robes. And not everyone got a shot off either, but the sides had been drawn by then," Reece said quietly.

"There are few autopsies carried out during war," Stewart replied.

"We could have the bodies exhumed for a thorough investigation," said King. Stewart shook his head. "Or just let sleeping dogs lie…"

"What?" King shook his head. "What about justice?"

Stewart swept a hand towards the precipice. It was a two-hundred-foot sheer drop to rocks below. "You're looking at it, son. What good would it do to bring all of this up again, the families knowing their loved ones had been murdered for money and greed? There would be suspicions over who wanted to keep the money and who wanted to do the right thing. More hurt, and it would feel like those men were dying all over again" Stewart paused. "And then there's Britain's image. Like it or not, that's what men like us are paid to keep intact."

"Please, don't kill me…" Reece's words seemed to hang in the air like a thick fog or a bad odour. Considering what they had just heard, the words sounded feeble and in poor taste.

"I tell you what I'm going to do," said Stewart, looking at King. "You saw how leaving that kid alive worked out for Piers. You made a judgement call. You were wrong. Actions have consequences." He paused. "Down in France on the operation against the IRA, you lost the asset and the money."

"And I killed a dirty agent!" King snapped.

"You left loose ends!" Stewart replied vehemently. "That boy in the jungle was a loose end and so was Simon Grant! Loose ends trip us up!" He looked at Reece, then back at

King. "This man double-crossed us when we all depended on each other. People died as a result. He stole money from the government, and he fed a bullshit story to the MOD and the families of the men who died, just so he could keep the money."

"I still have most of the money from Iraq and half the bounty that the South Africans were paying me, say the word and it's all yours!" Reece pleaded. "I can wire it to you..."

Stewart ignored the man and stared at King. "You make the call, son," he said. "Do what you think needs to be done." Then he turned and walked back to the vehicle. He got back inside, slipping into the passenger seat.

The sun had risen above the distant horizon and the mountainside was bathed in a rich hue of gold, its lustre slowly diminished by the growing dawn light. He looked up and saw King returning with the Makarov in one hand and the handcuffs in the other. King opened the door and tossed the handcuffs onto the back seat.

"How did he die?"

"He fell," King replied tersely and started the engine.

Stewart nodded, then after King had turned the vehicle around, he asked, "Did he scream on the way down?"

"No."

Stewart nodded sagely. "No. They never do..."

EPILOGUE

R eading, England
One month later

LEANNE JEFFRIES REREAD THE LETTER. It had been hand delivered through her letterbox, neither stamped nor franked. She supposed it had been delivered by courier, but there were no indications of a company stamp either. When she had rung the telephone number in the letter, the receptionist at the solicitors had made the appointment, and the train ticket that had accompanied the letter had been an open return from London Waterloo to Reading.

"Miss Jeffries," the receptionist said, distracting the young woman from her thoughts. "Mister Montgomery will see you now."

Leanne slipped the letter back inside her handbag and stood up. She had never been in a solicitor's office before, but as she looked at the receptionist in her two-piece trouser suit and hair pulled back so tightly in bun that it would likely have taken a decade off her face without the need for a surgeon's scalpel, she felt woefully underdressed in her leggings, high-top trainers, and denim jacket. She was also aware that her large hoop earrings from Elizabeth Duke at Argos were out of step with the receptionist's single pearls adorning her delicate earlobes. Leanne followed the receptionist as she opened the side door and saw her into the lawyer's office.

"Ah, Miss Jeffries, so glad you could come. How was your train journey? Good, I trust? Of course, it was, you're here and looking well and spot on time," he smiled warmly, gesturing her to the chair at the table in front of his mahogany desk. Behind him, the wall was adorned with all manner of qualifications and certificates including his Oxbridge degree and accreditation from the Law Society and SRA. "Take a seat, take a seat. This is the work of but a moment, and you will leave here in a much preferable position than you came in." He smiled. "If not for the tea and slice of Mrs Montgomery's delicious flapjack. I trust you take your tea white?"

"Yes," she replied nervously.

"Cynthia, two teas if you would be so kind, and two slices of Mrs Montgomery's best." He patted his not inconsiderable waistline and smiled. "If I didn't save it for our very best clients, I would, I fear, be as big as a house!" He held up a hand as his receptionist left the room, closing the door behind her. "Anyway, I digress." He looked at the young woman's expression and smiled warmly. "Don't look so nervous my dear."

"The letter said I would get two-hundred and fifty pounds just for attending," she said quietly.

Montgomery nodded, although his smile was fixed and not as sincere as it had been up to now. Money was money, and he knew that the young woman in front of him had none. "Of course, Cynthia will pay you the agreed sum in cash."

"Can I have it now?"

Montgomery steepled his fingers resting his wrists on his chest. "I feel you may take the money and run." He paused. "Which is your prerogative. But if you can bring yourself to stay and listen to what I have to say, drink a cup of tea with me and try some of the best flapjack you'll ever taste, then I will have Cynthia pay you one-thousand pounds instead."

Leanne Jeffries frowned. "This is a scam!"

"No, dear, I assure you it is not."

"What are you? A pervert?"

Montgomery laughed and leaned back in his chair. "I have something for you. From your brother, Mark."

"Mark?"

He nodded. "Mark Thomas Jeffries."

"What?"

"A legacy," he replied. "It's taken a while because what shall we say? Your brother skirted the wrong side of the law? That would be the best description. So, to legitimise my client's wishes, some things had to change, get lost, get found again, and well, I won't bore you with the details, but it hasn't been easy. I suppose what I'm trying to say is that things needed cleaning. And now, that cleaning has been done."

"But I don't understand. Mark died escaping Dartmoor Prison. At the inquest it said that he had assets seized after his arrest and that he had not left a will or anything."

"No official last will and testament, that is correct, yes. But I handled many of Mr Jeffries affairs, and trust me, this is what he wanted."

Leanne looked up as Cynthia entered with a tray of tea, milk, and sugar and two of the most enormous slabs of flapjack she had ever seen. She hadn't eaten today and could barely contain herself as the secretary placed the items on the table, unloading the two plates of flapjacks last. She smiled as Leanne swiped one, then left the room as discreetly as she had entered. The flapjack was sweet, sticky, and sumptuous. Back at her council flat the cupboards were bare, and her bank account was as empty as her stomach.

Montgomery smiled as he watched her eat and he cast a hand towards the other flapjack. "Please, take another. As many as you'd like, I'll get Cynthia to bring more. I shall also tell Mrs Montgomery that she has another fan." He smiled. "Great baker, but she can't cook for toffee. Her roasts are the stuff of unimaginable nightmares."

"I'd eat one," Leanne said with her mouth full. "It's a nightmare when there's no food, not if the food just isn't up to your expectations."

Montgomery's expression dropped perceivably as he realised that she was truly on the poverty line. "Of course, my dear." He paused, opened the file on his desk and looked back at the young woman opposite. "Without any further procrastination, I shall take you through Mr Jeffries' final wishes. Mark had a property in Southampton. Or just outside. It's a three bedroomed semi-detached house on a quiet cul-de-sac on the outskirts of Eastleigh. A nice property with a small garden and parking." He shrugged. "And it's yours. However, I would suggest you live there for a few years before you think about selling. Like I said, these bequests have been cleaned. But not to the extent they are sparkling like diamonds."

"A house? Really?"

"There's more, Miss Jeffries. Your brother bequeathed

fifty-thousand pounds to you. He expressed his wishes that you help any one of your siblings who so needed financial support, but other than that, there was no obligation, and the money is yours. Again, I would suggest not going on a spending spree, but since you would be moving to a new location, financially comfortable and in essence, venturing into a new life, then I suppose who would know?" He chuckled and marked where she needed to sign. "As I said earlier, we will advance you the thousand pounds, but the rest will be paid only once you have moved into your new abode. Moving costs can be billed to us directly, and it will be deducted from your final legacy."

"I don't know what to say..."

Montgomery smiled. "There really is nothing for you to say, Miss Jeffries. But I suggest that you plan for moving immediately, and I would warn you that money is the route of all evil. Nobody in your current social circle can be trusted. Your friends will not be your friends when they realise you have fifty-thousand pounds in your bank account." He paused. "Miss Jeffries... this is the first day of the rest of your life. Mark wanted you to go far. With this legacy, you can go back to education, train for something worthwhile and make something of yourself. He was always scared that you would go the way of your mother because of a lack of options, and there really is little chance of that now. He has given you a great gift from beyond the grave."

Leanne wiped a tear from her cheek and dabbed at her eyes with her sleeve. "I get it," she replied croakily, trying to hold back the tears. "I really do."

Outside, with the paperwork complete and her new life ahead of her, Leanne Jeffries headed to the train station with relatively little spring in her step and a heavy heart. She would never see her brother again. She had been patient. She knew he would have shown himself if he could, but she knew he had been watching her. Her guardian angel. He always had been. But whatever he had done, however he had escaped prison and faked his own death, it was over now. She had seen him watching, his face covered by the hoodie. She had felt his presence and when she had turned and watched the man walk away, she had known that her brother was alive. She had been patient, hoping he would contact her and take her away from the life of misery, the constant threat of living among the gangs and dealers. But now it was over. She had a new life. But she knew she would never see her brother again, and so would have to grieve a second time.

KING WATCHED his little sister all the way down the street. His chest ached and his legs felt heavy, leaden. Leanne reached the end of the street, stolen from view by the curvature of the buildings. And then she was gone.

"Happy?"

"Far from it," King replied.

"We're in the shit if this ever gets out," Stewart said gruffly.

"It won't."

"Shifting a conflict diamond wasn't your best move, son."

King shrugged. "It needed to be done." He paused, still craning his neck for another glimpse that would never come. "I've given her every chance. It's hers to fuck up, now."

"You couldn't have done more."

King nodded. He'd chosen this life, taken it as a way out of the mess he had made for himself. There was still a hundred thousand left from the sale of the blood diamond to the dealer he had found in Amsterdam. But he had already planned where he would send that, and the families and widows of the men he had taken from them on that drunken night of bravado, ego, and misadventure in Portsmouth just a few long years ago would lend a little respite, but he doubted it would ever alleviate his guilt. That was his, and his alone to carry, and if he was truthful, he didn't want to relinquish the burden of guilt. It was his penance and a reminder that he could and would be better.

"When does this all get wound up?" asked King.

"The actors have all been paid. The rent is up at the end of the month, and I have a couple of blokes coming to clean up and bin everything."

"I'm surprised they agreed to it," said King. "Hardly goes towards Equity cards."

"Grifters use actors all the time as extras in their cons. And jobbing actors seldom turn down work." Stewart paused. "We've used actors in stings as well."

"And they didn't know they were working for SIS?"

"Wouldn't go down well in some circles."

King nodded. There was nothing else to say. Another chapter in his life had closed, and when he walked out of this anonymous office, he would open the page on another.

It was both as simple and as complicated as that.

AUTHOR'S NOTE

Hi – thanks for reading and I hope you enjoyed the story as much as I enjoyed writing it! If you don't want to miss news of new releases, the chance to win giveaways or hear about promotions I'm running, then you can sign up to my mailing list here: www.apbateman.com/sign-up-now

As the reader you've already done your part and read this story. However, if you have the time to leave a short and honest review on Amazon, you'll make this author really happy! I'm hard at work on another thriller as you read this, so I look forward to entertaining you again soon.

A P Bateman

Printed in Great Britain
by Amazon

78154462R10174